*Is she getting a second take at her Hollywood ending?*

Despite her leading lady looks, Tamara Pierce has always been happiest out of the spotlight, especially since a painful breakup drove her away from her society friends. Now she's happily managing a magnificent, historic old movie house that's in danger of being torn down. It's good news when a billionaire buyer shows interest. If only the billionaire in question weren't Gregory Blanchard, who once fueled her fantasies of happily after ever.

Known for his reckless endeavors in romance and business, Gregory's determined to prove his worth with this new project. And he knows how to do it: making Tamara the public face of the Ellen theater. She's poised, passionate—the perfect partner on his arm at fundraising events. Once he lures her into the limelight, the shy beauty gets under his skin in a way no woman has before. But will a heartbreaker like him be the one to lead her back to love?

**Visit us at www.kensingtonbooks.com**

I0677548

# Books by Maggie Dallen

*The Chance Series*
The Accidental Engagement
The Accidental Boyfriend
The Accidental Elopement

*Reel Romance Series*
Her Leading Man
His Leading Lady
Her Leading Hero

**Published by Kensington Publishing Corporation**

# Her Leading Heo

*A Reel Romance*

## Maggie Dallen

**LYRICAL PRESS**
Kensington Publishing Corp.
www.kensingtonbooks.com

Lyrical Press books are published by
Kensington Publishing Corp. 119 West 40th Street New York, NY 10018

Copyright © 2017 by Maggie Dallen

All rights reserved. No part of this book may be reproduced in any form or by any means without the prior written consent of the Publisher, excepting brief quotes used in reviews.

All Kensington titles, imprints, and distributed lines are available at special quantity discounts for bulk purchases for sales promotion, premiums, fund-raising, and educational or institutional use.

To the extent that the image or images on the cover of this book depict a person or persons, such person or persons are merely models, and are not intended to portray any character or characters featured in the book.

Special book excerpts or customized printings can also be created to fit specific needs. For details, write or phone the office of the Kensington Special Sales Manager:
Kensington Publishing Corp.
119 West 40th Street
New York, NY 10018
Attn. Special Sales Department. Phone: 1-800-221-2647.

Kensington and the K logo Reg. U.S. Pat. & TM Off.
Lyrical Press and the L logo are trademarks of Kensington Publishing Corp.

First Electronic Edition: December 2017
eISBN-13: 1978-1-5161-0143-6
eISBN-10: -5161-0143-X

First Print Edition: December 2017
ISBN-13: 978-1-5161-0146-7
ISBN-10: 1-5161-0146-4

# Chapter 1

Tamara had never been a fan of parties, particularly ones thrown for the rich and powerful, which was why she found herself hiding behind a conveniently placed column in the old movie theater's lobby. The costume party was to raise money for The Ellen, the theater she ran—it was for a good cause, and if the event was successful, it would be worth the multiple panic attacks she'd suffered getting ready tonight.

Still, even that fact didn't help to keep the memories at bay.

And oh Lord, did she have memories.

She took another lengthy gulp from her champagne glass and let the bubbles work their magic. *Mmmm.* The champagne was dry and crisp, the tiny bubbles making her tongue tingle. The catering company had broken out the good stuff. Her mother or father would have been able to name the brand with just a sip. A smile tugged at her lips at the memory of her parents with their wine tastings, which inevitably had been followed by crate-loads of champagne or pinot noir arriving on their doorstep.

If there was one thing her parents had loved, it was a good party. Tamara looked around at the decadent costumes. Her parents would have loved this party. A familiar pang of guilt nagged at her. It had been six years since she'd seen her parents. Six years since she'd run away. The last time she'd sipped bubbly at a charity function, she'd been a ballerina, engaged, and miserable. Funny how much could change in six years.

She shook her head to clear away the guilt that memories of her parents always stirred up—it was ancient history, and those memories had no part in her new life. She focused on the champagne instead. It had also been six years since she'd had the good stuff, so she might as well enjoy it.

It might have been years, but the effects of high-end champagne hadn't changed, thank God. She eyed her glass, which was already half empty.

These days she and her friends drank the cheap stuff, which amounted to a killer headache the next day, but even with a pounding head, she was happy—happier than she'd been back then, at least.

She risked another peek around the column. Yep, the party was still in full swing. She hadn't recognized anyone from her parents' circle of friends—not yet at least—but the crowd looked eerily similar to the ones who'd shown up at her parents' functions. Her family's estate was often packed with these stuffy, hoity-toity types.

She supposed she'd been just like them, once upon a time. Spoiled, entitled—though she hadn't known it then. Time and distance had given her that perspective, and for that she was grateful. Back then, she'd been too caught up in that world to see it clearly. She'd attended every one of her parents' parties and kept quiet in the corner, like the good little girl she was—always seen but never heard. Her brother, on the other hand… Older and far more rebellious, he and his friends would get drunk right under their parents' noses before sneaking out to a party of their own.

"What are you doing back here?" The sound of her roommate's voice behind her cut into her memory and had her jumping back with a squeak. A splash of champagne sloshed over the side of her glass as she spun around to face Marc.

Thanks to tonight's theme of classic movie stars, her roommate and best friend was clad in a black tuxedo, his normally curly brown hair slicked down beneath a top hat. Taking the glass from her hands, he downed it in one gulp, ignoring her gasp of outrage. "You're hiding," he said, as he shoved the now-empty glass back into her hand.

She eyed the glass mournfully. "My champagne," she moaned.

He took her free hand and tugged her toward the center of the lobby where a bar had been set up by the caterers her friend Alice had hired. "My dear, there is an open bar a mere fifteen feet from where you're standing. Now be a brave little girl and come out from your hiding spot."

Tamara dug in her heels and scowled up at her friend, who clearly thought he was hysterical, judging by the smirk. But then, he had no idea how hard this party was. He'd never met Tammy Vanguard… He only knew Tamara Pierce.

"I'm not hiding," she snapped, as she struggled out of his grip to return to her hiding place.

"Mmm-hmm." Marc raised one brow as he studied her. The plan had been that Tamara would dress as Ginger Rogers to Marc's Fred Astaire, but Marc's boyfriend, Alex, had other ideas. The head costume designer at the dance academy where Marc worked, Alex had taken one look at her long blond hair and delicate features and shook his head. Before she or Marc could protest, he had called out to one of the interns in the costume department for a change of dresses and gotten down to business on her hair and makeup,

Tamara, he'd decided, was going to be Veronica Lake. As he'd put it, "with hair like yours, denying your inner Veronica would be a crime."

She'd been too stunned to tell him that she had no inner Veronica, and then it was too late. He and his intern had gotten to work.

Marc was thrilled with the results and Tamara had been too polite to argue. But now, out in public, she was keenly aware of how tightly the gown fit her curves and how the makeup made her look like a film noir femme fatale rather than the good girl next door as planned.

Parties made her uncomfortable to begin with, but add a revealing costume that screamed sex symbol, and it was all Tamara could do not to turn tail and flee back to their East Village apartment. What she wouldn't give for her comfy pajamas and a black-and-white movie.

Unfortunately, even if she wasn't duty bound to stick around as the movie theater's general manager, there was no way in hell Marc would let her leave.

As if to prove her point, Marc grasped her arm, which was covered in an elbow-length black satin glove. He nudged her forward again. "Alex would kill me if he learned you hid his masterpiece all night long. Now go, scoot!" He tried to push her again, but she clung to the column with all of her strength.

"Don't make me," she whimpered. Was her fear pathetic? Yes. But pride be damned. It would be a hell of a lot more pathetic if she had a breakdown and started hyperventilating in front of this crowd of potential donors.

Marc's expression remained firm as he peeled her fingers off the pillar one by one. When he was done and she was pouting at him, properly shamed by her juvenile attempt to stay hidden, he nodded toward the bar. There was no denying the challenge in his tone as he said, "Champagne is that way."

Dammit, he knew how badly she needed a drink, tonight of all nights. He didn't know all the sordid details of her past—his respect for her privacy was one of the many reasons she loved him so dearly. But he knew enough to know that this party was excruciating for her. The only way she would survive was with the help of some liquid courage.

She cast a quick glance toward the bar where the champagne beckoned. She needed a drink. Maybe two drinks. Double fisting it might not be classy, but it was efficient.

With a sigh she headed toward the bar, Marc at her side. "Cheer up, Buttercup," Marc said. "This is a party, not a funeral."

Tamara ignored him. She kept her gaze focused on the bar and tried to scope out the best way to get to the bartender while avoiding small talk with the other patrons waiting for drinks. She hadn't recognized anyone from her former life yet, but it was only a matter of time.

Alice, a public relations manager as well as volunteer at The Ellen, had invited the crème de la crème. They were targeting deep pockets, which meant that for the first time in six years her worlds were in danger of colliding. Her old life seemed so far away from her current minimum wage job. But tonight, thanks to Alice's guest list, her blissfully anonymous new life was in imminent danger of unraveling. All it would take was one person who recognized her.

But it had been years since she'd been a member of high society. She'd changed in appearance just as she'd changed everything else about herself when she'd started this new life. She'd let the white-blond highlights grow out, leaving her hair a darker shade. Gone was the perfect little bob, and in its place was an unruly mane that she let hang in front of her face like a barricade. She'd replaced the wire-rimmed glasses with contacts, stopped wearing makeup altogether, and adopted a clothing style that Marc lovingly referred to as hobo-chic. Her former friends would be horrified at the lack of style in her everyday wear. But this wasn't a normal day. Her well-meaning friends had unwittingly transformed her back into a princess. All it would take was one person from her past to recognize her.

She tugged at her black skin-tight gown where it clung to her hips as she sashayed up to the bartender. In a dress like this one, the only way to walk was to sashay. It wasn't intentional, and she sure as hell didn't mean to look sexy or attract stares.

"That's it, girl. Own it," Marc said, leaning down so no one but her would hear. Despite herself, Tamara bit her lip to keep from laughing. That was another reason she loved Marc—he could make her laugh even when she was terrified out of her mind.

*Success.* They reached the bar and Marc placed their orders while Tamara kept watch for ghosts from charity balls past.

"Who are you looking for?" Marc handed her a full glass of champagne, and she didn't hesitate before taking a gulp.

"No one."

Marc pursed his lips in disbelief, but he didn't push it. Instead, he brought up his favorite topic—Tamara's love life. Or lack thereof.

"You need to get out there and mingle," he said as he linked his arm through hers, a chummy gesture that also kept her from retreating to her hiding place.

"I don't want to mingle," she said. "You know I hate parties."

"Mmm, one of the many mysteries that is Tamara," he teased. "But tonight it's necessary, my dear. Whether you like it or not, you're the only representative for The Ellen and the only one who knows the full history."

Her sigh sounded tragic even to her own ears. It was the truth and they both knew it. The Ellen was more than a movie theater; it was her home. She'd taken the managing job six years ago when she'd moved to the city, alone and desperate. Here at The Ellen she'd found a safe space to start fresh. Soon enough, she'd met friends here as well, and they'd formed a bond over their shared love of the theater and the old movies she played.

Much as she hated this party, Marc was right. She had to be here. The owner had no interest in restoring the theater or even in ensuring it stayed a theater—he was actively looking for buyers and would be just as happy to see it torn down as restored to its former glory. Which was why it was up to her—she had to do everything in her power to help save it.

The imminent threat was over—they'd had a scare when her friend Caitlyn's boyfriend nearly bought the place and tore it down to make way for overpriced condos. Luckily Ben had come to his senses and withdrew the offer before the owner could sell.

But the threat was still real. The owner couldn't care less about history or classic films. He was still looking to sell, and her attempts to get the theater passed as a city landmark had been mired in red tape for months. Until it passed—*if* it passed—it was up to her to keep the history alive and the integrity intact. And that meant getting the repairs it so badly needed so it stood a chance of wooing a buyer who could see its true potential. And it *did* have potential. The theater was a living, breathing work of art, as far as she was concerned. The classic architecture alone would have made it unique, but the fact that it was still functioning as a cinema and that the movies played were from the theater's heyday made it a rare gem.

Marc continued to give her a lecture as he steered her none-too-gently toward the center of the lobby where she couldn't avoid the guests. "Alice drew the deep pockets, my love. Now it's up to you to convince them to invest."

Tamara moaned softly under her breath before taking a swig. Right. She could do this. It was for a good cause.

She repeated that mantra as she followed Marc's lead, mingling with the potential donors and dutifully answering their questions about the theater's history as she surreptitiously kept downing her drink.

Marc may have strictly enforced her mingling, but he also made sure her glass was always full. After drink number three—or maybe it was four—Tamara began to loosen up. She continued to regale the patrons with the theater's history, but she was removed from the situation. A hazy tipsiness had her watching the night unfold as if she was watching a soap opera on her couch at home.

And there was more than enough drama going on around her to satisfy any soaps fan. First Caitlyn's love interest appeared to declare his love—about time, as far as Tamara was concerned. They all knew Ben was head over heels for Caitlyn, but he apparently had been the last to know. Then there was Alice, who'd disappeared from the party she'd organized after a run-in with her mystery man. Then Marc's boyfriend, who was supposed to be working tonight, had shown up to surprise him, making Marc light up like a Christmas tree with excitement. And then there was Alice's sister, Meg, and her husband, Jake. Actually, there was no drama there, really. Just the usual lovefest that would be sickening if Meg and her husband weren't such awesome people who deserved the happily ever after that the rest of them struggled to find. No, the only drama from those two would be if Meg went into labor during the party, but a quick glance at her short, frightfully round little friend showed she hadn't succumbed to labor yet. It was just a matter of time though.

Between all of her friends, it was starting to feel like something was in the air. Maybe it was a full moon. Whatever it was, Tamara watched it all unfold around her through the hazy filter of champagne.

As usual, Marc seemed to be on the same wavelength, and not just because he was tipsy too. Coming up behind her with a fresh glass of courage, he leaned down to whisper in her ear. "You've got to admit it, for a party you claimed to dread so much, tonight has been pretty epic."

Tamara nodded as she took the glass. "I'll admit it. It has been eventful."

"Eventful?" Marc repeated the word too loudly, drawing attention from the group of partygoers next to them. "That's an understatement. Love is in the air, *ma Cherie.*"

She rolled her eyes, but he ignored her as he wrapped an arm around her bare shoulders. "Methinks you're the next target of Cupid's arrow."

Her snort of disgusted amusement was also ignored. This was an age-old topic for them. Her dear, lovable, romantic roommate could not get it through his thick head that she had no interest in finding love. But then, he still had no idea that she'd already had her so-called fairy tale romance—and she would never fall for that crap again.

Instead of delving into all that, she just muttered, "Unlikely."

Marc made a tsking sound. Her head was tucked beneath his chin, making his voice reverberate in her ears.

"You do realize that's how every good love story starts, don't you?"

When she didn't respond—there was no need to encourage him when he was like this—he continued anyway. "It always starts with someone who says they don't want love. You know what they say: love finds you when you're not looking for it."

She tilted her head to look up at him. "Is that what they say?"

He nodded once in confirmation, and she noted just how unfocused his eyes were. Oh man, they were going to pay for this champagne binge in the morning. In the meantime… She searched her brain to remember what exactly they were talking about.

Nope. Her fuzzy mind drew a blank.

And then it didn't matter what they'd been talking about. She no longer knew where she was or why she was there, because for one brief, terrifying moment, her entire world came to a screeching halt.

*He* was there. Gregory Blanchard. The man, the myth, the legend. He was there, in person, in *her* theater.

* * * *

Gregory had no idea what he was doing at this theater. It had been a dumb impulse, really. He'd known his best friend was going to come here and make a fool of himself over the woman he loved, and Gregory had felt compelled to witness.

If nothing else, he now had ammunition to embarrass his friend for the rest of his life.

But now the fun was over and he found himself at a formal affair fundraiser, the type of event he typically went to great lengths to avoid. But here he was. Voluntarily sipping some watered-down whiskey cocktail and making small talk with the partygoers he recognized. Or, more often than not, the ones who recognized him.

He did his best to come up with the names that went with the vaguely familiar faces. His father's friends, no doubt. Or perhaps his stepmother Elena's. Between the two of them, it was impossible to attend any social function without playing a game of six degrees of separation. *Of course I remember you. You're Elena's friend's daughter's husband!*

He supposed he could technically make his getaway at any point. No one was forcing him to stay. But no one was expecting him at home either. He took another long drink.

His ex had moved out several weeks ago, but their relationship had been over for ages. Hell, it had been over before it had even begun. Their relationship had followed the same pattern as every other relationship he'd ever had. Passion, followed by drama, followed by resentment, capped off with a bitter, disillusioned parting of ways. Or rather, *he* walked away—a fact his ex and his father were always quick to point out.

And now there was one more failed relationship for his father to throw in his face the moment he got his chance. Another bit of proof that he was incapable of committing.

*Just like his mother.* That part was typically unspoken but understood. She'd taken off when he was five years old, and his father loved to remind him of his many similarities to his flaky runaway mom.

It wasn't like he missed having Vanessa in his home—he sure as hell didn't miss the fighting. But he'd gotten used to having someone there, and now the silence was unnerving. It had never bothered him before, but then he supposed he'd thought that at some point along the way he'd find the real deal. He certainly hadn't expected to be thirty and single.

But he supposed he should have. Maybe after more than a decade of dating it was time to admit that his father might be right. Maybe the ability to commit just wasn't in his genes.

He shook his head in annoyance and stared down into the ice. He'd been spending too much time with the old man, clearly. Just because his father believed he was a flake didn't make it true. So maybe his relationship with Vanessa had been on-again, off-again—it had still lasted two years. That was something. He had a feeling he could be in a relationship for a decade and it wouldn't sway his father's opinion. Not as long as he shared his mother's dark looks and served as a constant reminder of her betrayal.

He'd long ago resigned himself to his father's condemnation of his love life—he'd never find a woman his father approved of or be in a relationship long enough to prove himself. But what bothered him more was his father's belief that Gregory's commitment issues extended as far as his business dealings, and there he couldn't have been more wrong.

Business was another reason he was at this ridiculous party. As a favor for Ben, he'd stuck his neck out for this little theater, using his connections on the landmarks committee to have it designated a landmark so it wouldn't be torn down or completely gutted.

It wasn't official yet, and he highly doubted the do-gooder volunteers who'd thrown this event even knew about it. But he'd put his name behind this place, and he'd figured he might as well check it out. See what all the fuss was about.

He spotted his friend standing near a wall, watching his new girlfriend, Caitlyn, as she chatted with a strange man.

Gregory came to stand beside him. "You do know you look like a stalker standing over here leering like that, don't you?"

Ben spun around. "What are you doing here?"

*Watching you make a fool of yourself over love.* He resisted the urge to say it. Instead he pointed at Ben with his glass. "Thanks to the favor I did for you, I am this theater's biggest champion. How could I refuse an invite when this is my new pet project?"

"Have I said thank you yet for that favor?"

"Only about twenty times," Gregory said. He didn't make a habit of throwing his family name around, and he wouldn't have done it for just anyone. But Ben wasn't just anyone. They'd met back in college and had hit it off from the start.

He and Ben were total opposites—Ben was British, loud, crude, and constantly disheveled, as if he was forever on his way home from a raging party. He, on the other hand, dressed well and spoke with the kind of elocution that came from attending elite prep schools for twelve years. Not a likely friendship, to be sure, but then maybe that had been the initial appeal.

Ben was exactly the type of guy his father didn't want him to consort with, which was exactly why he'd befriended him. He used to get a kick out of pissing his father off with his choice of friends and girlfriends.

Still did, he supposed. What other explanation for why he had stuck with Vanessa for so long other than the fact that her brash demeanor and the tasteless television show she was famous for drove his father nuts.

*Ugh.* That thought was disconcerting. Surely he'd had other reasons for putting up with Vanessa for so long—reasons that had nothing to do with sticking it to his father. He just couldn't think of them right now.

Ben's gratitude at the current moment was unnerving. Ben wasn't one to say thank you; he was more inclined to bust his balls over something. When it looked like he might continue with his thank-you speech, Gregory brushed it off. "Don't worry about it. Besides, you were right. This place does have character."

He'd been so consumed talking with the people who recognized him earlier that for the first time since walking into the lobby, he took a good look around. Sure, it was on the shabby side, but it had class, from its faded carpeting to the ornate sconces. He'd become something of an expert on real estate, and this building was the real deal. With some sprucing up, this place would be a rare gem, a remnant of a time gone by.

He scanned the lobby idly, noting the details with an experienced eye—but then his gaze was caught. Ensnared, really. Fixated on something on the far side of the lobby. No, not something—*someone.*

Holy hell, she was lovely. Blond hair fell in waves over half her face, giving a teasing glimpse of the delicate features it hid. He caught glimpses of siren red lips and smoky eyes. But there was no hiding that figure. She was short but perfectly built, with dips and curves in all the right places. Her dress was black, but she stood out in the crowd like a neon sign. "Who's that?"

Ben followed his gaze to a small group of costume-clad men and women gathered near the bar. "Which one?"

Which one? As if it wasn't obvious. There was only one who stood out in this crowd, and anyone could see that. To Ben, he said, "The blonde."

Ben squinted at the woman who was the spitting image of Veronica Lake...albeit pint-sized. "I don't know—oh, wait. Is that?" He leaned in a little closer. "That's Tamara Pierce. She runs this place."

*Tamara Pierce.* There was something familiar about her, but he couldn't place it. He would remember a woman like her. Maybe she resembled someone he knew. Someone other than Veronica Lake, obviously. He'd become a fan of the old film noir movies back in his college days. Ever since then he'd had a thing for the femme fatales, and this woman looked like she'd just stepped off the screen to bring his fantasies to life.

Ben's voice in his ear brought him back to the present. "Who's leering now?"

He ignored the jibe but did look away. Good God, he didn't want to be caught staring like some creeper. He'd approach her like a man when he saw an opportunity. Ben was staring at him, his eyes narrowed with suspicion.

The last thing he needed was his friend interfering. Ben was head over heels for his girlfriend, and he would bet good money that his friend would feel the need to spread the love around. As if he needed or wanted his friend's assistance. To get Ben off the scent, he kept up his steady perusal of the theater. "This place has potential. You were right to help save it."

Ben shrugged off the compliment.

"It was a risk," Gregory added. "But it looks like it could pay off."

Ben's response was so quiet he almost didn't hear. "The best things always are."

Somehow he suspected they were no longer talking about architecture. Ben was most likely referring to his new relationship—quite the risk for a guy who didn't believe in happily ever afters. But Gregory was in no mood to be lectured on how love conquered all. He was here to drink and maybe meet some pretty women to take his mind off his latest run-in with Vanessa.

His gaze scanned the crowd. Okay, so maybe he was hoping to meet one pretty woman in particular....

# Chapter 2

Tamara was frozen, but Marc followed her stare. "Oh. My. God," he whispered. "Is that...?"

She was too paralyzed to speak. Gregory looked like he'd just stepped off a magazine cover. Square jaw, straight nose, and razor-sharp cheekbones. The man didn't have to dress in costume to look like a matinee idol—he was one.

Tamara's stomach heaved. The champagne sloshed mercilessly. Oh God, she was going to be sick.

She heard a gasp beside her. "Holy crap, it's Gregory Blanchard." That came from Alex, who'd joined Marc on his other side so now the three of them stood silent and frozen, gawking at the celebrity in their midst.

"I know him." The words came unbidden through frozen lips.

*This couldn't be happening.*

"Of course you know him. The man is a living legend," Marc said.

It was true; as the ranking most eligible bachelor in the city, Gregory graced the cover of magazines regularly, his chiseled jaw forever popping up in the gossip section of the local papers.

Yes, she recognized him. But that's not what she'd meant. *She knew him.* Tamara opened her mouth to say just that but shut it quickly. What she'd been about to say would only lead to questions she didn't want to answer. Questions she didn't have *time* to answer, not if she wanted to get out of here without being seen.

Some of the panic started to ebb as that realization set in. It wasn't too late. He hadn't spotted her yet. He was talking to Ben near the front entrance, his profile to her. Unable to look away from Gregory, she clutched Marc's arm.

It was a struggle to keep her voice level when everything in her wanted to freak out. "Marc, could you make my excuses to Meg and Caitlyn? Tell them I'm sorry but I've got to get out of here. I have a, um…a headache."

Lying had never been her forte. She glanced up to see Marc frowning down at her. "A headache? Since when? Tam, what's up? You look like you've seen a ghost."

A ghost—that was the perfect word. He was a shadow from her past. She would be able to spot him in a crowd even if he'd never graced a magazine cover. With his black hair, olive toned skin and tall, broad build, Gregory Blanchard was impossible to ignore. Good looks aside, he had a presence about him, a charisma that had made him the center of attention even when he was young.

He'd been just as handsome back then, but in a boyish way. One of her brother's friends, he'd always been close but untouchable. Older and much, much cooler—he might as well have lived in a different world, even though they moved in the same circles. But he'd never noticed her existence, and she'd been content—well, maybe not content—she'd *settled* for watching him from a distance. Just like she was doing right now….

She blinked at his profile and looked away. What was she doing wasting time staring at the man? She could stare at his picture online for as long as she wanted once she was home and safe from recognition.

"Please, Marc. Just tell everyone I had to bail, okay? I'll explain later." That was a lie and they both knew it, judging by the way he cocked his head to the side and leveled her with a glare. Marc respected her privacy, but that didn't mean he was terribly fond of her penchant for secrecy.

"Please, Marc," she said again. She glanced toward the entrance and froze as her gaze connected with a familiar and stunning pair of dark brown eyes.

In the time it took for her to plead with Marc, Gregory had spotted her across the room as if her fear had summoned him like a beacon. He didn't look away, and she couldn't drag her gaze away from his if her life depended on it. And her life might depend on it, because his stare had her heart beating so fast and hard she was dimly aware that she might have a heart attack—or faint, at the very least.

Her mouth went dry and the blood rushing in her ears washed out the sound of the crowd around her. This was it. It had happened. Her worst fear had been realized. Someone from her past had found her.

And not just anyone—Gregory Blanchard. The prince of high society himself.

Two things seemed to happen at once—Gregory started walking toward her and the rushing sound in her ears cleared long enough for her to hear Marc say, "Oh my God, he's coming this way."

The excitement in Marc's voice was preposterous given the circumstances. A small part of her wanted to turn and smack him. *This man could ruin everything, idiot!* But of course, he didn't know that. Besides, she was frozen. She could no more turn and smack him than she could run away.

And that's what she should do, she told herself. *Run. Run now!*

But her traitorous body stood still, mesmerized into a catatonic state by the intensity of Gregory's stare. He stalked toward her, a panther approaching his prey. She was dimly aware of the crowd parting around him, of the stares and the whispers that followed in his wake. If he noticed, it didn't show. His expression was unreadable, and his attention was fixed on one thing. On one person.

Marc whistled beside her, and his voice was filled with laughter. "Nice work, Tamara. Looks like you've reeled in New York's white whale."

"You're welcome," Alex chimed in over her shoulder. The two of them laughed behind her as they prided themselves on getting their "little hermit" out of her shell.

They thought he was coming over to flirt with her.

Gregory was a few steps away when that thought registered, and its sheer absurdity was enough to puncture the panicked trance she'd gone into. She couldn't have this conversation here, in front of Marc and Alex. Not here in her theater... Her home. If she had to face her past, she would do it outside or anywhere else. *Just not here.*

She turned on her stiletto heel and bolted.

She didn't get far.

"Tamara?" His low voice cut through the music and the chatter, stopping her in her tracks.

The original cold fear returned and a shiver raced through her at the sound of his voice.

She turned slowly. There was no escaping it now. Resignation at her fate had her steeling her spine and squaring her shoulders. She had known this day would come eventually.

He was smiling down at her, and the sheer sex appeal behind it stole her breath away. Sweet Jesus, he'd always been hot, even as a teenager. But now, he was literally breathtaking. He'd filled out, his chest and shoulders molding the suit to perfection. His jaw was even more defined, if that was possible. He'd matured into the aristocratic features that had made him seem older as a teenager. Now they made him look like what he was: a whip-smart, highly educated leader in the city. One not to be trifled with by enemies and whose cool elegance made him a favorite match for supermodels and actresses. Last she'd read, he'd been linked to someone famous. Who was it?

What did that matter? A distant voice mocked her for obsessing over his looks and love life at a time like this. But now that the moment she'd feared was finally here, an odd calm came over her. It was almost… Relief.

Maybe that was why she was able to summon a smile when he said her name again. "Tamara Pierce?"

He'd lowered his head a bit and leaned in so they could speak over the noise of the crowd. It was an oddly intimate gesture, like they were part of an exclusive club. She could smell a warm musky cologne as he drew even closer, his eyes fixed on her and filled with warmth.

It was then that his words hit her. *Pierce.* He'd called her by her mother's maiden name, the name she'd been using ever since she left Boston.

She blinked up at him as the significance of that one word sank in.

"Ms. Pierce," he continued, apparently not thinking it odd that she was staring at him like a mute idiot. "I'm a friend of Ben's." He gestured over his shoulder toward Ben, who was leaning against a wall glaring at the poor man who was speaking to his girlfriend, Caitlyn.

Was it possible Gregory didn't recognize her? A flicker of hope had her breath quickening and her smile broadening. She looked to Ben—of course, he was a friend of Ben's, hadn't Caitlyn told her that? He could be here to support Ben. Or maybe Caitlyn invited him….

Gregory started to speak again, and she turned her attention back to him. She instantly wished she hadn't done that. His eyes were unnerving. His gaze was too direct. Too intense. Too…*sexy.*

"He told me you were the expert here," he said. A smile hovered on his lips as he shoved his hands into his pockets and ducked his head again, in a charmingly self-effacing gesture. As if he was just another guy looking to learn some history and not a freakin' billionaire playboy.

A billionaire playboy who didn't recognize her.

There was no doubt about it. His eyes were direct and intense, sure, but there wasn't so much as a flicker of recognition there. She finally allowed herself to believe it. Gregory Blanchard had no idea who she was.

The flood of relief was so overwhelming she nearly laughed. A giddy dizziness had her beaming up at him, her breath coming in short, choppy bursts as she stifled her excitement. *Focus, Tamara.*

The theater. He wanted to know about the theater. "Yes," she forced herself to say. "I'm the general manager, so I guess that makes me the resident expert."

"Excellent." His smile, slow and charming, triggered a sweet warmth that spread through her limbs like molasses. She was drowning in those eyes, that look, the cocoon-like effect his closeness had on her. Like they were the only two people in the room.

Until Marc came into view over Gregory's shoulder and the bubble popped. With a look of horror, he mouthed the words, "Are you okay?" Clearly her attempt to flee hadn't escaped his notice. She gave a short nod and turned her attention back to Gregory.

History. Right, he wanted to learn about the theater. Grasping at the safe topic, she launched into her spiel by rote, starting with the theater's construction in the '20s and ending with its current fate, which remained an unknown since she hadn't heard back from the landmark committee and the owner was still intent on selling.

She waited for him to make a benign comment—maybe admire the architecture or, even better, offer a donation to the fundraiser. But he didn't do either.

"Have we met before? You look so familiar."

Her heart stopped. *No, no, no.* There was no way he was just now beginning to recognize her. She struggled to maintain her smile. What should she say? Before she could come up with the appropriate denial, he answered his own question.

"What am I saying? Of course we haven't met. There is no way I would have forgotten a face like yours."

Her heart resumed beating, in double-time now at the flirtatious tone.

The threat was gone. He truly didn't recognize her. The irony of it all nearly made her burst into hysterical laughter. Her former self would have been crushed if the great Gregory Blanchard didn't recognize her, but now? Being forgettable was her saving grace.

Another wave of relief had her relaxing a bit under his warm gaze. Even if he thought she looked somewhat familiar, he'd clearly convinced himself that he had never seen her before. She was well and truly in the clear.

"I guess I just have one of those faces." She lifted her glass to her lips to keep from laughing out loud. The gesture had her gazing up at him through her eyelashes. With a start she realized that the move was unintentionally flirtatious. A fact that he didn't seem to miss.

"No," he said, his eyes sparkling with mischievous laughter. "Trust me, there is nothing common or forgettable about your face." He leaned a little closer. "Or anything else about you."

His appraising look, from her head to her stiletto-clad toes, was openly seductive. Her breath caught in her chest as tendrils of desire followed in the wake of his gaze, bringing her body to life. Or at least that's how it felt. Like she was waking up from a long sleep. Her senses heightened to a new level thanks to one sexy look.

Maybe it was his smile, the rush of adrenaline fear had brought on, or maybe it was the ridiculous costume—more than likely the alcohol had something to do with it—whatever it was, Tamara did something one hundred percent out of character. She flirted.

Treating him to the same head-to-toe ogling, she tilted her head to one side and leaned in, placing her hand on his bicep. "Trust me, if we'd met before... You'd remember."

The fact that he had met her before—many, many times—made the lie that much more amusing. For her, at least. She bit her lip to hold back a laugh.

The implication was clear, and at any other time in her life—any time when she wasn't three sheets to the wind—she would have blushed furiously at the overt innuendo. But thanks to the champagne, she felt as though she was watching it all from a distance. Like she truly was Veronica Lake and he was Alan Ladd, and for one magical moment she truly was a femme fatale. A far cry from poor, weak Tammy Vanguard of the Boston Vanguards, hiding herself away in an East Village movie theater.

His low laughter was headier than any champagne. He gestured toward her glass. "Can I get you another drink?"

She looked down and noted with surprise that it was empty. Again. "Sure, why not?"

He held out his arm and she slipped her hand through, allowing him to escort her through the crowd and back to the bar. Dimly aware of the eyes that followed them, she had to fight through the fuzzy haze to think of something to say. "So, Mr. Blanchard, why the interest in The Ellen theater? Or did Ben drag you along for moral support?"

She glanced up to see Gregory grinning at her. "Oh, he didn't need my help for that performance. In fact, I'm pretty sure he'll give me hell later when he realizes I witnessed his public humiliation."

"It wasn't humiliating," she said. "It was romantic." The words came out, but she hardly recognized them. Since when did she stick up for grand romantic gestures? Since they made her friend so supremely happy, she supposed. As long as she wasn't in the midst of it, romance wasn't such a terrible thing. It just wasn't for her.

Clearly it wasn't for Gregory either, because he openly scoffed at that. "Romantic," he repeated with clear disdain. When he looked down at her, there was only a hint of bitterness in his eyes, but it was there, tempered with self-deprecation. "Don't mind me, Ms. Pierce, I suppose I'm not one to weigh in on romance at the moment."

She blinked at him, trying to figure out what that meant. He had a knowing tone, like he'd made a joke she was supposed to get, but it flew right past her. His self-mocking smile faltered in the face of her blank stare, and he quickly added, "Never mind. Tell me, how did you come to be an expert on old movies?"

It was funny—no one had ever asked her that before. For such a huge part of her life, she had no prepared lie. The truth would have to do—minus some key details. "One summer when I was twelve or so, I was at the beach with my family." *And yours.* "I got severe sunstroke and was ordered to stay inside all day while all of the other kids played in the sun."

For a moment, a nervous flutter made her stomach clench. What if she triggered a memory? Their fathers had been friends since college and the two families had been close for as long as Tamara could remember, even though her family was based in Boston and Gregory's spent most of the year in New York. They'd spent countless holidays and vacations with the Blanchards, including their son. He'd been there on that summer trip to the Hamptons. She remembered it all so clearly. But then, she'd been younger than Gregory and all but invisible to the then-teenaged heir. He wouldn't have paid attention to the fact that she'd been forced to stay inside. He probably hadn't even been aware that she had joined her parents in the Hamptons that summer. He'd had a girlfriend—a blond bombshell who'd filled out a swimsuit in a way Tamara would never have been able to do, not even when puberty struck and she developed curves of her own.

Gregory leaned in, his eyes filled with amusement. "And?" he prompted.

She nearly stumbled in her ridiculously high heels, and his arm tightened around her, holding her steady.

How much had she had to drink? Alarm bells started going off in the part of her brain that could still function properly. Too much. She'd had far too much to drink.

She looked up to find him grinning. Oh crap, he knew she was drunk. "You stayed inside all day...."

Swallowing down a wave of nausea, she plodded on. "With nothing better to do but lie on a couch and feel sorry for myself, I discovered this old movie channel. It was love at first sight."

That much was true. She still remembered her first black-and-white movie and the way it had made her feel.

A tantalizing smile hovered over his lips, and his fixed gaze was flatteringly attentive. "What was it that you loved so much?"

For a moment she forgot she was supposed to be monitoring her words, carefully hiding any clues that might let him draw a line between Tamara Pierce and Tammy Vanguard, the so-called loony debutante who'd come unhinged. No, for one moment, she was just a woman and he was a man who showed an interest in something she loved. That, it turned out, was even more intoxicating than champagne.

"It was like I'd discovered a way to escape to another world." She remembered that day like it was yesterday. For a shy young girl with few friends, the black-and-white world had been an enchanting new world that no one else seemed to know about, least of all her peers. Which meant it was her place—hers and hers alone. Now that she was older, she knew she wasn't the only one who liked old movies, but they still gave her that comfortable feeling of slipping away to another world. When bad memories came back to haunt her, or the guilt of how she'd run from her former life grew too great, there was always an escape at this theater.

He leaned down closer, and once again she forgot about the crowd. It was just the two of them.

"Film is an incredible means of escape," he said.

She nodded. "All films are, I guess. But the classics... They come from another world. They have a different way of speaking, of acting."

She was babbling and she knew it, but she couldn't seem to stop because he was leaning in so close and her head was one hundred percent clouded by his warm male scent, a musky cologne that left her addled.

"And black-and-white movies," she continued. "It's like you're entering a world where everything is clear. It's another reality, one with right and wrong and good and bad. The heroes are...well, heroes. Real heroes, you know? And the romance..." She sighed as her brain conjured up her favorite scenes, ones she knew by heart. "The romances are pure. Untarnished. Nothing at all like real romance."

Oh crap. That came out sounding far more bitter than she'd intended. But it was the truth. There was a silence, and she looked up to find him staring at her with an unreadable expression. The only thing she knew for sure was that he was studying her. Analyzing her. Warning bells went off again. That could not be good. She was supposed to be avoiding attention, *especially* from someone like him—someone from her past.

"So that's why this theater is so important to you?" he asked.

*Yes!* Yes, this was about the theater. He was a potential patron. She latched on to that idea. "It's important that these films be remembered, don't you think? They deserve to be shown in full and to be preserved for future generations."

There. She was back on track. It was one of few topics she could easily talk about, even with strangers. She'd gotten into classic film trivia as a kid—it was a natural side effect of her passion for the movies. Her parents bought her tons of books on the topic until her shelves were filled with biographies and texts on the history of the film industry. Honestly, it had never occurred to her back then that she might turn her hobby into a career—she'd been far too focused on ballet.

But when she'd run away to New York City, she'd seen an ad in the *Village Voice* for the manager position. The owner had been impressed by her arcane knowledge and hired her on the spot. It had seemed like a good sign at the time. A sign that maybe her life was about to turn around. It was here that she'd met her close circle of friends, and it was at this theater that she'd found a new home for herself—one without an abusive ex-fiancé or a family that believed his lies.

She launched back into her donor spiel, once again on even footing now that she was talking about the theater and its history. A safe topic, unlike her foray down memory lane. *Stupid, Tammy. So stupid!*

They were next in line at the bar, and Gregory turned to her. "What can I get for you then, another champagne?"

She forced a smile to match his. "Why not?"

*Why not? Because you're drunk and two sips away from making a fool of yourself.* The voice of reason reared its ugly head, dispelling some of the magical champagne haze.

One night. Surely she could allow herself one night to flirt with a hot guy. One she'd had a crush on for so many years…

When he handed her the glass, he gave her the smile she'd seen so many times from afar—first as a girl at their parents' parties, then as an adult on televised interviews and in magazines.

From afar it made her heart race—up close and directed at her? She was a goner. Done for. Stick a fork in her, because she was finished. At least that was how it felt for one split second as her brain melted into a bemused puddle and her heart threatened to jump out of her chest.

"Shall we?" He nodded toward the double doors that led to the theater. Partygoers were encouraged to tour the theater itself but the food and drinks were kept to the lobby, and the vast majority of the crowd was grouped around small standing tables set up nearby.

The theater, in comparison, was quiet—some of the music piping through the lobby filtered into the space but was muted by the seats, carpeting, and high ceiling. Some couples sat in the seats, their heads lowered toward one another, while others roamed the aisles on the sides, getting an up-close view of the old stage with its hidden wings and small, overlooking balconies.

Gregory came to a stop in the back. Taking her hand, he tugged her toward the dark shadows near the sound and lighting booth. He moved with such ease, it was almost as though he, not her, were the one familiar with this place.

*They shouldn't be back here on their own*, the sober portion of her brain called out. She should steer him away, back toward the lights, the music… the people. But he smiled at her over his shoulder, and the flirtatious promise in his eyes spoke volumes. "Come on," he said, tugging her closer. "I want a behind-the-scenes tour from the expert."

She was lost. The teenage girl in her was deliriously happy. This couldn't be happening. Surely it was a dream brought on by binge-watching too many old romantic comedies. Because in real life men did not whisk Tamara Pierce back into the shadows. They didn't gaze down at her with open longing.

And they sure as hell didn't kiss her.

But that was exactly what Gregory did. She saw it coming as if in slow motion—the dip of his head, the dark intent in his eyes, the way his gaze sought hers, silently seeking permission.

She didn't move. Didn't blink. Couldn't think, let alone breathe.

And then his lips were on hers, warm and insistent, but gentle. Sweet. There was no wild passion, just a tender touch that was perfection in and of itself yet left her aching for more.

He pulled back and she blinked up at him. Why was he stopping? *Don't stop.* The disappointment cut through her, and she stopped herself just before the protest slipped from her lips.

With a wince of regret, he pulled his phone out of his pocket, and she belatedly realized that it had been ringing.

Oh God, she really was out of her mind if she hadn't even noticed that shrill sound. He held up a finger and mouthed, "Sorry," before murmuring into the phone.

She couldn't so much as summon a smile or say "no problem" before he turned slightly so he could speak in semi-private. Her mind was too busy chanting one phrase over and over. *Gregory Blanchard kissed me.* The obsessive thought made it impossible to do anything but stand there like a statue—a statue that was just waiting for the kiss to resume.

The great Gregory Blanchard would have awed anyone, but for Tamara, this was everything she'd dreamed of as a tween, and then fantasized about as a teenager, and then told herself not to think about once she grew up and realized that dream men were just that—a dream. A myth. A fantasy. Certainly not something she should waste her time thinking about as a grown woman with a career and a new life—one that did not include Gregory and everything he represented.

A wave of horror managed to cut through the girlish response to Gregory's kiss. It would have been bad enough if she'd let herself get so wrapped up in any man—but Gregory?

She stared at his back as he spoke to the caller on the other end. This wasn't just any man she'd kissed. It wasn't some average Joe she'd been flirting with—it was Gregory Blanchard. A shadow from her past. Someone from her parents' world. From Billy's world.

She wasn't just flirting with a sexy man at a costume party. She was flirting with danger.

His back was still toward her when she did what she should have done the moment she'd spotted him across the room. She turned on her heel and ran away.

# Chapter 3

Gregory couldn't stop thinking about her—the one who'd gotten away.

Even at an executive meeting for his family's company, his mind kept wandering back to that night as it had been doing for the past week.

His father droned on, making the perfect background noise for his Veronica Lake fantasies. It was annoying, really, how often he found himself thinking about her. Though it was better than the alternative, which was stewing over his breakup with Vanessa.

Maybe that was why he couldn't let go of that night. That brief tease of a flirtation with a Veronica Lake look-alike had been just the distraction he'd needed. But she hadn't been in black and white—she'd been vivid, electric. And not at all in keeping with the description he'd gotten from Ben when he'd asked about her the next day. Quiet, shy, timid. That was how his best friend had described her, but those descriptors seemed so... *boring*. As if anything about that woman was plain.

One other tidbit his friend had mentioned when he'd casually brought Tamara up in conversation—apparently his mystery woman did not date. Ever. At least that's what Ben had heard from Caitlyn, who apparently was good friends with her.

That was fine by him, since he wasn't in the market anyway. That much he'd decided after the final blowout with Vanessa. Clearly he was doing it wrong. Vanessa had been the longest relationship to date and even that had been more off than on, and no one would have called it healthy.

Until he could figure out why his love life was such a disaster— regrettably, a very *public* disaster—he was out of the relationship game.

It seemed everyone in the universe had heard about his latest breakup with Vanessa—everyone except Tamara. She hadn't even blinked when he'd tried to joke about his most recent disaster, which had been widely published in the tabloids. The press loved to follow his love life. Add a popular TV star like Vanessa, and they were perfect tabloid fodder. But it seemed Tamara didn't read tabloids. Either that or she was an incredibly good liar.

If his gut was anything to go by, his Tamara was honest to a fault. She was guileless, open. Her smile when he'd approached her had been a breath of fresh air, radiant and pure. And that kiss…

"Are we boring you, Gregory?"

His father's nasally voice interrupted the latest mental rundown of this fascinating woman's appealing traits. He hadn't even gotten to her physical attributes yet, and he'd made something of an obsession out of cataloguing those.

All eyes turned to him—his father's lawyer and a few of his other lackeys along with senior members of the company. Gregory paused deliberately. Nothing annoyed his father more than when his attempts to publicly put him in his place failed spectacularly.

"Not at all." He let his tone fall flat with insincerity. "Hearing you recite the quarterly earnings is always stimulating, Father."

That earned a few snickers from his friends in the group, but the majority of those present, namely his father, scowled back at him. "You should pay attention; this information might prove useful one day. But then again, perhaps not."

Gregory met his father's gaze and refused to flinch. His father's threat was subtle in front of this group, but Gregory didn't miss his meaning. It stung as intended. Gregory had done well for himself with the trust his grandfather had set aside for him, doubling the amount in less than a decade and building a brand of his own. Despite that, his father still controlled the family business—and though tradition dictated that he should be taking over soon, or at least officially be named next in line, his father refused to admit that Gregory could handle the responsibility.

A few rebellious years in his late teens and early twenties and his father had forever labeled him weak, fickle. Every failed relationship since merely added to his father's certainty that he had inherited his mother's lack of steadfastness, her tendency to run in the face of commitment. He'd given up trying to prove his father wrong—every time he tried, it backfired.

Not to mention the gossip pages seemed to have their own take on his love life. A fickle playboy apparently sold more papers than a homebody who happened to be unlucky in love. Gregory couldn't care less how the tabloids portrayed him, but his own father should have been able to see the truth.

Of course, that would have meant that his father open his eyes and see his son as the living, breathing man he was today and not merely as the offspring of the woman who'd broken his heart and left him. Left *them*. But his father never seemed to realize that Gregory had been a victim of her actions just as much as he was. She'd left her son as well as her husband, but somehow he was always being judged for her actions. His father assumed that by inheriting her dark looks, he was also innately unable to be loyal. In his father's eyes, he lacked the dedication necessary to own a pet fish, let alone run a company.

*But then again, perhaps not.* His father's words rang in his ears, a barely veiled reminder that he was not the leader of this company now, nor would he ever be unless he earned his father's approval. A task that some might call herculean. He just called it impossible.

Impossible but necessary. The company was his family's legacy, goddammit. It should be his, even if he was the flunky his father professed him to be. Which he wasn't. But even if he was…

"How is your project coming, son?" His father was the only person he knew who could make the word "son" sound like an insult.

His project… *His project?* He glared at his father. Surely he didn't mean that demeaning request at the last meeting. His father's thin lips were pinched together in a smirk. Yes, that was exactly what he'd meant.

The request had come after another long, not so thinly veiled battle in the boardroom over the company's direction—Gregory stressed the need to diversify while his father argued that they stay on the tried-and-true course. He discounted every argument Gregory presented, tossing them aside with thinly disguised disgust, claiming his son relied too heavily on his emotions and instincts rather than facts and figures. Never mind the fact that his gut and his instincts had made Gregory a financial success in his own right. When it came to his son, his father had never been able to see reason, only his ex-wife's face.

It had come to a head when Gregory had outright challenged his father, asking him to give him responsibility, let him use his instincts and give him a chance to prove himself. His father's response was to assign Gregory responsibility for the company's pro bono division—another way of saying he was the head of the "charity league," a role typically filled by one of the stuffy old matrons on the Upper East Side who had nothing better to do than plan teas and organize fundraisers.

He'd honestly thought his father had been joking. Not to be funny but to make a point, show who had all the power and put him in his place.

Now, as he glared at his father across the boardroom, the eyes of every senior executive riveted to them, he realized it—his father hadn't been joking.

*Shit.*

The sanctimonious bastard's expression was filled with mockery and amusement. He most likely guessed, correctly, that Gregory had walked out of that meeting and shrugged off the insulting gesture. There was no way he would give his father the satisfaction of knowing that he was right—or worse, that he'd won.

He'd asked to be put in charge of something, to prove that his instincts were good. Why the hell not in charity? He could only imagine the horror on his father's face if he took the ridiculous assignment and made a success of it. Turned his father's trick against him.

Unbidden and unwelcome, the face of his mystery woman came into his mind. Her passion when she spoke about classic film, the sincerity in her eyes when she spoke of its meaning to her.

Hell, he'd already helped that old theater by pushing it through the landmark committee. Why not take it one step further? Why not save the thing in the process?

And if the gesture won him the girl…

No, this wasn't about her. Hadn't he just declared himself out of the dating game? What he needed post-breakup was a serious timeout. Time to figure out what he was doing wrong and what he really wanted.

Again he saw Tamara in his mind's eye, but he shook his head, dispelling the tempting sight.

Okay, yes, clearly he wanted her—at least his body was clear on that. But he hated that his father had been proven right, yet again, with his latest romantic failure. His father had moved on from his mother and had been happily married to his stepmother, Elena, for decades.

He wanted that. So what was his problem?

Shifting in his seat, he steered clear of that train of thought. Now was not the time for personal reflection or self-therapy. His father was watching him, displeasure written all over his smug face.

This wasn't about Tamara. Hell, it wasn't even about the theater, not really. This wasn't personal. It was business.

His gaze collided with his father's as his plan of action fell into place. Who was he kidding? This wasn't just about business—the old man was right; he did tend to let emotions get in the way. But this time the emotion had nothing to do with romance or passion.

He smiled at his father. It had everything to do with hate.

\* \* \* \*

Tamara's friends were staring at her, waiting for her to speak. Too bad. They'd be waiting all day. As if tormenting her at home all week hadn't been torture enough, now Marc had started grilling her on what had gone on between her and Gregory, and his interrogation took place in front of all of their friends at the latest Operation Petticoat meet-up.

Operation Petticoat was the name Caitlyn had given the group, thanks to her obsession with Cary Grant. They met bright and early every other Saturday morning to do some cleaning and minor repairs that helped keep the theater running since the current owner couldn't be bothered to care.

So now she faced Meg, Jake, Caitlyn, Alice, and Marc like a prisoner facing a firing squad, though this particular squad was scattered around the theater doing chores.

"She totally went off alone with him," Marc was explaining to the group at large. "And she won't spill on what happened with the hottie."

Tamara rolled her eyes and forced out the lie she'd been telling all week. "Nothing happened. You are obsessed with something that didn't even occur." She playfully patted Marc on the head as she walked past the chair where he was sitting. "I think they call that delusional, Marc."

Marc narrowed his eyes at her. "I know what I saw." Then again to the rest of the group, "I know what I saw! She was flirting. Our little Tam-Tam was a little vixen." Turning back to Tamara, he jabbed a finger in her direction. "Don't try to deny it."

With a wry grimace, she stated the partial truth. "I wouldn't dream of confirming or denying anything that happened that night. In case you hadn't noticed, I was three sheets to the wind."

"That's true," Caitlyn called from the ladder where she was perched trying to take down the last of the decorations from last weekend's event. "Tam was in rare form."

Tamara gave Marc a look that said "See?" He couldn't deny it—they'd recuperated together the next day with plenty of fried food and a Netflix binge of some horrifically terrible '80s movies.

"I still say there's more to it," Marc mumbled. "I saw the way he was looking at you. That guy was ready to pounce like he was starving and you were his favorite meal."

Meg, ever the caretaker, came over to intervene. "Leave the poor girl alone, Marc. If she said nothing happened, nothing happened."

She flashed Tamara a smile. Tamara tried to return it without collapsing from the crushing guilt at lying to her friends.

She was the worst.

But after all these years of keeping secrets, what was one more? To tell them about Gregory would open too many doors. It would mean having to tell even more lies, like that she'd never met him before.

No, it was best to close the door on that night and never think about it again.

*As if she hadn't been replaying their interaction on a loop for the past week...*

But this obsession had to come to an end sometime, and today was the day. She'd had a week to relive that magical night—one week to let her inner tween revel. Now it was time to face reality again. A reality that included an emergency meeting with her boss, the owner, this afternoon. Her stomach had been churning all morning, ever since she'd received his text. Whatever news he had, she highly doubted it could be good.

She and the owner had been at odds from the day she'd started. He'd made it clear he had little interest in old movies or the theater's history. But he trusted her and loved that she took matters into her own hands to ensure the theater did well—even if it meant working for free on her off-time and helping to promote and host events that might save its future.

She had a horrible feeling in the pit of her stomach. Like maybe today was the day that he pulled the rug out from under her feet and informed her that the theater had been sold.

She was so caught up in worrying about what the owner had to tell her that she'd finally managed to temporarily put Gregory Blanchard out of her mind.

Until Caitlyn brought him up again, that was.

"It would make sense that Gregory was flirting," she said. "I mean, Tamara looked hot as hell in that Veronica Lake outfit, and you guys saw the headlines, right? He and Vanessa Davies are finally done for good."

Tamara did not want to listen. She didn't want to think about it. And she sure as hell didn't want to admit that she'd read every gossip article she could find that had to do with Gregory and his love life.

She'd even sneaked a copy of *Us Weekly* in with her groceries and smuggled it past Marc so he wouldn't see it when she got home. Her crush was officially mortifying.

"She's right," Jake called to her from across the lobby. "You were insanely hot. You should dress up as old movie stars more often."

Clad in her typical oversized flannel shirt and jeans, she rolled her eyes. "Yeah, I'll get right on that."

"She doesn't need sexy dresses to be hot," Meg admonished. "Besides, who said she even wants to attract more male attention? We all know her stance on dating."

Tamara gave her friend another grateful smile. She had a sneaking suspicion that Meg believed she was a closeted lesbian, but she'd never outright asked. But she was right enough about her stance on dating.

She didn't do it. Ever. That was a promise she'd made to herself when she'd left Billy. She couldn't put herself in that position again. No amount of happiness was worth that kind of pain.

Gregory's face loomed in her mind—the look in his eyes as he'd leaned toward her. The warmth of his breath on her cheek just before his lips met hers.

She inhaled quickly as heat scorched through her. It had been ages since she'd had such a vivid reminder of what she'd been missing. But she would forget about that night and that tease of a kiss.

And even if she couldn't forget completely, she would put it out of her mind.

There was no room in her life for a man. And Gregory? He was out of the question. It was one thing to flirt with him when she was in costume and using a pseudonym. But she'd been lucky that he hadn't recognized her, and she wouldn't push her luck.

It was decided. She wouldn't think of him anymore. Starting now.

Caitlyn called out to her. "When you and Gregory were flirting, I sure hope you thanked him."

Oh for the love of God, how was she supposed to forget about him when her friends wouldn't stop saying his name?

"Thank him," she repeated. "For what?"

Caitlyn stopped her work. "Didn't I tell you? He's the one who helped Ben get The Ellen pushed through as a landmark."

Tamara froze in the middle of wiping down the concession counter. "What?"

Caitlyn and Ben had told them the good news Monday, when the landmarks committee had made it official. All she'd known was that Ben had made it happen, but she hadn't thought to ask how. Or who else was involved.

"Gregory Blanchard," she said slowly, as if maybe there were some other Gregory in the mix.

Caitlyn grinned. "Of course, Gregory Blanchard. He used that fancy name of his as a favor for Ben."

Tamara released the breath she'd been holding. Of course, Gregory. Who else had the family legacy to influence the landmarks committee?

She should have guessed. It was something her family and the Blanchards had always been good at, using their influence to curry favor. Her family and his wielded money like a weapon, using it to open doors and smooth over any hardship to come their way.

She was the first to admit that she and her brother had been spoiled as children, her parents using their money and their power to give her and her brother the best of everything. Once upon a time she'd been naive enough to believe that meant something. She'd mistaken their generosity for understanding, mistaken financial backing for true support. It wasn't until shit hit the fan that she'd seen how little comfort money could provide when it was trust and love that she'd needed.

Annoyance had her scrubbing the counter a little too hard. She supposed she owed Gregory her thanks—but that wasn't going to happen. Because he was back in his world and she was in hers, and she had no intention of letting those worlds collide again.

# Chapter 4

"You sold it?" It was the third time Tamara had repeated the phrase. After going home to shower, she'd come back to The Ellen to meet the owner. His news had stunned her into incoherence. Like a parrot, she latched on to that phrase, ignoring the current owner, Oliver Paley, as he went on a tangent.

Short and squat, the man Marc referred to as the Oompa Loompa went on as if she hadn't spoken. "I should take legal action against you. How dare you go to the landmarks committee without telling me?"

Tamara barely listened. She couldn't be bothered to deal with his anger. Not when he'd dropped life-changing news in her lap.

"Who did you sell to?" Her mind was scrambling to make sense of the sudden turn of events. Were the new owners aware of the landmark status? He'd have had to legally, right? But she wouldn't put it past the owner to sidestep the law. Even if the new owners were aware of its status, that just protected the building itself and its interior—new owners could come in and use the space to do whatever they wanted. No status could force them to show old movies or keep the spirit of the theater intact.

Fear had Tamara frozen in her seat as Oliver kept talking. What would she do if the new owners didn't need her around? Where would she go? She'd been battling that fear ever since she discovered Oliver intended to sell, but now it was a reality. Her life was about to change. Again.

The difference was, this time around she actually liked her life. She'd built a real home for herself, and now with one twist of fate it could all be taken away.

Oliver strode across the office, sifting through files on his overcrowded desk as he started to pack up his belongings. It seemed he couldn't get out of there fast enough. "I should fire you right now," he muttered as he tossed aside a folder.

"Why don't you?" It was an honest question. What she'd done in going behind his back had been a fireable offense. She'd known that but still had done it, rationalizing she wouldn't have a job anyway if he sold the building to a company that wanted to tear it down.

She'd thought she'd bought herself some time with the landmark status. A couple of nights ago, she and the other volunteers had celebrated their win at Cagney's, the bar owned by Meg and Jake next to the theater.

But now... Maybe they'd celebrated too soon. When the Oompa Loompa spoke again, she almost forgot what she'd asked.

"They asked that I keep you on."

She frowned. "What? Who?"

He glared at her over his desk, which was shoved into a corner of the too-small office space next to the room that held the projector. "The new owners," he said slowly, as though talking to an idiot.

"Who are *they*?" she asked. *And why on earth would they specify that she be kept on?*

True to form, Oliver wasn't paying attention to her or her questions; he kept talking to himself. "They came in here and made a good offer. What could I do? I mean, especially after the predicament you got me into. Do you know how much I could have sold this place for if I could sell to developers like I wanted to?"

Yes, she knew. Ben's company and the client he represented had been willing to shell out big bucks to turn this place into a condominium. But that was before Ben realized he had a heart—and that he'd lost it to Caitlyn.

"Who did you sell it to?" This time Tamara's voice was loud—well, loud for her—and she matched his slow I'm-talking-to-a-moron tone. Frankly she was starting to annoy herself with the repetitive questions. She needed answers before she lost it.

She'd never once been so assertive with her boss—now former boss, she supposed—and he stared at her as if just realizing she was there in the room with him. "The Blanchard Group."

"Blanchard. As in Gregory Blanchard?" No. *No, no, no.* It couldn't be. There was no way.... Was there?

Oompa Loompa shrugged. "I don't know, I just talked to the lawyers. They made a good offer and I took it."

"Why? Why would he do that?"

Oliver stared at her as if she'd grown a second head. "How should I know? You can ask them yourself when they get here."

"When? And who?"

He shoved the last folder on his desk into a briefcase. "They're coming today to check out the place. I'm guessing they'll want to meet with you."

"'They' who?" She tried to keep her voice level, but even she could hear the rising panic in her tone.

A low voice behind her confirmed her worst fears.

"'They' meaning me, Ms. Pierce."

She froze, staring at Oliver as if by ignoring the voice she could make the man disappear. But she felt his presence, an electrical current in the room that had her skin tingling and a shiver racing down her spine.

Finally, she turned to face him. "Gregory." The name slipped out on a whisper, which was all she could manage. After thinking about him nonstop for more than a week, she found his sudden presence in her office surreal. Like a dream had come to life. Except that this was no dream. He was flesh and blood...and taking up entirely too much space in the cramped room.

She couldn't breathe. Clutching the back of her chair, she forced herself to meet his gaze.

He still didn't know who she was, she told herself. She could keep it that way.

But the exposure of her true identity was no longer the only danger this man posed. He'd gotten under her skin that night at the party. She'd tried to blame it on the alcohol, but he had the same effect on her now when she was stone cold sober. He made her forget who she was, who she'd become. He made her think of things like romance...and sex. Things she hadn't cared about at all in the past six years, not since she'd left behind a love life, along with everything else.

He smiled at her, but it wasn't a friendly gesture. It was the smile of a predator who had its prey in its grip.

She stayed quiet, practically hidden in a corner as Oliver spoke with Gregory, who had apparently come on his own to size up the place. She barely heard their small talk as she struggled to breathe normally.

*Do not panic. Do not panic. Do not—*

"Tamara will show you around," Oliver said, interrupting her pep talk. "Isn't that right, Tam?"

She hated when he called her that, like they were friends. And now she hated that nickname more than ever. It was too close to the name she'd been called. Tam. Tammy. Way too close. Why hadn't she changed her first name as well as last?

But there was no time to regret past decisions, because Gregory had moved to the doorway and turned back as if waiting for her to join him.

As she walked to his side, the full force of the situation hit her. Gregory was the new owner. She was either going to have to leave this place—her home—or work beside him, hoping against hope that he never figured out her secret. Praying he never got too close.

* * * *

By the end of the tour, Gregory had learned every bit of history and film trivia he could ever hope to know. He was left with only one question—where the hell was the woman he'd met the week before?

It was with something close to horror that he found himself staring at this stranger who bore a startling resemblance to the mesmerizing, charismatic young woman with the sexy gown. They stood in awkward silence in the theater's lobby. Oliver had long since left and the tour had come to an end. Gregory knew he should take some time, think of a diplomatic way to address the situation. He knew that was what he should do, but—

"I'm curious. Do you always require a case of champagne to interact with people, or is it just me?"

That got her attention, at least.

For the first time since he'd arrived, Tamara lifted her head enough so he could see her entire face and not just glimpses through her long, blond hair.

"Excuse me?"

There. He could even hear her voice now that she wasn't speaking softly with her head tilted down like some sort of servant from another era.

He took a step closer and watched as she backed away. A wall was two feet behind her, and he experienced a pang of guilt at the realization that she was scared of him. People were not scared of him.... Well, maybe business rivals, but certainly not his employees. And definitely not women.

Shoving his hands in his pockets, he stopped advancing and forced himself to loosen his posture. *See? Nothing intimidating about this guy.*

He even attempted to soften his tone. "I merely meant..." What? That she'd been a sassy, confident vixen the other night and had apparently transformed into a shrinking violet. How to put it delicately...

But she seemed to know what he was thinking, because her cheeks turned a violent shade of crimson and her tongue slipped out to lick her lips in a nervous gesture that made him more aroused than he'd care to admit.

"I-I'm sorry," she said, her hands twisting together as though she were wringing out a rag. "I had too much to drink the other night, but I assure you—"

"What? No." He bit back a sigh of annoyance. Was she deliberately being obtuse? For the love of God, he wasn't *complaining* that she'd been a charismatic siren. "You have nothing to apologize for. I just meant..." Oh hell, he was making a mess of this. "I liked the woman I met the other night."

She stared at him from beneath lowered lashes, her gaze inscrutable.

Guilt kicked in once again. That had sounded like a come-on. And maybe it was, if he was being honest. He would have given anything to see that flirty little temptress again. To be so close to her and be stuck with her shadow was beyond frustrating.

But he had to remember where he was. At the theater...her workplace. Which meant she was now his employee. Of course she wouldn't flirt with him, and he shouldn't be forcing the issue. That didn't mean he had to accept her role of self-conscious wallflower, however. But this was about business, so he tried a different tack. "Look, I need someone who can be a spokesperson for the theater."

Her chin tilted up, and he caught a flash of interest in her blue eyes. A china doll, that's what she reminded him of with those big eyes and tiny features. Everything about her seemed delicate, fragile. The other night that delicacy had been tempered with strength—a rare and intoxicating combination of vulnerability and indomitability. But today, there was just fragility. The need to scoop her up in his arms and protect her from the world threatened to make him do something stupid.

When she spoke, her voice was only slightly louder than it had been, but there was more strength to it—more substance. "I'm afraid I'm not much of a spokesperson, Mr. Blanchard."

Her formality in calling him "Mr." was duly noted.

"I'm not very good at speaking in public and..." She pressed her lips together for a moment, as if summoning up courage. "Despite my behavior the other night, I am not typically good at speaking with strangers."

He studied her for some time, trying to reconcile the woman before him with the one from the other night. "I think you're wrong," he said. And then dared to add, "Either that or you're lying."

He'd merely meant to tease, but her instant and over-the-top reaction was intriguing.

"I'm *not* lying!" Her cheeks flushed again almost instantly and she dipped her head. "Why would you think that?"

Pausing to consider her reaction, he finally explained, "I merely meant that perhaps you were lying to yourself. Doing yourself a disservice, at the very least."

She peeked up at him, and he could have sworn her eyes were filled with suspicion.

"You were brilliant the other night when you spoke about the theater and its significance."

Her cheeks couldn't grow any redder without her head exploding, he was sure of it. It was charming, really. Perhaps Vanessa and his other exes had taught him that modesty and humility were a thing of the past—a remnant of another time—but Tamara's embarrassed reaction made something in his chest tighten.

"I wasn't brilliant," she murmured. "I was drunk."

His head fell back as a loud laugh escaped him. He hadn't expected that response. When he looked at her again, he was pleased to see a small smile hovering over her lips.

"Trust me, you were brilliant." He caught her self-deprecating eye roll and added, "You convinced me to buy this place, didn't you?"

Her head shot up and her eyes narrowed on him. "Now who's lying?"

Laughing softly, he admitted, "Okay, maybe it wasn't entirely your sales pitch. But you and your enthusiasm for classic films did get me thinking." That much was true. He'd already committed to donating to the cause, at the very least, after that night. And the theater wouldn't have been so high on his priority list that fateful day at his father's office if he hadn't been so hung up on his Veronica Lake mystery woman.

With the mood between them infinitely less tense, he laid it out for her. "Look, I'm taking a gamble on this theater. If it were just my money going into this, it would be one thing, but I've invested in the property through my family's company, and there's quite a bit of pressure on me to make it a success."

He could no longer see her eyes, as she'd tipped her head back down, but her posture was tense, and he knew she was paying close attention.

"The theater doesn't bring in enough money to warrant me hiring an employee who will be the spokesperson for the theater, but that is exactly what I need."

That had her looking up, and now her eyes were wide with fear. He was tempted to take it all back and pull her into his arms, assuring her he wouldn't pressure her. But she was his employee, dammit, and he'd seen her play the role he needed her to play. It wasn't like he was asking her to sell her body to turn a profit; he was merely asking her to be the face of the organization.

"I'll do my part, obviously," he added. "But I have other obligations and can't make the theater and its success my only priority."

She nodded slowly, and he smiled in relief. "Is that a yes? You'll be the face of the company?"

Her big eyes grew even bigger. "No! I mean, that's not what I meant when I nodded. I just meant..." She shrugged, and her voice faltered. "I meant, I understand your predicament."

His smile faded. Hell, he didn't want to have to threaten her job, but that was exactly what he was going to do. This was business, after all. He had a point to prove to his father, and even if he didn't, Gregory Blanchard never did anything in half measures. If he put his name behind this theater, he was sure as hell going to make sure it was a success. "This theater can't afford to hire someone new," he said again. Before he could finish, she beat him to it.

"I understand. If I won't do it, you'll replace me with someone who can."

His silence was answer enough. Shit, he didn't want to be the bad guy here. This was not how it was supposed to go.

* * * *

That had not gone as planned. Not that she could ever have planned for her theater to be bought by her former crush and current... Well, current *crush*, she supposed. It was humiliating, but it was the truth. His presence still had the exact same effect on her that it had had when she was a teenager. It turned her into an addlebrained moron. And one who blushed way too easily. It was just as bad as the last time she'd seen him when she was sixteen. Maybe even worse, because she couldn't act on it or even allow herself to daydream that her fantasies would come to life.

"So how did you leave things with him?" Marc was sitting next to her at Cagney's, and they each cradled a hot toddy as they watched Jake work. Meg leaned across the bar from her, and Caitlyn leaned against the bar beside Marc.

Alice was supposed to join them so the whole volunteer crew could hear about the new owner and his plans for the theater. Meg's younger sister was running late again, as usual, and Meg said they could go ahead without her since she'd been acting weird lately over some guy.

The rest of the crew had listened attentively as she'd told them about her run-in with Gregory.

Now, though, everyone wanted to know what she'd tell Gregory. She'd told him she'd think about it even though every instinct told her to run screaming in the opposite direction. Working with Gregory would be bad enough, but to go public and let herself be the face of the theater, as he'd put it? Disaster waiting to happen.

"What does he mean by 'face of the theater'?" Caitlyn asked.

She sighed. "He wants me to go to social functions with him and talk up the theater. Give some history and a pitch on why film preservation is important." In theory, it sounded like a cushy gig. In reality...what he was asking was her worst nightmare. Interacting with the general public was one thing. But when he said 'social functions,' she knew exactly what he meant. Whether he realized it or not, he was asking her to revisit a world she'd left behind.

"So he wants you to convince his friends and acquaintances to donate money?" Caitlyn guessed.

She shook her head. "Not exactly. He's hoping to turn the theater into a legitimate moneymaker." At their confused looks, she added, "Alice did too good a job with the gala. He saw the potential of this place and he wants to exploit it by expanding the services that the theater offers—"

"Ugh, he doesn't want to show current movies, does he?" Meg asked.

"No." There was an audible sigh of relief amongst her friends. They were all purists in that sense. Classic film deserved to have a dedicated theater. She cleared her throat and told them the rest. "But he does want to use the space for events, screenings, that sort of thing."

Caitlyn pursed her lips. "He wants to make it trendy, doesn't he?"

Tamara nodded. That was the gist of it. She didn't want to delve into just how he intended to do that. To her it was obvious; he planned on tapping in to his influential circle. The movers and the shakers of Manhattan— though he hadn't called them that. Where Gregory Blanchard went, press followed. Where the Blanchards were, so were the rest of the elite. He was hoping to cash in on his name and his crowd to make their little world hip.

Marc laughed. "Why do you have to make 'trendy' sound so horrible, Cait?"

As her friends teased one another about who was more of an old lady— Caitlyn with her knitting store or Meg with her new urge to nest—Tamara quietly panicked. The urge to drown the problem with another cocktail was tempting, but drinking too much was part of the reason she was in this mess in the first place. She sure as hell couldn't show up at his office drunk, much as she'd like to. And she had to go—he'd given her forty-eight hours to decide, and her time was nearly up.

Her heart was aching, and much as she wanted to talk to her friends about it, she couldn't. Marc had tried to talk her into the role last night as they'd watched TV on the couch together. But even then, she'd kept her

mouth shut. It wasn't that she didn't trust Marc or the others; it was just...
embarrassing. She didn't want them to see her differently. And finding out
she'd been committed to a mental facility? That had a tendency to change
the way people saw her.

She hated the idea of explaining the surrounding circumstances,
defending herself like she was some sort of criminal on trial. Even her
parents hadn't believed her side of the story. How could she expect
anyone else to?

After the institution she'd spent a miserable few weeks back at her
parents' place attempting to pretend nothing had happened, pretending
she didn't hear the whispers from her former friends or the embarrassment
in her parents' voices when they had to explain why she was back, why
she'd left New York and all of her dreams of being a ballerina.

*I'm afraid the stress was too much for her*, she'd heard her mom say
in a hushed, apologetic tone. *We should have known better than to let her
go off on her own. She's always been sensitive, you know.*

She'd decided then and there that she'd needed a new start. Somewhere
where her ex's words weren't haunting her, where she wouldn't be a source
of shame to her family. Somewhere she could get her head on straight and
meet people who liked her for who she was. A place where she wouldn't
be judged or manipulated.

She wouldn't go back. She would rather lose her job at the theater than
go back to the world she'd left behind. She'd come too far to go back now.
And even if she wanted to, how could she? Too much time had passed. Her
family would never forgive her even if she wanted to return to their world.

Tears threatened to spill, and the effort to hold them back had her throat
aching and her head pounding.

*This was her home now; she couldn't just walk away. Not again.*

But what other choice did she have? That plaintive inner voice had to
be silenced. Ruthlessly, she forced herself to face facts. She'd gone six
years without seeing her family or the people she'd considered friends
once upon a time. If she did as Gregory asked, she'd be forced to reenter
that world. She couldn't do it.

*Coward.*

But it wasn't just that. She had to think about the theater and its future. If
she became the face of The Ellen and the people Gregory wanted to impress
remembered her—and they would—the theater would be tainted by her
history just as surely as she was. No, it was better that she walk away now.

She watched her friends laughing and chatting and tried not to get too
maudlin. It wasn't like they'd disown her if she stopped working at The

Ellen. But who knew if her replacement would continue Operation Petticoat on Saturday mornings, and what if she wasn't welcome—

"So what are you going to do?" Jake had taken a break from his customers and joined them, interrupting the conversation and drawing all attention back to her and her dilemma.

Marc seemed to see her answer written all over her face. "Nooo," he wailed. "Please tell me you're not going to wuss out just because he wants you to talk to people."

She swallowed down a bitter retort. It wasn't like she *wanted* to say no. But anything she said would open the door for questions. Judging by the way Marc was watching her, she figured she'd already be in the hot seat when she got home that night. But for now...

She pushed her stool back and started donning her winter coat and scarf. "I'm sorry." She didn't trust herself to look up at her friends as she said it. Their answering silence made her guilt intensify. She was letting them down. But it was better this way. Or it would be better in the long run.

She had to believe that; it was the only way she could bring herself to do what needed to be done.

* * * *

Gregory had given her the location of his office at Blanchard Group headquarters, which was housed in one of the many high-rises in Midtown. It had been ages since she'd been anywhere so posh and corporate looking— she'd gotten used to working in a run-down theater where the dress code was typically an oversized sweatshirt. Riding up in the noiseless elevator, watching the numbers fly by, she was painfully aware of how underdressed she was with her knee-high winter boots, jeans, and heavy but unfashionable winter coat.

Everyone around her was dressed to perfection in pencil skirts and suits. Fidgeting with the strap of her messenger bag, she reminded herself that she wasn't here to look good. There was no one to impress. She was merely here to quit her job. Which she loved.

Another round of tears had her swallowing thickly. It wouldn't be the first time she had to start a new life. At least this time she had Marc and the others at her side. They'd forgive her for leaving the theater, that much she knew.

The doors opened on floor thirty-one, and Tamara entered through thick wooden double doors to find herself in the pristine lobby of The Blanchard Group with a view that rivaled the top of the Empire State Building.

She was vaguely aware of a perfectly coifed blonde heading toward her with a bright smile but couldn't tear her eyes away from the view. God, how did anyone get any work done here with this view?

"Can I help you?" the blonde asked.

"I'm Tamara Pierce. I'm here to see Gregory Blanchard."

If the blonde thought it odd that an unkempt woman who looked like she came from the wrong side of the tracks was here to see the billionaire playboy, she didn't let on. She merely tilted her head in acknowledgement and told Tamara to follow her.

She should have left bread crumbs. The woman led her through a maze of hallways before stopping in front of a corner office. Of course the heir apparent had a corner office. The blonde knocked once before opening the door and gesturing for her to go in. No sooner had she stepped foot in the office than the blonde shut the door behind her. Gregory's head was down, and the door's soft click made her jump.

Crap, what was she going to say? Inexplicable nerves made her mouth dry, and for a moment she stood there gawking at the top of his head. She'd had it all planned out, but now those words had scattered and she couldn't think of anything, let alone a coherent sentence to explain herself.

Then he looked up, which didn't help matters. This conversation would have been difficult with anyone, but that it had to be with Gregory, of all people? Sometimes life just wasn't fair.

*As if that was news.*

He smiled and shut his laptop, leaning back in his seat looking quite pleased with himself. Her stomach clenched painfully. He must have thought she'd come to accept the position. She shifted in place, clasping her hands in front of her, and watched as his expression shifted. The smile fell a bit, and he crossed his arms over his chest. "You're turning me down."

It wasn't a question, but she nodded anyway.

"Why?"

Her throat closed up. God, he made her too nervous to breathe. She cleared her throat and tried to remember the speech she'd prepared. "I don't think it would be in The Ellen's best interests—"

"Bullshit."

She blinked in shock. "Excuse me?"

"This isn't about the theater; this is about you." He pushed his chair back and stood. Had he always been so tall? Had his shoulders always been so broad? She didn't remember ever thinking he filled up an entire room the way he did as he stalked toward her.

He came to a stop a foot in front of her—close enough for the conversation to feel suddenly intimate but not near enough to be intimidating. There was no reason for her to feel this rush of nerves that bordered on terror.

"What are you so afraid of?" His voice was low and his gaze intent, as if he was trying to read something in her eyes.

She looked down at the floor. "Nothing." *Everything.* She couldn't stand his stare any longer. "It's just that I'm not the right person for this position. I'm not what you need."

"You are exactly what I need." His words seem to hang in the air between them. She couldn't stop staring at her feet, as if her boots might be able to explain why that phrase hit her so deeply. The simple sentence echoed through her even as she told herself he didn't mean it like that. Clearly, he hadn't meant to imply—

"Oh hell."

His low growl had her looking up, the shock of the guttural sound enough to break her boot fixation. She shouldn't have looked up. He was closer now, and his gaze had gone from intent to predatory.

When he was so close she could barely breathe, she managed to whisper, "What are you doing?"

"What I wanted to do that first night I met you before you ran away from me." His voice was a growl, and it sent shivers racing through her. "What I couldn't do yesterday when you were still my employee. But now…"

She found herself holding her breath and forced herself to exhale. "Now?"

His answer came in the form of a kiss. Hot and possessive, his lips moved over hers insistently. This was nothing like the gentle, sweet kiss at the theater. This was everything that kiss had hinted at—it was the fulfillment of that promise. This kiss was hard, demanding, filled with passion. The shock of it had her brain going blank, and then sensations took over. Blissful, hot, sweet, and torturous all at once. A craving she hadn't known she'd harbored was unleashed with that kiss, and the onslaught of desire made her incapable of doing anything other than surrendering.

In one heartbeat she'd gone from passive victim of the kiss to passionate participant. Her lips clashed with his. Their tongues tangled. His arms wrapped around her waist, pulling her tight, just as she slipped her hands into the hair at the nape of his neck, holding him close.

His body was hot and hard against hers, and for the briefest of moments, it didn't matter who she was or that he was a blast from her past. The only thing that mattered was that this kiss was devastating in its intensity, washing away her history and making her new again. She was in the moment, and the moment was everything.

Until a cough came from the doorway behind her.

They both froze before pulling apart slowly. Gregory kept his hands on her waist, a reassuring touch even as blood rushed to her cheeks. *What had she done?*

But there was no time to go down that rabbit hole, not when someone had witnessed her lapse of sanity. Someone who worked for The Blanchard Group, clearly.

"So sorry to interrupt, son," the voice from the doorway said.

*Son.* Her stomach pitched and rolled. She knew that voice. It was a voice that used to intimidate the hell out of her when he'd come over for dinner parties and bridge night. It couldn't be… But even as she tried to tell herself she was being paranoid, the rational part of her brain reminded her that he'd called Gregory "son."

Oh hell. This was Gregory's father—one of her parents' best friends and the man who could ruin everything. Panic had blood roaring past her ears, making it difficult to hear. Oh God, the rush of blood was making her lightheaded. *Don't you dare faint.*

"No, clearly you're not interrupting anything." Gregory's voice dripped with sarcasm. To her horror, he took a step away from her, and she heard his father walk into the office. Seconds later he was standing next to them.

She forced herself to focus on her breathing. Passing out in the middle of Gregory's office would not help matters. She needed to focus. Concentrate. She had to get out of here before he recognized her.

"Aren't you going to introduce me to your new *friend*?" He'd addressed the question to Gregory, but he turned to her, and Tamara resisted the urge to look him in the face. It had been years since Gregory's father had visited her family home…. Or at least years since she'd been there to help entertain him and his wife. If she walked away quickly, she could escape without being recognized. *Move. Move now.*

She started to turn, but his voice stopped her cold.

"Tammy?" His tone was incredulous. "Why Tammy Vanguard, what a pleasure to see you again."

# Chapter 5

Gregory watched in horrified fascination as Tamara—*his* Tamara, as he'd come to think of her for some unknown reason—blanched at the use of that name. *That name.* He recognized it, but he couldn't jar loose the connection.

But clearly his father knew the name...and her. That fact made him blind with rage. She was his, not his father's. But that was ridiculous. She didn't belong to either of them, and he certainly wouldn't stand by and watch her squirm in misery under his father's cold, watchful gaze. Not even knowing what he was doing or why, he interceded on her behalf once it became abundantly clear that she was frozen silent at the mention of her name. Her real name, apparently.

"Father, Tamara was just on her way out. If you'll excuse us." Grabbing Tamara by the elbow, he led her out of the office, trying not to wonder at her icy rigidity or the sudden change in her demeanor.

At the doorway, he let her go and she finally broke out of her silence to look up at him with impossibly wide eyes brimming with tears. "Thank you. And I-I'm sorry."

With that she turned and fled, her big winter coat disappearing around a corner—the wrong corner, he dimly noted. Hopefully one of his colleagues would find her and lead her back to the elevator. In the meantime, he had a father to contend with.

He turned slowly, taking a moment to swallow the bitter emotions that always threatened to cloud his judgment when his father was around, and especially so today. It killed him that his father knew more about his mystery woman than he did.

"Well done, son. You've gone from melodramatic arm candy straight to the insane asylum."

The rush of blood to his head had Gregory quite literally seeing red. He'd gotten used to the jabs his father took at the women in his life. His father was of the mindset that Gregory, as usual, failed in his love life as he did everything else. The older man's complaint, which covered all of his failures, it seemed, was that his son was too emotional. Not rational enough and definitely not level-headed or committed. In short, he was his mother's son—destined to disappoint, at best. At worst, he was doomed to hurt the ones he loved.

In business, his father saw this as a danger. His tendency to follow his gut rather than the spreadsheet was a constant source of concern. And in his private life, his father saw his tendency to date women based on something so crass as attraction and passion as even more of a danger. Not necessarily to the company's bottom line, but to something even more precious, if that was possible—the family name.

From the time he was old enough to speak, the monumental significance that was "the family name" had been drilled into him. It went without saying that his mother had tarnished the name. And the family name was certainly not honored when he tainted its pristine image by associating with women of a lesser caliber.

In short, his family was a bunch of snobs and his father was the worst of them. He still believed in ancient notions of good blood and marrying for breeding rights as if they were aristocracy and not just stinking rich.

So yes, he was used to his father's insults when it came to the women in his life—and to be honest, he sometimes wondered if that wasn't what drew him to the women he dated. They were almost always loud and vulgar to some extent. Famous and beautiful, yes, but they were miles away from the blue-blooded proper maidens his father paraded past him at family functions.

He'd grown almost immune to his father's insults on that front. Except for today. Except for Tamara...and she wasn't even his girlfriend.

"Don't talk about her like that," he snapped. He cursed himself for it a moment later as his father's grin turned cold and knowing. Shit, he'd shown his hand to his opponent as if this were their first go-round and not their millionth showdown.

"You don't remember her, do you?"

*Vanguard.* The last name clicked. Memories of a giant house in the Hamptons. A family just as dysfunctional as his. Christmas parties, family dinners. They were friends of his parents. He'd hung out with their son, John, at the obligatory social functions. A fun kid who'd liked to party and hit on girls. And the Vanguards had a daughter. John's little sister. A quiet girl who'd clung to her parents' shadow rather than go off to parties with her brother and his friends.

*Tammy.*

He had a vague idea that there'd been rumors around her, but for the life of him he couldn't remember what they were. He and John hadn't been close friends, and they didn't keep in touch after John was sent off to some boarding school in the Alps. By the time whatever scandal had occurred, he'd been off to college, out of his parents' grip, and had wanted nothing to do with their social circle, let alone their gossip.

He racked his brain to remember something. Anything. The fact that his father knew more about her than he did was infuriating.

"It was a shame, really," his father said, shaking his head in a blatantly phony display of empathy. "She was such a sweet girl. You never would have thought that she'd be so..."

What? Be so *what*? But he wouldn't give his father the satisfaction.

"I wonder if her parents know she's here," his father continued. He walked over to the liquor cabinet and helped himself to a drink. "They were worried sick when she ran away. Mortified, really."

He noted with a heavy dose of black humor that his father seemed to think being worried and mortified were one and the same. If her parents were anything like his father, "worried" was a nice way of saying that whatever she'd done, they'd been embarrassed by it.

It was just now starting to register that she'd used a different name. Tammy Vanguard had run away? Why?

He could break down and ask his father to explain—it would give his father pleasure, which was annoying, but his curiosity would be satisfied.

Or he could ask her himself.

Without pausing to think it through, he walked away from his father, out of his office, and went after his mystery woman...who was turning out to be more of a mystery with every passing minute.

\* \* \* \*

One of the perks of working at a movie theater was that Tamara could escape into an old movie whenever she needed to. For now, at least.

As she curled up in one of the seats, alone in the dark theater, she realized it might be the last time she could indulge herself with a private screening. She threw some M&Ms into her mouth to keep from crying.

She had a feeling there would be a lot of tears in the days to come; she could hold off for a little while. Let herself pretend she really did live in the black-and-white world where every story had a beginning, a middle, and an end. Where it all made sense and where it all came together in a satisfying conclusion.

*The Ghost and Mrs. Muir* may not have been the best pick. It was one of her favorites, but right now it was too romantic. She didn't want to think about love or romance or fate. She should have gone with something far more cynical. *Double Indemnity,* maybe.

The door to the theater opened and closed behind her, and she braced herself for Marc's line of questioning. She hadn't responded to his handful of texts since leaving Cagney's earlier that day, and he was the only one who knew where to find her when she wanted to be alone.

He didn't seem to understand that being alone meant he was not welcome. Or rather, he did understand, but he ignored the silent message. Probably for the best. More often than not, his forced conversations made her feel better. Less lonely, at least.

"I'm more of a film noir guy myself."

She sat upright with a start at the sound of Gregory's voice in the row behind her. "What are you doing here?" Turning in her seat, she found him settling into a seat behind her and to her left, stretching his legs out in front of him.

"I own the place, remember?"

Right. Crap. So many emotions threatened to overwhelm her that she couldn't speak. Humiliation seemed to be leading the pack. He knew who she was and had most likely heard all of the rumors. Anger, at herself mainly. She should never have tempted fate by flirting with Gregory or even contemplating going to work for him. But it was helplessness that had her hands shaking, and she clutched her candy tighter. *What would she do now?*

Gregory was staring at the screen as if he'd just dropped by to catch a film. "I wouldn't have pegged you for such a romantic," he said.

She looked from the screen and back to him. "I guess I'm just full of surprises."

He looked at her and let out an appreciative laugh. "I guess you are. *Tammy.*"

Flinching at the sound of her own name, she turned back to look at the screen. "Look, I know I don't technically work for you anymore, but I have to clean out my office, so I figured it would be all right if I watched one last film."

He was silent for a moment. "Do you really believe I came here to get your keys from you?"

His voice, low and knowing, felt intimate in the theater's darkness. She heard him move, and seconds later he was in her row, sitting next to her. Risking a glance at him, she inhaled sharply. He looked hot in everyday life, but the flickering light from the screen seemed to exacerbate the sharp angles of his face, and his eyes were unfathomably dark as he watched her.

"What do you want from me?" There, she'd asked the question nagging at her. Surely by now he knew who she was...and if he hadn't heard all the rumors, he must at least know the most damning one. The rumor that had sent her running. She was unstable, crazy even. She flinched in the darkness. *Crazy.* She'd always hated that word. It was how Billy had described her, not how she'd felt. That was one thing she'd learned at the institution. She wasn't crazy, and neither were any of the other patients. She and everyone else there just had issues they'd needed to address. Getting that kind of help had been the sanest thing she'd done in years. It was there that she'd figured out the truth and seen her relationship for what it had been—abusive.

Still, the gossips didn't care about the reality. They just liked a juicy story, and labeling one of society's preppy little debutantes "crazy" had apparently been too good to pass up.

"I'd like to know the truth."

*Ah, the truth.* He made it sound so simple.

"I'm sure your father would be happy to fill you in." She tried to keep her tone steady, but some of the age-old bitterness seeped in.

"The truth," he repeated. "Not rumors."

That distinction—the fact that he was actually willing to hear her version and not just believe whatever gossip still swirled about—that made her respect for Gregory skyrocket. Some pressure in her chest loosened—just slightly, but after so many years she suddenly felt like she could breathe.

"You don't have to tell me, obviously," he continued. And honest to God, he sounded bored by it all. Tamara bit her bottom lip to keep from laughing at that. Here she was so caught up in her old drama, it had never occurred to her that this man might not even take an interest.

They'd shared a couple of kisses and toyed with the idea of working together—not exactly a meaningful relationship. She didn't mean enough to him for him to care about her sordid past.

That should be a relief. And it was. Sort of.

When she remained silent, he said, "I remember you, you know."

She'd been staring at the screen, but those words had her looking over in disbelief. "Liar."

He laughed. "I didn't recognize you at first, obviously, but once my father jogged my memory, some of it came back. The quiet daughter of my parents' friends. She would tag along at the beach sometimes but was too shy to play along."

"Mmm," she said. "That sounds like me."

He continued softly, his voice hypnotic. "A dutiful daughter, if memory serves. I have a hazy memory of a little Goody Two-shoes. Good grades, perfect manners... A dancer, wasn't she?"

"A ballerina," she said softly. She was surprised to find the corners of her lips tugging up into a smile as the memory of dancing took hold. She hadn't allowed herself to remember her dancing career in far too long. To hear her former self talked about like this—in the third person, like she was a distant memory—it was oddly cathartic. Because that girl *was* a distant memory. It all felt like a lifetime ago now that they were sitting here at The Ellen. They were two adults now.

The chemistry she'd felt between them at the party—that electric energy that made her frighteningly aware of his body next to hers—it was back. A physical presence that hung between them in the darkness of the theater.

Or maybe it was just her.... All she knew was her heart was pounding and she was achingly aware of his arm brushing hers. Of his quiet, steady breathing in the silence between the film's dialogue.

Despite the fact that her worst fears had just come true—she'd been discovered and she'd lost her home at the theater—all she could think about was his kiss. Thank God for the dark of the theater, because her cheeks were on fire, along with the rest of her body.

As if reading her mind, he reached across the armrest and took hold of her hand. It wasn't a sexual gesture, but try telling her body that. Aching awareness had heat pooling between her thighs, her body aching for his touch with a desperation she'd grown so accustomed to that it was the norm. But with one kiss, one touch, this man had made her realize how lonely she'd been all these years.

"You don't need to tell me what happened back then," he said again. She forced herself to listen despite her fiercely racing heart. "But the woman I met the other night... It would be a shame if she walked away from this place she loves over rumors and scandals that happened a lifetime ago."

"It was six years," she whispered.

His laugh was deep and seductive. "That's a lifetime in gossip years, trust me."

She wanted to trust him. There was a part of her that wanted that to be the truth. Maybe no one cared anymore. And with that thought, a flood of other hopes reared their heads. Like maybe she wouldn't have to leave The Ellen after all. And maybe she didn't need to hide herself away in fear. And maybe the fact that Gregory's father recognized her wouldn't lead to yet another scandal.

She found herself asking the question again because as much as she wanted to hope, years of distrust were hard to shake. "What do you want from me?"

"Say you'll work with me," he said. Maybe it was her imagination, but the husky voice and the dark lighting made his words seductive, in more ways than one. They made her want to close the distance and continue that kiss. They also made her want to say yes—to being his partner and to being the face of The Ellen.

"Say you'll put the past behind you and come work with me, for The Ellen. This theater needs your passion and your knowledge."

She turned to look at him, but all she could catch was the outline of his profile as he stared up at the screen. His words were tempting. So tempting…

"Don't let a bunch of nosy old gossips like my father come between you and your dream."

*Not my dream—my home.* But she didn't correct him. She'd walked away from her dreams of dancing professionally years ago. *They'd* done that to her. Her parents and their little world. But mainly her ex. They'd stolen her dream a long time ago. Or maybe she'd let it go too easily. Maybe she should have fought harder.

But now it was her home that they threatened to take away from her— if she let them.

She couldn't let them have her home on top of everything else she'd lost.

Taking a deep breath, she squeezed his hand in the dark. "Okay. I'll do it."

# Chapter 6

*What had he done?* Gregory blinked in the daylight, absurdly bright after the dark theater. He'd left Tamara there with her thoughts, but leaving had been torture. Her hand in his had been slight and cool, nearly impossible to release. And she'd been so close. Close enough for another kiss, surely.

But now she was off-limits.

He supposed he should feel proud of himself for talking her into staying. But the truth was, as glad as he was to have her working for The Ellen, he was pissed as hell to have her working for him.

There was no way he would abuse his position as her employer by kissing her again, much as he might like to.

*Goddamn moral high ground.*

Still, he should be glad he'd gotten through to her. And he *was* glad, he told himself. It would have been a shame if his father and his friends kept that remarkable woman from working for a cause she was clearly passionate about.

Passionate, that word described her to a T. She buried it beneath a well-constructed armor of quiet anonymity. Seeing her at the costume gala was like watching a swan fit in amongst a flock of ducks. Tamara was unique and vibrant…. When she chose to be. Or, more often than not, when her guard slipped and he caught a glimpse of the real woman. The mystery woman, as he still thought of her.

But despite his noble thoughts that afternoon, he couldn't deny that curiosity still plagued him. He'd set out to ask her for the truth, but when push came to shove, he hadn't been able to force the issue. She'd looked too vulnerable and had seemed too relieved when he'd let the topic drop.

Which was why, when he met his stepmother for their weekly dinner that evening at her favorite restaurant on the Upper East Side, he didn't wait till the main course to dive into the subject he wanted to hear about.

"Ah," she sang softly, her French accent barely there after so many years of living in the United States but adding a hint of the exotic to her speech. "I was wondering when you would bring up the lovely Ms. Vanguard."

He sank back into his seat. "He already told you, didn't he?"

Since Gregory had reached puberty, he and his father had been engaged in one battle or another. His stepmother, who'd married his father after his mother walked out on them when he was a toddler, somehow managed to be Switzerland throughout it all. He shouldn't have been surprised that she nodded as she took a sip of her wine. "Of course, dear. It's not every day your father walks in on you canoodling in the office." Her brows arched over the rim of her glass. "And with the Vanguard girl, no less."

He bit back the urge to badmouth his father. If his efforts to sway his stepmother to his side of their little war hadn't worked thus far, no amount of whining about his father's gloating about Tamara would sway her.

"Just tell me her story, Elena."

Her smile was smug—she loved nothing more than to be in the know when it came to gossip. Even if that gossip was nearly a decade old. "It all started with that boyfriend of hers," she said. "Little Tammy left her parents' home in Boston to attend a ballet academy." She set her glass down. "She was very talented, you know."

Gregory struggled not to let his impatience show. "I'm sure 'little Tammy' was wonderful."

His stepmother continued as if he hadn't spoken. "Tammy fell in love. That Braden boy. You remember him, don't you?"

Yet again, the name sounded familiar, but he couldn't place it. His parents had far too many friends.

"He was in the grade below you," his stepmother added.

*Billy Braden.* There it was. Recognition was followed by disgust. "She dated Billy?" Billy had been an asshole back in high school. A bully and a kiss-up, the worst possible combination, as far as he was concerned.

His stepmother made a noise of agreement. "He was never a gentleman," she said with a sniff.

Gregory almost laughed out loud. "Never a gentleman" was putting it mildly. "So, she was dating *Billy Braden.*" He said the name with all the disgust he felt and gestured for her to continue.

His stepmother shrugged gracefully. "All I know is what I heard from her mother, you understand. But it seems Tammy couldn't handle life in the city on her own. Billy tried to help, it seemed, but it was no use."

The vagueness of her story was nearly as annoying as the idea of Billy being the one there to help Tamara when she was having a rough time. "That's all? She had a tough time transitioning to living in the city? She was what...eighteen or so? That doesn't seem all that outrageous."

His stepmother's eyes widened. "Oh, but it got so much worse. Her parents were rather vague on the details, understandably, but it seems Tammy spiraled dreadfully."

"Spiraled how?" He was speaking through gritted teeth, partially because he hated imagining Tamara in such dire straits but also because the longer this conversation went on, the more he hated himself for participating in it. Hadn't he told her he didn't care about the rumors?

And he didn't. Not really. But how could he defend her if he didn't know the accusations?

Still, that line of reasoning didn't altogether alleviate his guilt.

His stepmother raised her glass and resumed drinking. "They were rather stingy with the details, but I still say her family overreacted when they had her committed."

He nearly spit out his whiskey. "They had her...what?"

Elena nodded with a sigh. "I adore her parents, you know that, but I have to say, her tragic downfall was most likely their fault as much as anything else. She was always so sheltered. They were overprotective to the extreme. Was it any wonder she couldn't make it on her own?"

He'd stopped listening after the "committed" part. "Where was she committed? For how long?"

And there Elena grew intensely unhelpful. "I don't know, dear. The Vanguards were awfully tight-lipped on the subject. It was embarrassing for them, as you can imagine."

He bit his tongue at that. *Yes, how terribly embarrassing to have a daughter in pain.* "Then what happened? Did she get the help she needed?"

Elena sighed again, this time louder and more dramatic. "That's what was so very sad. After she was released, she disappeared. Ran away."

Hence the new name and the job at the theater. The pieces fell into place there, at least. But the rest of it... He hated himself more than ever for listening to rumors rather than letting her explain eventually, if she trusted him enough.

Until then, it was none of his business. He was just her employer.

His mind flashed on that kiss—the one that had turned his life upside down in the course of minutes. Hell, even that first chaste kiss at the theater had thrown him for a loop. He hadn't been able to stop thinking about her since. And then he'd had to go and kiss her again in his office—a true kiss this time. That had been the real kicker. For a man who'd kissed as many women as he had, that kiss might as well have been his first. Nothing else came close.

With one kiss he'd experienced the kind of all-consuming fire he'd only read about. The kind of passion people wrote poetry about, sang songs to honor.

And now he was just her employer.

*Just her employer. Who did he think he was kidding?*

The waiter refilling her wine glass briefly distracted Elena, but once he left, she returned to the topic with a shake of her head. "The whole thing was blown out of proportion, if you ask me. But you know how gossip works. One whiff of a scandal, especially within a family as spotless as the Vanguards, and a feeding frenzy begins."

"Sounds like you have a soft spot for Tamara," he said.

She nodded, but her eyes narrowed with suspicion. "Why do I get the sense that you need something from me?"

"Because you know me too well." He grinned as she rolled her eyes.

"All right, out with it. What do you want?"

"I'd like you to help Tamara." Before she could reply, he hurried on, explaining her new position at the theater. "I need her help talking up the theater and its mission. I've heard her spiel myself and I think she'd be a natural if she could just get over her fears of returning to her parents' circle of friends."

Elena nodded slowly. "Are you sure she's ready? It would just be a matter of time before word spread to her family." She held her hands up in a helpless gesture. "She can't avoid them forever, much as she might want to."

"How she handles her family is up to her, but I do think she's ready to come out of hiding." She just needed a nudge. Or a shove. He kept that part to himself. Elena was giving him enough questioning looks; he didn't need her wondering why he'd taken it upon himself to be Tamara's personal champion. He had a hard time explaining it to himself. If she weren't his employee, he'd say it was because he was developing feelings for her.

But she was his employee, so that excuse wouldn't fly. Better to avoid Elena's questions altogether and try not to take too close a look at his own motives while he was at it.

"So, will you help?" he asked. At Elena's raised brows, he continued, "You understand this world better than anyone. You know who she should talk to and can help pave the way."

"Ah," Elena said, her eyes flashing with mischievous laughter. "So you'd like me to be her fairy godmother, is that it? Help the prodigal princess return to the fold?"

He let out a huff of laughter at the mixed metaphor. "Yes, something like that."

"Of course, my dear. I'd be happy to help Tammy reinvent herself in the eyes of society."

Gregory resisted the urge to roll his eyes at her dramatic flair.

"We can start Friday night," she said. "Why don't you bring her along to our little Christmas gathering?"

He choked on laughter at her description. The annual Blanchard holiday party was anything but little. But it would be the perfect place for Tamara to start meeting the right people for their cause.

* * * *

Tamara paused with one fry hovering in front of her lips as Gregory informed her of Elena's plan. "So I'll be…"

"My date," Gregory finished. He took a bite of his burger, looking completely at ease with the fact that he was turning her world upside down over a casual working lunch at Cagney's.

Tamara clamped her mouth shut to keep from hyperventilating. Date. He wanted her to be his *date*. At a famed Blanchard holiday party. *Breathe, Tamara. In, out. In, out.*

She'd agreed to meet him to brainstorm ways they could get more funding and use the space to bring in more of a cash flow. Most of all, Gregory's plan seemed to hinge on changing the perception of the theater from a struggling relic to a trendy, retro taste of glamour.

Tamara had to admit that as a backdrop for the costume fundraiser, the theater had been easy to envision as a classy, elegant venue. A place where sophistication was still in style and people still dressed up for the theater. How to promote that image was the problem. Money and influence were the solutions, according to Gregory.

Specifically, money via patrons of the arts and influence via the city's best trendsetters.

Gregory had made it sound so easy as they'd made notes in the tiny office above the theater. But now, over lunch, she was beginning to see what a challenge this would be. And by challenge, she meant "mistake on a monumental scale." She couldn't do this. No way, no how.

Why the hell had she agreed to this?

"I remember the Blanchard holiday parties," she said. It was all she could think to say. She was trying too hard not to panic to think of anything more worthwhile to add to the conversation.

"You do?" His lips curved up in amusement, and she tried not to stare.

Of course she remembered. Her parents went every year, and up until she'd moved to New York, she'd joined them. "I remember your mother, too," she added.

"Stepmother," he corrected. "She's hard to forget." He was full-on smiling now, and it made his eyes glow with a warmth she felt to her core.

What she didn't add was that she remembered *him* at those parties. She could vividly recall watching him with whatever girlfriend he'd invited that year and trying not to be too jealous.

But that was ages ago, when he was just her crush. Now he was her boss. Big difference.

Sitting up a little taller, she forced herself to stay on task. She'd agreed to this, hadn't she? Now she had to suck it up and do her job. But that was so much easier said than done.

This party would be filled with the type of people her parents were friends with. What if word got back to her parents? The guilt she tried so hard to avoid nearly crippled her as a vision of her mother's face flashed in her mind. She wore the disappointed look Tamara remembered so well. She couldn't bring herself to think about what her mother's expression would be if she learned from one of her friends that her runaway daughter had not only surfaced but had shown up at one of her friend's parties.

She might have been angry with her parents—okay, maybe she was still angry when she thought of the way they'd betrayed her trust, taking Billy's word over her own. But that didn't mean she wanted to hurt them. At least, not any more than she already had.

She swallowed the sick taste of guilt, but a terrifying thought had her freezing in place. "What if my parents are there?"

He stopped eating and looked over at her, his eyes wide with surprise. "They won't be."

Panic had her clutching the edge of the table, her knuckles whitening as she struggled to remain calm. His word wasn't good enough. They went every year—at least they had when she'd still lived with them. If they were there…oh God, what would she say? How could she explain?

There was every possibility they didn't want to see her. She couldn't just surprise them at a holiday party after six long years.

Gregory was eyeing her warily.

She leaned over the table, hoping for some sort of reassurance that he would never be able to give. This man couldn't tell her if her parents hated her after the way she'd fled. She wasn't even sure she believed him that they definitely wouldn't be at the party. "How do you know they won't be there? They always go."

He resumed eating his fries as if they were discussing the weather and not the family she hadn't seen in six years. "They'll be in Florence with the Rutneys for the holidays, according to Elena."

"Oh." She should have felt relief, but instead her stomach was churning—a physical reaction that had a tendency to happen when topics she avoided like the plague reared their ugly heads and forced her to face her past.

She stared at the table and mindlessly toyed with her food, for lack of anything better to do. She tried not to focus on the fact that a relative stranger knew her parents' holiday plans when she did not. And now, knowing where they'd be and who they'd be with, it would be more painful than ever when she thought of them this holiday season. That first year after she'd left her family behind, she'd told herself it would get easier. And in some ways it had. She'd gotten better at shoving unwanted thoughts aside. She'd learned how to escape her thoughts through old movies and new friends. But in other ways, the longer she was away from her family, the harder it was. The distance between them seemed to grow exponentially. The things they should have talked about—the things she should have said—weighed on her, and the weight grew heavier with each passing year.

She should have talked to them before she'd left. That was her biggest regret. She'd been so hurt, so confused, so angry. Her ex was the one to blame—he'd been the one who'd worn away her confidence, manipulated her trust, and beaten her down with his emotional abuse.

Yet at the time, she'd been far more hurt by her parents' betrayal. At least that's how it had felt. She'd expected them to trust her and her judgment, not believe that sociopath of an ex. She'd hoped they'd support her and be strong on her behalf, but instead she saw their embarrassment and shame because their daughter had been drawn into scandal.

She'd prayed they would stand by her side and help her to sort through the mess that her life had become. But they hadn't. They'd shipped her off to a mental health facility where she'd known no one.

She forced herself to shove those thoughts into the sealed-off cave in the back of her mind. At this point it was ancient history. Except that it never seemed to truly go away.

Something else nagged at her. Gregory had talked to his stepmother about her. She did remember his stepmother—she'd always liked her. Elegant and kind, the woman had been good to Tamara when she was a girl. She tried not to think about what his stepmother had told him about her, but it was hard not to. Because as much as she'd like to think it was ancient history, people remembered. And people loved to talk. She had to imagine that Elena had filled Gregory in on more details. Maybe she'd heard Billy's version of events and had told Gregory that she'd cracked under the pressure of the big city. Or maybe she'd told him how she'd run away from her family without a word.

"Hey, are you okay?"

She was surprised to look up and find him leaning over the table, his hand reaching out, almost as if he was going to grasp hers, but he stopped short. The concern in his eyes made her heart squeeze. Here was a guy who knew about her past—or enough rumors, at least, to get the gist—and he was not only still here, he was helping her. Supporting her. Hell, he was practically holding her hand through it all.

Which made the words that much more difficult to get out. "I'm sorry."

His brows drew together in confusion. "Sorry for what?"

She shook her head. "I can't. I just can't."

Understanding filled his gaze, and she looked away before she could see his disappointment in her. It was too similar to the look in her parents' eyes when they'd made excuses for her to their friends. She couldn't stand to think about that look, let alone see it in Gregory's eyes. "I know I said I could do this—be the face of the theater. And I will, I promise. But I need some time."

His silence lasted so long that she finally looked up to see his reaction. To her surprise, a hint of a smile played on his lips as he watched her. There was no hint of the disappointment she'd been so afraid of seeing.

"We'll see," he said. Reaching out a hand, he brushed back a strand of her hair, and she shivered at the intimate contact.

"We'll see?" she repeated.

"We've got a little time, and I think I can change your mind."

He was serious, she realized. Whatever it was he had planned, he seemed confident that he'd be a success. But why? He was going to so much trouble when most people in his position would have given her up as a hopeless cause on day one. His attention was sweet and humbling at the same time.

"Why?" It came out unbidden, but once it was out there she found she needed to hear his answer.

"Why what?" Some of the concern faded, and he was grinning at her now in amusement.

She cleared her throat. "Why are you helping me like this?"

His smile broadened and he shook his head. "I told you, I need your help."

"But why? Why do you even care about this theater in the first place? And why do you care that it's a success? And why do you care that it remains true to its original purpose? And why..." *Why do you care about me?*

She let her words trail off before she said too much. He leaned back in his seat. "Contrary to popular opinion, I do care about things other than making money and dating TV stars."

Tamara felt heat rising in her cheeks. She was still mortified at the way she'd devoured all the gossip on his latest romance. "I didn't mean to imply—"

He held up a hand to stop her apology. "I know you didn't. To be honest, I was intrigued by the theater and its history after the fundraiser, and..."

She dropped her head to avoid meeting his gaze. Memories of that night still made her embarrassed. When he didn't continue, she looked up. "And?" she prompted.

He sighed. "Okay, I'll admit it. I may have bought the place to spite my father."

Tamara's mouth fell open. *Who the hell buys a theater as an act of vengeance?*

He laughed at her reaction. "Believe me, I know what a spoiled brat I sound like."

Laughter won out. "You really do."

He shrugged. "I can't help it. My father brings out the worst in me."

A memory rose of Gregory getting in trouble for taking his father's car out when he'd been told not to. "I remember that, too."

His eyes narrowed on her as he gave her a teasing smile. "That's some memory you have there."

She kept her mouth shut. Her ridiculous crush might have been ages ago, but it was still embarrassing to bring up now. Especially because he could take that to mean that she was still attracted to him.

*Which she was.*

Yeah, but he didn't have to know that. She wanted to ask him more—what his father had done this time to provoke him into buying a theater—but before she could, they were interrupted.

Ben and Caitlyn came through the front door and headed straight for them. "Well, look who we've got here," Ben said, sliding into the booth next to Tamara.

"It's everyone's favorite hero," Caitlyn finished, as she sat down next to Gregory and gave him a peck on the cheek.

Ben looked to Tamara. "I'd be jealous about that kiss if I wasn't tempted to kiss the man myself for swooping in and saving the theater from some developer's dastardly plans."

Tamara giggled at her new friend's over-the-top tone.

Gregory rolled his eyes at the praise. "Dastardly developer? You wouldn't be referring to yourself, now would you, Ben?"

Ben waved away the accusation. "Ancient history, my friend. Besides, you're the man of the hour now, don't try to be modest."

"It's true," Caitlyn said, leaning over to help herself to one of Tamara's fries. "Pushing the theater through the landmarks committee was help enough. No one expected you to actually *buy* the place."

He shrugged. "I just made a couple of calls."

Tamara bit her lip to keep from laughing. *Just a couple of calls.* He made it sound so easy. He made *everything* seem easy. With that cool confidence and natural charm, Gregory would never have run from his problems. He would never need to find power by manipulating the people around him. He would never exploit their weakness or make a woman his prey.

For the first time in a long time, Tamara found herself wondering "what if?" What if she hadn't met Billy all those years ago. What if Gregory had been her first boyfriend, like she'd always dreamed?

She shook her head and forced a smile as Ben and Gregory teased Caitlyn about Operation Petticoat. Their little ragtag group of volunteers wouldn't be needed for much longer if Gregory's plan was a success and they got the funds to restore the place properly.

"We'll still meet," Caitlyn said. "Won't we, Tam?"

Tamara forced away the melancholy "what if" thoughts and smiled at her friend. "Of course we will, we'll just have to skip over the gum-scraping and get right down to the fun part."

"Mmm," Caitlyn agreed. "We do like to have our post-work drinks." Her face brightened. "And no more early morning Saturdays!"

"Thank God," Ben groaned.

Caitlyn smacked his shoulder. "What are you moaning about? You've only been to one Operation Petticoat meet-up." Turning to Tamara, she added, "He's slept right through every other one."

"Exactly," Ben said. "Now I won't have to feel guilty about skipping the work part. I am still invited to drinks, right?"

"Not so fast, my lazy friend," Gregory said. "We won't be hiring more staff until the theater starts bringing in money. So for the time being…"

"Operation Petticoat is still in effect," Tamara finished for him.

Ben groaned as Caitlyn laughed. "We'll be there bright and early."

Ben turned to Gregory. "Does that mean you'll be part of the Saturday crew?"

Gregory shook his head. "Sorry, buddy, I'll be out of town on business this week."

Tamara looked down at her plate full of food and hoped her disappointment didn't show. He was her boss, nothing more. Even if the memory of that kiss made her lips tingle every time she thought about it. Which, it seemed, was every other second.

"We'll let you off the hook this time," Caitlyn said. "There should be more than enough of us to get the work done quickly."

"Yeah, and our ranks keep growing," Tamara added. At Caitlyn's questioning look, she explained, "Marc was going to see if Alex wanted to join."

Ben added, "And I wouldn't be surprised if Alice showed up with a date one of these days."

"Seriously?" Tamara asked.

Caitlyn nodded. "Sounds like things are heating up with her and that doctor."

Ben leaned over and donned a ridiculous old-timey accent. "So what about you, Tam-Tam. When are you going to bring a fella to the party?"

All eyes were on her—including Gregory's. *Please do not blush, please do not blush.* Too late. She felt the telltale heat creeping into her cheeks at the unwanted attention.

Caitlyn jumped in, probably thinking she was helping. Reaching across the table, she smacked Ben on the arm. "Don't be an idiot."

"Ow! What?" he whined as he rubbed his arm.

"You know Tamara doesn't date, and that's her prerogative. Leave her alone," Caitlyn scolded.

That led to another round of teasing bickering as Tamara tried to fade into the booth. But her attempt to become invisible didn't appear to work. She felt Gregory's gaze on her even before she looked up.

What must he think after that pronouncement? That she was a frigid freak, most likely. Or maybe that she was even more screwed up than he'd heard. Because, really, what grown woman didn't date?

*One who'd been burned by love.*

But not every guy was like Billy. And maybe, just maybe, she'd matured enough to know a good guy when she saw him. She'd been so young back then. So naive and gullible. But she'd learned her lesson, hadn't she?

She met Gregory's gaze, and her stomach quaked at the intensity of it. The memory of their kiss came back to her so quickly and vividly it took her breath away.

His smile was slow and seductive and meant just for her.

For one crazy moment she thought he must have read her mind. Or else his mind had wandered to the same place.

She gave her head a little shake and turned her attention back to her friends, forcing a smile though she had no idea what they were going on about.

Gregory was her boss, and even if he wasn't, he was out of her league. *And if he wasn't?*

The fluttering sensation in her chest was so foreign she almost didn't recognize it. How long had it been since she'd felt anything close to hope?

\* \* \* \*

It was late afternoon the following day when Gregory finally reached the end of the files Tamara had pulled for him.

She was sprawled on the floor opposite him in the tiny office above the theater as she had been all day. At some point, she'd thrown her hair up into a topknot that reminded him every time he glanced her way of the fact that she'd been a ballerina.

He could see her long, slender neck bent over a stack of papers, her brow furrowed in concentration. A few wisps of hair had escaped her bun and were hanging around her face, framing her delicate features.

His throat closed up for a moment with some unknown emotion. He couldn't place it, but it was overwhelming in its intensity. Some mix of yearning, regret, and hopefulness. All he knew was it was more emotion than he was used to dealing with, so he did what he did best—he focused on business.

"What did you do with last year's tax statement?"

Tamara pointed to a stack of papers to his left. Running a hand through his hair, he asked, "Did the former owner just not believe in computers or what?"

She shrugged, a hint of a smile tugging at her lips. "He was a bit of a technophobe."

"Wonderful."

Shifting so she was sitting upright across from him, she gave him a winning smile. "Don't worry, we'll get it all sorted soon enough. I'm sure you'll be able to turn this place around in no time."

Was she kidding? His father's cynical voice from their call that morning rang in his ears, and he stared at her for a long moment before realizing she was being serious. He found himself smiling back.

"I appreciate your confidence," he said. "But as the proud new owner of this delightfully dilapidated theater, I think I'm the one who's supposed to be giving pep talks to my team."

He looked around pointedly at the "team" of one, and she burst out laughing, a sound he wished he heard more often.

"The next pep talk is all yours, oh noble leader." Her grin was contagious, and for a brief moment he caught a glimpse of the young girl he'd once known—innocent, sweet, defenseless. Whatever had happened to her to make her so guarded and afraid—he wished he could go back in time and save her.

He nearly laughed out loud at the thought. Who the hell did he think he was? A knight in shining armor? If only his father knew what he was thinking. The shock would kill him. After a lifetime of telling him he didn't care enough, wasn't committed enough, wasn't good enough—he'd be stunned if he found out his only son had suddenly developed a hero complex.

He did laugh then—a short, humorless laugh filled with all the bitterness his father brought out in him. He should never have taken his call this morning; now his day was tainted by his voice.

Tamara's voice interrupted his dark thoughts. "What's so funny?"

He shook his head. "Nothing." When she didn't look away or change the topic, he told her a version of the truth. "I was just thinking about my father."

She tilted her head to the side. "What about him?"

How much did he remember about the old man? Or, more importantly, the way he'd always criticized him? It didn't matter. The past was the past.

Except one part of his past was here, watching him. Waiting patiently for him to explain.

"I was just thinking how hard my father would laugh if he could see us now." At her frown of confusion, he added, "See *me* now."

"Why?" Honest curiosity filled her eyes, and though he opened his mouth to make a flippant remark, he found herself telling her the truth.

"Because he thinks I can't commit to anything—namely women and business endeavors, but I'm pretty sure his assessment covers all aspects of life." He forced a smile to lighten the mood. "I bet he wouldn't even trust me to have a pet."

"But why?" she asked. "I thought you were really successful." He watched with amusement as color filled her cheeks at the blunt remark.

"I've done well for myself with the trust money I was given," he admitted—though it wasn't much of a secret. "But my father never fails to point out that my success was built on money I inherited. I didn't exactly build anything with my own two hands."

"Maybe not, but it's not your fault you were given an advantage. And the fact that you took that money and made it flourish says something. You could have just accepted the money and sat back and lived like a spoiled prince for the rest of your life."

Gregory found himself temporarily stunned by the compliment. When he realized he was grinning like an idiot, he gave his head a little shake and got back on topic. "I wish my father saw it that way."

"How does he see it?"

Yet again, he contemplated deflection. He could think of any number of quips to make light of the topic and move on to something else. But he found himself compelled to tell her the truth. It must be something in those eyes. They were too guileless and way too perceptive.

"The way I made my money was in quick turnovers and hedging bets."

"So?"

He ran a hand through already mussed hair. "So, these ways of making money are what my father likes to call 'fly-by-night.'"

Her lips quirked up in a half smile. "What does that mean?"

"That I'm flaky, shallow, unable to commit, can't see things through, not serious enough for real business, don't know the meaning of hard work—"

She cut him off as he recited his father's list of poor attributes. "And *are* you those things?"

The question was so simple, he laughed again. "No," he said slowly. No one had ever asked him what he thought on the subject. He barely asked himself anymore. "I think I have it in me to see things through, in relationships and in business."

She tilted her head to the side again, and he could practically feel her eyes searching his face. "So that's what this is about for you?"

For one moment he was so transfixed by the intensity of her gaze that he couldn't figure out what she was referring to. For a second there, he thought she was talking about her. About them. But that wouldn't make any sense—there was no "them." Maybe there had been a chance at some point but not any longer. And her next words confirmed she wasn't thinking about relationships but about The Ellen.

"You need to make this theater a success to prove to your father that you're serious," she said. It wasn't a question, just a statement of fact. And somehow when she put it like that, it sounded ridiculous. Juvenile. He was a grown man, for God's sake. Still, he couldn't deny it.

He gave her a short nod. "What do you think, Tamara? Do you think I have what it takes to see this through?" He'd meant it to sound teasing. He'd intended to lighten the mood. But the question came out far too serious, and he tensed as he waited for her answer.

Her smile eased the tension in his body, and warmth flooded him at her words. "Of course you can," she said. "I know you're capable of it—you always have been." Her eyes sparkled with laughter. "Maybe you just need the right project."

He couldn't bring himself to reply. His brain was too stunned by the thought that flashed through it, unbidden and unwelcome.

*Maybe I just need the right woman.*

# Chapter 7

Something in the air had shifted, Tamara would have sworn it. One minute they were talking about the Oompa Loompa's terrible filing system and the next they were sharing secrets. Well, he was sharing, at least.

There was a vulnerability in his eyes when he talked about his father that made her heart ache on his behalf. She remembered his father and the two of them together. It wasn't a stretch to imagine that his father pushed him too hard and was too critical. But to hear Gregory admit it was a different story.

*He was confiding in her.* The knowledge was heady and endearing. Somehow it put them closer to equal footing. Now she wasn't the only one with baggage and a past; he had his issues too. And he was sharing them with her.

The silence that fell between them was thick with tension. Not uncomfortable, but nerve-wracking. Like there was more going on under the surface… She just had no idea what she was missing.

She never had been any good with subtext. Maybe that was why she'd always gravitated toward black-and-whites.

The work for the day was done, and she filled the silence by coming to a stand and dusting off her jeans. "Okay, well, um… I guess that's all we can do for today. I'll tackle that stack over there in the morning."

He stood too, his hands tucked in his pockets. "Sounds good. But before you run out of here, there's someplace I want to take you."

"Where?"

He smiled in lieu of an answer. "Just tell me this—are you free for the next few hours?"

She studied him with open curiosity but gave in with a nod. "Yeah, I'm free. Where are you taking me?"

He took her by the hand and pulled her after him. His obvious excitement at whatever surprise he had lined up was contagious.

\* \* \* \*

Tamara's whisper echoed off the walls of the Metropolitan Opera House lobby. "Gregory, what are we doing here?"

She tugged her oversized, puffy winter coat closer around herself, hoping to hide the pilled sweater and faded jeans. Only some ushers lingered in the lobby, but she was fairly sure she sensed their disapproval as they looked in her direction. Pulling on his sleeve, she whispered again. "What are we doing here?"

She'd asked the same question when their cab pulled up in front of Lincoln Center and again when an usher met them outside the main doors with a pair of tickets in hand.

Now, as Gregory led her into the packed theater, he turned to her with a smile. "We're seeing *The Nutcracker.* I would have thought that was obvious by now."

"But...but..." Too many questions tried to come out at once as she followed him down the aisle toward their seats near the stage. "But this has been sold out for months." Of all the protests and questions, the most logical won out.

"I made a call," he whispered. Leaning down, he quietly asked the elderly couple at the end of the row if they could squeeze past.

He had made a call. Of course. As if that answered anything. The lights dimmed as they took their seats, and the rest of her questions were put on hold as the orchestra started up and the curtains rose.

Tamara couldn't tear her eyes away as the first ballerinas poured onto the stage. *This.* This was everything. It was why she'd left home at sixteen. The beauty, the elegance, the transformative power.

Ballet had been the focus of her world from the time she could walk until the day she walked away from her family and her ex. She'd given this up along with all the rest, and seeing it now... It was sweet torture. Bittersweet memories rose to the surface, but they were drowned out by the sheer joy of immersing herself in this world once again. Only six years, but it felt like a lifetime.

Her gaze drank it all in greedily—the costumes, the symmetry, and the graceful movement. She let herself forget about everything else—Gregory, the theater, the party, and her family. The music washed it all away, and in its place was a brilliant peace. The coming-home sensation she'd always reveled in when she danced.

By intermission she was breathless with excitement. She forgot to ask Gregory all the questions she'd been meaning to ask and instead chatted his ear off about the techniques, the choreography, and the orchestra. He gamely encouraged her enthusiasm, asking questions and giving his opinion, though it was clear that going to the ballet was not his typical pastime.

The rest of the ballet passed in a dream. This wasn't escape—not like when she lost herself in movies—this was magic. She'd nearly forgotten how powerful the ballet could be. How it transformed the everyday world into something beautiful. For so long now she'd classified dancing as part of her former life and locked it away along with all of the negative experiences that had made her flee. How stupidly simplistic she'd been. There was nothing innately bad about ballet—it just happened to be linked to some bad memories. But it was also tied to some of the best memories of her life. Like the first time her mother had brought her to the ballet. They'd gone to see *The Nutcracker* when she was five years old, and it had been love at first sight.

She'd been hooked. Her father encouraged her love, even splurging on season tickets just to make her happy. He and her mother never missed her recitals—not once. The memories blindsided her, but the graceful movements on the stage combined with the beloved music softened the blow.

When at last the curtain call ended, the lights turned up, and the house began to empty, Tamara couldn't bring herself to move.

"Are you all right?" Gregory asked. He was sitting beside her, giving her the space she needed.

Was she all right? She was better than all right. "Perfect," she said, turning to face him. She realized then that they were nearly alone in the theater. "Sorry to keep you." She sat up straight, ready to get up and head toward the aisle, but Gregory made no move to leave.

"I'm in no rush," he said. "Did you enjoy yourself?"

She couldn't suppress a wide smile. "I more than enjoyed myself. This…" She gestured around the theater. "I'd almost forgotten how much I loved the ballet. How much I miss it." The last part she added softly. She didn't want to linger on the sadness of having given up her life in ballet or the reasons behind it. Not now, when she was so utterly content and…happy. Yes, that's exactly what this feeling was. The emotion felt like hearing a forgotten language. She recognized it but wasn't entirely comfortable with it.

"Good," he said. "I'm glad." His gaze met hers, and she couldn't look away. His eyes were warm, soft. The look was understanding. More than that… It was intimate. Her lips parted as if she were going to say something, but she couldn't think of anything to say. The silence went on too long, giving it a heaviness—a significance. But for the life of her, she didn't know what the silence meant.

Swallowing thickly, she finally managed words. "Thank you."

To her surprise, he grabbed her hand, tugging her to her feet alongside him. "Don't thank me yet. There's one more thing I want you to see."

She followed him blindly, allowing him to pull her along. She should be wondering about what this next surprise could be, but she found herself entirely focused on the feel of his large, warm hand enveloping hers.

It felt good. Amazing. A simple touch shouldn't be such a turn-on. But her reaction wasn't just the sexual chemistry she felt around him. There was another element to this touch.

It made her feel safe. At home. Like she belonged somewhere… Like she belonged with him. Hand in hand.

He came to a stop in the lobby, where a fair-sized crowd was still gathered. She stopped short beside him and looked up with raised brows. "What are we doing?"

A group of older women stood in a cluster near the door, most likely waiting for their car services or their chauffeurs, judging by the high-end dresses.

"Take a look at them." Gregory said it quietly in her ear, and she shivered slightly in response. It was hard to focus on anything other than the feel of his warm breath on her neck or his scent, which wrapped around her like a cocoon, but she did her best to block him out and do as he asked.

The women all seemed to be in their late forties or well into their fifties. Some clearly had had work done, while some had had better work done that wasn't nearly as obvious. All of them were outfitted in tasteful, elegant dresses that would make her mother proud. Their shoes cost more than her monthly paycheck. All of this was to say—they were exactly the crowd she'd expect to see at the Met. For the life of her, she couldn't spot anything out of the ordinary.

Finally, she gave up and turned to Gregory for help. "What exactly am I looking at?"

He leaned down again so his chin was resting on her shoulder and they were both looking toward the group by the door. "Those women," he said slowly. "Are they scary, do you think?"

Her initial reaction was a quick snort of amusement. "No, of course not."

"Do you feel intimidated by them?" he asked. His face was so close to hers that it took all of her willpower to focus on his words and not turn her head and plant a kiss on his neck. But even with the distraction of his physical proximity, she heard the teasing in his tone and knew exactly where this was headed.

"No," she said, a soft sigh escaping with that word. "I wouldn't say I'm intimidated by them."

She heard the smile in his voice. "Were a fight to break out right this minute, do you think you could take them on?"

She burst out with a laugh that was too loud, and some of the women in question turned to stare. "Yes," she said through muffled laughter. "I could probably take them in a fight."

Only then did Gregory pull back, and a damp chill replaced his comforting heat. He turned so he was facing her and took both of her hands in his. "You do realize that these women are exactly the sort who will be at my parents' party on Friday, don't you?"

She nodded, pressing her lips together to stifle another laugh.

"The only difference being, you may or may not remember some of the partygoers, just like you very well could have run into someone you knew once upon a time while watching the ballet tonight."

She nodded again. He had a point, and she knew it. She glanced over at the older women and had to admit that they hardly seemed intimidating at this moment.

"So," Gregory said. "What do you say? Will you come to the party on Friday?"

She looked into those warm brown eyes and she knew—there was no way she could refuse this man. Not now, maybe not ever.

"Yes," she said with a long exhale. "I'll go to the party."

His grin was triumphant and more than a little smug. He took her by the hand and led her past the group of women and into the cold night air. "Let's get a cab, I'll have him drop you at home before I head to the theater. I want to look over a few more files before I call it a night."

She couldn't help herself—the entire cab ride she found herself babbling away, reliving her favorite parts of the classic ballet. At his prompting, she told him all the parts she'd played in *The Nutcracker*.

"I bet you were an adorable Clara," he said.

She laughed. "I was a better Sugar Plum Fairy." It had been so long since she'd allowed herself to think about that time in her life, let alone talk about it. She found herself absurdly disappointed when the cab pulled up in front of her apartment building.

This night couldn't be over—not yet. Acting on impulse, she told the driver to keep going to the theater. At Gregory's questioning look, she shrugged. "You kept me company through a ballet, which I know is not your favorite thing in the world. Least I can do is help you finish up at the theater."

He didn't protest, and the laughter in his eyes was its own reward. He was happy she was joining him. She settled back against the seat of the cab with a sigh of pleasure. At the theater, they fell right back into a comfortable working relationship. It was so easy to be with him that sometimes she forgot how intimidating she used to find him. He was so down-to-earth, not at all what she'd expect of a notorious playboy billionaire.

After a while she looked at her phone and realized midnight was rapidly approaching. This day had gone on longer than anticipated—not that she was complaining. She stood up from where she'd been kneeling on the floor. "I should probably get going."

He picked up the coat she'd thrown over the back of a chair and held it out for her. "You shouldn't have stayed this late. What kind of terrible employer keeps his employee at work until midnight?"

She laughed as she slid her arms into her jacket. "A cruel slave driver. That's you to a T." When he wrapped the jacket around her, she was suddenly aware of how close he was. And the fact that they were alone in this small office.

That easy comfort vanished in a heartbeat. There was nothing comfortable about this silence. He didn't move as she turned in his arms. Memories of his kiss were all she could think of as she stared up at him. Those lips were so close. All she would have to do was stand on her tiptoes and—

"Can I walk you home?" Was it her imagination or did his voice sound hoarse? The atmosphere between them had shifted. Gone was the easy camaraderie, and in its place was an electric tension that was exciting and nerve-wracking all at once. It demanded a release in some form or another.

She nodded, suddenly too shy to speak. No, not shy. She tried to figure out what exactly it was she was feeling around him. Nervous, for sure, but not like she had been at the costume party. Her secrets—well, most of them—were out with this man. And there was a relief that came with that. True, she still had to face her harshest critics at the holiday party. And yes, there were still her parents to deal with. But in this moment, as he walked beside her the half mile to her Lower East Side apartment... A weight she'd been carrying for years was gone. A few simple reassurances that he didn't care about gossip and poof! He singlehandedly eviscerated the ghosts that had been plaguing her.

"What are you thinking about?" he asked. It was only then that she realized she was smiling to herself.

Habit made her want to clam up, but everything was different with Gregory. Maybe it hadn't been the champagne or the costume the other night. Maybe it had been his presence, reminding her of the optimistic girl she'd once been, or maybe it was his way of putting her at ease even as he made her nervous. It was an incongruous mix of excited anticipation and comfort at being with someone who knew her. Someone who didn't judge and who looked at her like she was still Tammy—not crazy Tammy and not the reinvented Tamara. But the Tammy she'd once been.

She struggled to put all she was feeling into words and failed. She said the best thing she could come up with. "Thank you."

He turned to her with his eyes wide with surprise. "For what?"

She shook her head with a soft laugh. How could she explain? "For believing in me. For not pushing me for information. For giving me a chance at the theater. For not letting me quit without a fight...." She trailed off with a sigh and threw her hands up for a lack of words. "For everything, I guess."

They had reached her apartment building, and when she turned to face him, she found that he was smiling softly. Almost tenderly. Her heart clenched in her chest. She'd watched this man from afar for as long as she could remember, but she'd never seen this smile before. This was special. It held genuine emotions that resonated within her. They struck a chord of...something. Not love, surely, but tenderness and caring and warmth—emotions she'd said goodbye to ages ago.

Fear reared up in her, instant and irrational, but there it was. She gasped softly, but when he gave her a questioning look she shook her head and forced a smile, shaking off the panicky feeling that had choked her with its intensity.

Now was not the time to delve into her emotional baggage—and that was what it was. Remnants of pain from the last time she'd fallen for someone.

Oh wow. Was she falling for Gregory?

She looked up at him, and the lights from the streetlamps sharpened his features, making him unbearably handsome. Her breath caught in her chest. Oh yeah, she was falling. Hard.

The question now was... Was he?

As if in answer to her question, he leaned toward her, his eyes riveted to her lips.

*Yes, please.* Her eyes started to drift closed automatically, instinctively. Her lips tingled in anticipation. She hadn't been able to shake the memory of his last kiss and all that it had stirred, physically and emotionally. She needed to feel that again. That kiss—his kiss—was the key to her courage. Not just her courage, but her former self.

He was so close, his breath warm on her lips when he cursed softly. Her eyelids fluttered open, and she saw him hovering over her, his eyes squeezed tight and his lips pressed together as if he was in pain.

"What is it?" she asked.

He shook his head but then, in the next instant, he reached out and clutched her arms, his head dropping so his forehead rested against hers. "God, I want to kiss you so badly."

For a second she thought she'd heard him wrong, he sounded so pained. But once the words sank in, she laughed as a giddy joy spread through her chest. He wanted it too. He felt it too! "Why don't you?"

He groaned, and the agony in that sound made her giddier than ever. He wanted her...bad. The realization was heady. It was a drug she hadn't tasted in years. The man she wanted was hers for the taking.

"I can't," he bit out. "Technically you're my employee, Tamara. I can't take advantage of that."

She remained quiet as she processed his words. For a moment, neither of them moved. They stayed locked in an awkward non-embrace for several heartbeats, their breath mingling in the frigid air. That surge of power gave her a rush even as excited anticipation left her shaky. Here, now, with this man—she was herself again. Confident, strong, and for the first time in a long time she wasn't confused or scared—she knew what she wanted.

She wanted this man.

"What if I take advantage of you?" she whispered. Closing the distance between them, she pressed her lips to his, and the length of her body molded against his strong frame. The heat was electric and instant, coursing through her limbs and stealing all reason and doubt.

For a moment it seemed he might not respond. Or worse, that he might back away. But he let out a low groan and wrapped his arms around her waist, pulling her so tight it was hard to breathe. "God, Tammy, you're undeniable."

When his lips moved to her neck, she allowed herself a smug smile. *Undeniable.* She liked that. That was exactly how she felt.

That was the last thought she had before his lips came back to hers and she lost herself in a kiss that melted her bones, leaving her putty in his hands. And his hands were everywhere—skimming over her back and her neck and up her sides. The bulky coat was a frustrating barrier between them, but then he moved his hands down and cupped her bottom, pulling her up against him until she felt his hard length pressed against her belly.

She moaned at the contact and he pulled back, his breath coming in short bursts. "Are you sure this is what you want?"

The break in contact made her shiver, and for the first time she realized they were still outside and in plain view of the rest of the world. Grasping his arm, she tugged him toward the front door of her apartment. "I've never been more sure."

The short walk up to her apartment was delayed by multiple stops to make out like a couple of teenagers in the stairwell. When she finally threw open the door, she had just enough time to say a prayer of thanks that Marc had gone out with Alex for the night before Gregory was behind her, pulling her back into his arms and nuzzling her neck as he stripped her of her winter jacket.

Spinning around, she helped him with his outer layers as they slowly stumbled their way through the apartment to her bedroom. Once there, they paused as if by unspoken agreement.

They were working together. She'd had a crush on him for as long as she could remember. She hadn't been with anyone since her ex. He didn't know the whole story of her past. There were a number of reasons why this was a bad idea, but none of them seemed to matter. Not to her, at least.

She waited to see if he would put an end to it, but after a few seconds of staring at her, his eyes dark with hunger, Gregory pulled her close. "I have never wanted anything more."

His growl rippled through her before he claimed her lips once more, his tongue thrusting into her mouth with a possessive urgency that made her ache for more. All thoughts about what this would mean in the morning were washed away by the sensation of his hands on her body. He seemed to be everywhere at once.

His hands were at her waist, unbuttoning her jeans before slipping up below her sweater, his touch scorching her skin from her stomach to her breasts. Through her bra he teased and pinched her nipples, his touch rough and urgent.

She let her head drop back as a desire she'd thought she'd lost forever took hold and washed away the past and the future. God, how had she lived without this for so long?

When he lowered her to the bed, she reached for him, grabbing his shirt and tearing it over his head as desperation had her arching against him. She needed to feel all of him against her. Inside her.

He pulled off her sweater, and his clever hands unsnapped her bra and tugged that off too as she ran her hands over his chest and back, absorbing his heat and his strength. When he lowered himself to her, her bare breasts pressed against his hard chest, she moaned at the unbearable sweetness of it. The perfect joining of hard and soft, of masculine and feminine… of old and new.

He was a symbol of her past and a beacon for the future. He'd given her hope and a new confidence. It somehow seemed so right that he be the one to open her heart again and remind her of her sexual nature. Something she'd thought she'd forgotten or discarded. Something she'd written off as a remnant of her former life.

She clung to his shoulders as he kissed his way along her neck, over her collarbone, and down to her nipples. When he pulled one into his mouth and sucked, she couldn't hold back the gasp of pleasure. Her hands moved to his hair, gripping him tightly against her as he sucked and licked, driving her wild.

"I can't wait," she whimpered as she arched her hips off the bed, pressing herself against him as she tried to slake the needy ache between her thighs. She felt his erection even through their jeans, and the need to have it inside her was almost too much to bear. God, it had been so long. Too long. She was empty and aching and so very needy.

In a heartbeat he had her jeans off, grabbed a condom from his wallet, and was tugging his own off to join hers on the floor. "I need you, Tammy. I can't—" He didn't finish, but he didn't have to. He couldn't wait either.

"Hurry," she moaned. He tore her panties and the rest of his clothes off and came back to her. Their joining was rough and urgent, as if he too had been celibate for years. In one thrust he filled her completely, and she cried out at the feel of him inside her.

For the first time in a long time she felt full—complete. Whole.

He dropped his head so his forehead was resting against hers, their breath joining in frantic pants as they moved together in a rhythm that was so natural they could have been lovers for ages.

His thrusts turned fast, insistent, and she cried out until her voice was hoarse. When the tension coiled so tight she couldn't take it anymore, she gripped his back and buried her face in his neck as the world spiraled out of control.

She was dimly aware of his climax seconds later but was too drained to do any more than lie there in his arms as he shifted so he was beside her. If he spoke, she missed it. Blissful sleep claimed her just as he nestled her against his side.

\* \* \* \*

When Gregory woke later that night, it took him a moment to realize where he was. As his memory came back to him, he found that he was grinning to himself like an idiot before he even opened his eyes.

That had been epic. Spectacular, actually. Like nothing he'd ever experienced. And no one would say he was lacking in experience.

Not that his performance proved anything. It had been a long time since he'd been so overcome with desire that he couldn't wait. Normally he took his time, ensuring that his partner was fully ready. But with Tamara—he'd lost himself in her like a goddamn teenager.

And it had been amazing.

When he was fully awake, he rolled over in bed to find the source of that once-in-a-lifetime experience. But there was one problem. She was gone.

Sitting up straight, he scanned the dark room, but there was no one there and her side of the bed was cold to the touch. Maybe she'd run to the bathroom. He waited a few minutes, and when there was still no sign of her, he threw off the covers and put on his jeans. Fear had him fumbling with the button.

Crap, he'd moved too fast. She'd seemed stronger since that night at the movie theater—without her secret weighing on her she'd been more open and talkative. More like the mystery woman he'd met that first night than the timid creature Oliver had introduced him to. He'd been starting to think that she trusted him, and last night had seemed to prove that she did. But maybe she wasn't there yet. And now he'd gone and ruined things with her by moving too quickly.

He made his way down the dark, narrow hallway and blinked rapidly as he stumbled into the brightly lit kitchen. Once his eyes adjusted to the light, he saw a disheveled and adorable Tamara staring up at him with wide eyes.

She looked…guilty. That was when he noticed the pint of ice cream in front of her and the spoon sticking out of her mouth. Relief rushed through him, and he couldn't help but laugh.

"I was hungry," she said around the spoon in her mouth.

His head fell back as he laughed harder.

She took the spoon out of her mouth, and he heard her mumble, "It's not that funny."

And it wasn't that funny, but he was overwhelmed with relief that she hadn't run away from him. And the fact that he was so relieved—well, that was the comical part. His exes always accused him of keeping his distance, of not letting them in. He'd just assumed that was part of his makeup. He didn't like peas and he didn't do intimacy.

Yet here he was, scrambling around in terror in the middle of the night because his woman wasn't cuddled up by his side. *His woman.* He liked the sound of that. She was still staring up at him, her long, blond locks in disarray and her freshly scrubbed face sweet and innocent.

She *was* his woman. It was as simple as that. After decades of dating and struggling and not being able to commit, this petite woman dressed up as Veronica Lake and slipped right into his heart. It was ridiculous. It sure as hell didn't make any sense. But at that moment, he couldn't care less. He merely wanted to enjoy this new feeling.

Besides, she looked so adorable with her knees pulled up beneath her oversized T-shirt, he couldn't help himself. She let out a little squeal of surprise when he leaned over and scooped her into his arms and headed out of the kitchen.

"Where are we going?"

While the bedroom was tempting, Gregory surprised himself by opting for the living room with its oversized couches. Lit only by the lights coming in from the street, he plopped onto one of the couches with Tamara snug on his lap.

With her nestled against him, Gregory's body responded as it seemed to whenever he was close to Tamara—like a pubescent teen with raging hormones. Her curves pressed against him just begging to be touched, but he forced himself to keep his hands on her back.

That was easier said than done when she turned her head and dropped kisses on his neck, her soft breath whispering over his skin. Resistance was futile.

But no. This wasn't any other woman, and waking up fearing that he'd scared her off had knocked some sense into him. If he wanted this to be real—and he did—then they needed to talk. He might not be an expert at relationships, but his gut told him she had to trust him fully and completely if this was going to be serious.

And holy crap, he wanted this to be serious. If his father could see him now—desperate for intimacy and commitment—he would die laughing. Hell, he could hardly believe it himself. He'd started to honestly believe he was not cut out for anything deeper than what he'd had with Vanessa—and that had been all about seeing and being seen. It was about how they were perceived by others rather than what they meant to one another.

He'd thought that was the extent of his heart's capabilities. But all it had taken was one woman to slip through the cracks of the armor he'd constructed to keep his father's criticisms out. It seemed the past decade had been spent trying to piss off his father or get his revenge. But now, here with Tamara, that bitterness seemed like something belonging to someone else. There was certainly no room for it in this cozy apartment, in this dark living room with this incredibly tempting woman.

Just like there was no room for secrets.

"Tammy—"

And just like that, she stilled. He'd noticed she had a tendency to freeze up at the sound of her former nickname.

She pulled back slightly to face him even though the room was so dark she couldn't have seen much. "You sound serious."

He chuckled softly. "I guess I am."

She groaned and leaned her forehead against his shoulder. "Don't tell me you regret what happened before. Just because we're working together—"

He cut her off with a kiss. Regret it? Never. "That's not it. I may be an ass for sleeping with my employee, but I wouldn't take it back for the world. That was incredible. *You* were incredible."

He felt her smile against his shoulder. "You were pretty great yourself." She kissed the corner of his mouth, and for a moment, he nearly lost his motivation. But then he remembered how scared he'd been that he'd thought he'd lost her when he'd woken up, and he knew without a doubt that he would never truly have her to lose if she didn't trust him with whatever deep, dark secret she was keeping to herself.

"I know I said I wouldn't pressure you," he started. When she stiffened in his arms, he added, "And I won't. But I need you to know that I'm here for you if you want to talk."

When she remained quiet, he added, "I want you to trust me."

\* \* \* \*

It was the rawness in his voice that finally jarred her into speaking. He was right; he deserved her trust. After all, he was taking a chance on her—in business and in his personal life. Surely he'd heard the rumors. Enough, at least, that most men would have run in the opposite direction.

She'd seen it with her own eyes after her stint at the clinic. Her friends had all disappeared when they caught the whiff of scandal that clung to her. But Gregory was right, that had been six years ago. Ancient history. And it didn't seem to bother him, so why not come clean?

After years of holding them in, the words were slow to start. But once she got underway, they tumbled out of her mouth, as if relieved to escape.

"When I first met Billy, my ex, he was really sweet." She felt him tense beneath her, but he didn't interrupt, so she cleared her throat and continued haltingly. "I met him when I moved to New York for a ballet academy. I was only sixteen and Billy was going to Columbia. His parents were friends with mine, so they hooked us up and it was…well, I thought it was love at first sight."

She listened to the street noise outside as her mind wandered back to that time when she had been so naive and innocent. She hadn't let herself think about those early happy days in ages, and the wash of emotions was bittersweet. "He was my first love. My first kiss. My first everything."

Between his silence and the darkness that hid them both, some of the tension eased in her body and the words came quicker. There was a small part of her that imagined she was in a confessional, baring her soul. She hadn't grown up Catholic, but in that moment she could see the appeal of unburdening a heavy load anonymously.

"I don't know if he changed or if he was always controlling and I just hadn't noticed because I was so in love in those early days."

His hand tightened against her thigh, but he kept quiet.

"The academy was strict, too. I don't think that helped matters. My every move was watched and critiqued; I had to be careful what I ate and how long I slept." She smiled in the dark at the memory of battered feet and endless rehearsals. "It was brutal, but I loved it."

She was quiet so long, lost in her memories, that Gregory finally spoke. "And then what happened?"

Her smile faded as the memories grew bleaker. "Billy and I moved in together. He proposed and I said yes. It was all very romantic except that I was so young."

She shifted on his lap. "My parents were happy with us as a couple. He always boasted to them about how he would take care of me in the big bad city." Her laugh was humorless. "I think he fooled us all into thinking that I was this helpless waif and he was my Prince Charming."

"But he wasn't," Gregory said, jumping to the punch line.

"He wasn't." For a moment she thought she couldn't continue. Her throat closed up on her as that lingering fear took hold. When Gregory reached for her hand and grasped it in his, she shook off the temporary paralysis. She was here, now. With Gregory.

"It started with him making simple decisions for me. He didn't like the way I was wearing my hair to rehearsals, so he suggested that I change it. He didn't like me wearing clothes that were too tight, too revealing." She shook her head in disgust at her former self for not seeing it sooner. "It wasn't like I dressed like a tramp or anything, but he started to shop for me and I let him clothe me like I was his little doll."

She swallowed a thick lump in her throat. Pity for the girl she'd been made her temporarily weepy. "I'm sure you can guess where this is going...."

He made a noise that was somewhere between a growl and a murmur of assent. Yet again she was glad of the dark. She wasn't sure she wanted to see the emotions playing over Gregory's face. It was one thing to pity herself, but she wouldn't have been able to handle it coming from him.

"It got worse and worse, but it happened so gradually that I managed to make excuses for him the entire time." She drew in a deep breath. "But then it got physical."

She felt his entire body stiffen beneath her and found herself stroking his chest as if he was the one who needed comforting. And maybe he did. She'd come to terms with the abuse over the years. Or at least, she'd grown used to it. It was part of her history, like the scar on her leg from when she fell out of the tree. It was always there, but it no longer stung the way it once did.

Maybe it was because of his reaction that she couldn't bring herself to go into detail. "It was never anything too serious," she said. Ugh, now it sounded like she was defending him. "I mean, I was never hospitalized or anything." Her stomach twisted and nausea settled in as the memory of those few incidents came back full force. The first time he'd backhanded her. He'd been drinking and she'd talked back. At least that's what he'd said; she honestly could never remember what she'd said that had set him off. He apologized after the first time. Told her it would never happen again.

She hadn't really believed him, but by that point he had her so firmly in his grip that she'd been half afraid to order for herself at a restaurant, let alone declare that their relationship was over. The few times he hit her after that he never left a bruise and he never apologized, either. He slapped her once when she wanted to stay home rather than sit by his side when he met his friends. Then there was the time he'd grabbed her arms and shook her. The memory of each incident was vivid, like it had happened yesterday.

The silence stretched between them, and she shoved the memories back where they belonged and licked her dry lips. "But between the physical abuse and his controlling ways..." She shrugged in the dark, as if the rest was obvious. And maybe it was.

She heard Gregory's ragged breathing in the dark. "I will kill him."

She pulled back at the dark growl. Then she shook her head, even though he couldn't see. "It's over now. He's been out of my life for years."

He pulled her back against him, and he cradled her in his arms once more. "Is he why you ran away?"

She almost laughed. No, but that would have made more sense. "I wish I had at that point." Licking her lips, she started in on the next part of her sordid tale. The part that hurt more than anything else.

"He made me doubt myself." He didn't respond, but then she hadn't expected him to. "I was so young and after two years of his manipulations and controlling ways, I just…" She shrugged again, at a loss for words. "I lost myself. And in the meantime, he took every opportunity to convince my parents and my friends that he was always right and I was…well, crazy. In their defense, they didn't see me often enough to know any better. They lived in Boston and we only saw them on holidays and the occasional weekend."

"But they knew *you*," Gregory reminded her.

She nodded. That was what had hurt the most. She'd thought her parents of all people would have seen through his lies. Part of her felt the need to defend them even though she had the same thought. They knew her; they should have known something was wrong. She'd been too cowed by Billy to tell them everything that was going on, but she'd hoped they'd see. He'd made her doubt herself to the point that she couldn't tell truth from his lies. He had her believing his lies that she couldn't handle life in the big city. That she needed him. That she was overreacting and that he was only trying to protect her. If he made her believe it, could she really blame her parents for falling for it too? She tried to explain it to Gregory. "They worried about me. They've always worried about me. I don't know if you remember, but they had always been overprotective."

"My stepmother said as much."

She bit her lip to keep from asking what else his stepmother had said. It didn't matter. She was setting the record straight now. "Anyway, they believed him. From the earliest days of our relationship he made comments about how difficult the ballet academy was for me. How I wasn't strong enough to take the challenges and criticisms. He said it so often, I started to believe him too. Then as our relationship progressed, he made my attempts to stand up for myself sound like…" She struggled to find the words to describe how confusing it all had been. "He made me feel like I was being melodramatic. Paranoid, even. I found out later that he'd been telling my parents the same thing."

Gregory tightened his grip on her, and she let herself sink against his chest, temporarily borrowing his strength. "By the end of it all, he'd manipulated the situation so no one believed me when I tried to tell them how bad things had gotten between us."

She couldn't bring herself to say the worst part out loud. The most shameful part. There had been moments when she wasn't even sure herself. She'd been told so often that she was being paranoid that she'd honestly started to wonder. She remembered clearly the feeling of not knowing whether she could trust her own mind. Nothing could compare to that terror.

"The more I fought against him, the more it looked like I'd gone off the deep end. That I'd cracked under the pressures of the academy and living in a new city."

After a moment of silence, Gregory filled in the ending. "So your parents thought it would be best if you got help."

She opened her mouth and closed it again. How could she tell him that it hadn't been solely their decision? Yes, it had been their idea, but she hadn't protested like she could have. She'd been so confused at that point that she'd honestly believed she needed that kind of help.

"They thought it would be for the best," she said. "In their defense, I think they honestly did think it would be in my best interests. And it *did* help. Thanks to that time away from Billy and my life in New York, I was finally able to see him for what he was."

She heard him mutter something under his breath. Enough to know that he thought they had been trying to sweep her under the rug. She couldn't bring herself to deny it. Their need to avoid public humiliation and scandal had certainly played a part in their decisions. They'd worked hard to create the image of a perfect family. A perfect daughter. One who made false accusations against one of their circle's favorite sons was not ideal. And to admit that she'd been sent out into the real world and couldn't hack it? Not an easy pill to swallow for her family.

But she didn't want to go down that cynical path with Gregory. Not tonight. Now that the worst of her story was out there, exhaustion took hold, and she buried her head in his shoulder, enjoying the feel of his strong arms around her.

For the first time in a long time, she felt safe.

Gregory buried his face in her hair. "I'm so sorry," he murmured.

She tightened her arms around his neck. "It's all history now." And for the first time in six years, that felt like the truth. Telling someone the whole story had helped her see that part of her past for exactly what it was—a story about her past. It no longer had any bearing on her current situation.

Except she would have to face the crowd of people she'd run away from. Next weekend, to be precise.

An annoying jangle of nerves threatened to disturb the cozy, peaceful feeling she was reveling in as she cuddled up to her new... What? Boyfriend?

*Nope, do not go there.* Her rational brain quickly scolded her. It was too soon for that kind of label. Still, the mere thought that this might be *more*—something special—was enough to make her stomach do backflips in excitement.

It went from backflips to molten lava as Gregory's hands wandered from her back to her waist and over her thighs. "I think we've had enough talking time for tonight, don't you?" she whispered.

His low laugh was answer enough as he stood with her in his arms and headed back to the bedroom.

# Chapter 8

Tamara sipped her coffee at the diner, hoping against hope that the caffeine would kick in soon. Marc and Caitlyn sat across from her, picking at their breakfasts.

"More coffee," Caitlyn muttered as she reached for the carafe on the center of the table.

"Don't get me wrong," Marc said as he bit into a piece of bacon. "I'm glad we got to visit Meg and meet her little munchkin. But I'm pretty sure we could have waited a couple of hours."

Tamara shrugged. "We were excited to meet her."

"And it was worth it," Caitlyn said staunchly. Then she yawned. "I think the adrenaline is wearing off."

They all nodded in agreement, but Marc was watching Tamara closely across the table. "Don't for one second think I'm too tired to grill you on the mystery man."

Caitlyn's head shot up at that, her eyes comically wide. "What mystery man?"

"Exactly." Marc gave Tamara a smug grin, his eyes alight with mischief. "I got home from Alex's yesterday and there was a giant bouquet of flowers in our living room, addressed to our little Tam-Tam."

Tamara ducked her head as she sipped her coffee. She was the only one of their friends who never dated, and being the object of this sort of scrutiny was not something she'd been missing in her life. "I was going to tell you," she started.

And she had been planning to, just as soon as she and Marc had a moment alone together. But he'd been at Alex's, and as soon as he returned, Meg had gone into labor. Tamara's news got lost in the excitement. She'd forgotten that the flowers Gregory had sent from his business trip to DC were still prominently displayed in the living room.

Thank God she'd thought to remove the note that thanked her for an amazing night.

"Oh my God, she's blushing," Caitlyn said. She and Marc seemed to forget all about their food as they stared at her, waiting for an explanation.

"Who is he?" Marc demanded. "Have I met him? Is he someone we know? Oh my God, did you put up a profile on Tinder without telling me?"

Tamara laughed. "Slow down, Marc. Yes, you've met him. Yes, you both know him—sort of. And no, still not on Tinder." Before Marc could ask again, she blurted it out. "It's Gregory."

Caitlyn let out a squeak that Tamara assumed meant she was excited. Maybe even happy for them. Since Caitlyn actually knew Gregory, and Marc was apparently stunned into speechlessness, she focused on Caitlyn. "Do you think I'm crazy?"

Her friends had no idea how much that question hurt her to ask. It had been a long time since she'd doubted her sanity, but now, with Gregory... she had this sense that she was waiting for the other shoe to drop. It was too good to be true. So yeah, maybe she was making a monumental mistake and she just couldn't see it. For the first time in a long time, she desperately needed an objective opinion.

Caitlyn blinked at her, clearly stunned herself, but then she leaned forward and her face lit up with excitement. "Are you kidding? Of course you're not crazy. Gregory is amazing—he's sweet, funny, loyal, and, you know..."

"Hot," Marc finished for her. He leaned forward too, so both of her friends had their elbows on the table and looked a bit like two detectives interrogating a hostile witness. Or maybe that was just her imagination.

"He is hot as hell," Marc stated, as if it was a fact that needed to be clarified. Then he broke out in a giant grin that had her sinking back in her seat with relief. She didn't need Marc's approval, by any means, but her best friend's opinion meant a lot to her, especially when she wasn't sure she could trust her own judgment. Like right now. Oh, she was still over the moon at the recent turn of events, but there was a little part of her that doubted it was real. It all seemed too good to be true.

When was the other shoe going to drop?

She didn't have time to go down that path, since Caitlyn and Marc were bombarding her with questions. For a few seconds she couldn't get a word in edgewise as her friends lobbed questions at her. Where to begin?

Finally, Marc said, "I mean, you two just met! How did this happen so quickly?"

Tamara's breath caught in her throat as a vague sense of guilt dampened her happiness. Taking one more fortifying sip of coffee, she met her friend's gaze. "Actually, we didn't just meet. I've known him for quite a while."

The silence that met that statement was deafening. She could sense the onslaught of questions and hurried to beat them. Looking from Marc to Caitlyn and back again, she launched into her story for the second time in as many days.

This time it was easier. So much easier. Somehow telling Gregory had unblocked the dam. His non-judgmental response and sympathetic ear had been exactly what she'd needed to overcome her fear of saying the words out loud. She still kept her eyes on the table—she didn't want to see their pity or their anger. But when she was finished, she looked up and found only support.

Funny how telling her story made her body feel lighter, as if her past abuse had been a physical anchor weighing her down.

They had questions—of course they had questions. They had opinions and comments and more than a little anger toward her ex. As their anger grew, some of hers seemed to abate. As they expressed their hurt on her behalf, her pain subsided. There was closure in telling her story. There was relief in sharing her pain.

*Huh.* It had taken six years for her to learn that lesson, and she owed it all to Gregory. Warmth spread through her. After so long feeling like she had to hide from the world, even from her own friends, he'd come along and shown her she didn't need to be afraid. He not only gave her the strength to tell her story but also showed her that talking about her past didn't hurt her—it actually helped. And that not everyone would judge her. The people who truly cared about her wouldn't look down on her.

Eventually, they got back to him. Not even her sordid tale could divert their interest in her newfound love life.

"I think it's awesome," Caitlyn stated.

"It is." Marc's tone was definitive.

But then there was a pause. Perhaps she was reading too much into it, but there was a definite pause.

"What?" she asked. "What's the problem? Am I missing something here? Am I being an idiot?" She looked from one hesitant face to the other, and her stomach plummeted. "Seriously, you guys, I need some perspective here. Am I setting myself up for disaster?"

Every fear she'd been suppressing since he'd left her apartment the day before came rushing to the surface. She wasn't pretty enough—God knew she wasn't nearly as beautiful as his exes, who were paid to be stunning. She wasn't stylish or sexy or worldly or any of those things.

It seemed her closest friends agreed.

"Are you sure he's serious?" Caitlyn asked, her tone gentle, as if she were talking to a child.

Her heart sank for a moment. Caitlyn was friends with him, and she didn't believe he could care about her.

Marc leaned in, his brow furrowed with concern. "We don't want to see you get hurt, Tam. And it's not like you have a lot of experience dating, let alone handling men like Gregory."

A sad sigh slipped out. Men like Gregory. Meaning someone incredibly attractive, worldly... And who didn't come with a boatload of luggage.

"You think he's out of my league," she said. She tried to keep any hurt out of her voice. It wasn't their fault. They were just being honest, and the truth hurt.

Marc sat back with his hand over his heart. "That's not what we're saying."

"Definitely not," Caitlyn said. After a brief pause, she continued. "I haven't known Gregory for long, but from what I've seen and what I've heard from Ben, he isn't exactly good at commitments."

Wasn't that what Gregory's father accused him of? Apparently that misapprehension was universal. But she knew better. If Gregory really cared about something or some*one*, he could be just as loyal as the next guy.

*If* he really cared. Did he really care about her or was she just a rebound after his latest breakup with that actress? Her friends clearly thought she was a passing fancy. She'd like to believe she was something more, but she had to face facts.

"We're just worried about you," Marc said. Once again he leaned forward. This time he reached out and grasped her hands in his. "You've clearly been through enough in your lifetime. You've had a rough go of it in the love department. I don't want to see you get hurt again."

Tamara swallowed. Neither did she. She honestly wasn't sure if she could go through another heartbreak. Wasn't that why she'd sworn off love all those years ago?

The new and improved Tamara didn't date, she didn't try to attract men, and she sure as hell didn't fall in love.

Shifting uncomfortably in her seat, she tugged her hands from Marc's. This was different. Gregory was different. He knew all about her past— he even had known her in her past. He knew where she came from and how she got here, and he hadn't run screaming. That had to count for something, didn't it?

But maybe her history was part of the novelty. Maybe he'd grow tired of her when it was no longer just interesting gossip and he realized it had changed her forever. That she had issues with trust that couldn't be overcome and that she had a history that would follow her wherever she went.

Her stomach twisted into a knot as another fear took hold. What if his show of caring was because of her past? What if he pitied her?

Her friends were watching her, and finally Caitlyn broke the silence. "Tam, we didn't mean to rain on your parade." She glanced over at Marc. "Did we?"

He shook his head. "We just worry about you. Friends do that."

She forced a smile. "I know, and I appreciate it. And maybe you have a point." She swallowed down the anxiety this conversation had stirred and tried to recall the relief she'd felt in sharing her story with Gregory. He'd done that. He'd helped to free her from her past. He hadn't judged and hadn't held it against her.

She could trust him.

For the first time in a long time, she could truly trust someone. That counted for something. Hell, it counted for *everything*.

"I appreciate your concern," she said again, this time with a stronger voice. "But I think we've got something good. I may not be in his league, but I come from the same world. I know him and he knows me."

Her friends' looks of surprise were almost comical. They clearly weren't used to the new and improved, confident Tamara. "I don't know how long this will last, but I know that I want to give it a shot. And so does he."

Marc and Caitlyn exchanged a wide-eyed look. "Well all right then," Marc said, a smile spreading slowly over his face.

Caitlyn was grinning too. "Maybe Gregory has finally met his match."

\* \* \* \*

By the time Gregory arrived back in the city, it was too late to stop by Tamara's. Much as he wanted to see her, their reunion would have to wait until the following day when she would be his date to his family's holiday party.

The wait seemed interminable. After nearly a week away from her, Gregory couldn't think of anything else. He couldn't remember the last time he'd been so smitten. His infatuation would have been amusing if it wasn't so all-consuming.

He'd acted like a lovestruck teenager during his business trip to DC—calling and texting constantly, seemingly unable to go more than a few hours without touching base with her. God, was that what happened to

Ben when he met Caitlyn? No wonder he'd acted like such an ass. Who could think straight when his brain, body, and heart were in a constant state of yearning?

He was so distracted that he nearly missed the visitor waiting for him in the lobby of his apartment building.

"Gregory."

He froze midstep on his way to the elevator. He would recognize that voice anywhere—as would most Americans who owned a TV, he supposed.

"Vanessa." Without turning he heard her stiletto heels tapping against the tiled floor. "What are you doing here?"

Her voice dripped with sarcasm. "Delighted to see you too, Greggy."

He turned then and found himself face to face with the woman who had made his life a living hell off and on for the last two years. It was his own fault for not breaking up with her sooner, but still… Now that he had ended it for good, he was rather hoping he would never have to see her again.

Her long, brown, perfect curls swayed as she moved toward him in a little black dress that left nothing to the imagination. More than one magazine had claimed she had the perfect curves. Women everywhere paid good money to get her perky boobs and curvy butt. Once upon a time that had appealed to him, but now it did nothing. Funny what personality did to one's looks. Let the rest of the world drool over his buxom ex. The only one he wanted was a petite blonde with an affinity for baggy sweaters.

Vanessa stopped a few feet away from him, her arms crossed over her chest and a familiar pout on her face. "I still have a box of my things up there. I need them."

He sighed loudly. After one of their last blowouts, he'd had the fantastically terrible idea that he should ask her to move in with him. As if that would help the fact that they could barely stand to be in one another's presence. That decision had been the deathblow to their sad excuse of a relationship.

She'd technically moved out more than a month ago, but "moving out" seemed to be a slow, torturous affair for Vanessa. It seemed she was constantly remembering "one last thing."

"How did you know I'd be coming home today?"

"Your office," she said as she led the way toward the elevator, acting for all the world as if she still lived in the building. Her sense of entitlement had always irritated him, but it had never seemed so obnoxious as it did now after getting to know Tamara. With her understated elegance, humility, and innate ability to laugh at herself, Tamara was basically the exact opposite of his spoiled, narcissistic ex.

He made a mental note to have another talk with the company's receptionist. A fan of Vanessa's, she'd caved to his ex's line of questioning on more than one occasion. "You need to leave that poor girl alone," he said.

She pushed the button for the penthouse suite as he stepped on the elevator. Turning to him, she gave him a fake smile. "Funny, I was going to say the same thing to you."

*He shouldn't ask. He shouldn't ask. He shouldn't—*

"What are you talking about, Vanessa?"

Her smirk had him cursing under his breath. Why had he given in to curiosity?

"I heard you've been seeing someone new." Her tone was taunting. What was this, grade school?

He tried to sound bored, but his heart rate automatically accelerated at the mention of Tamara. Not that their new relationship was a secret, but the knowledge in this woman's hands was dangerous. While Tamara might be paranoid about how vicious the gossips could be in their parents' circle, they didn't come close to the wrath and vindictiveness this woman was capable of. "Where did you hear that?"

"Does it matter?" she asked.

Her smug superiority was his answer. She'd been keeping tabs on him. The elevator doors slid open with a ding, and he gaped at Vanessa in disbelief. "Yes, it matters. Why the hell are you spying on me?"

She shrugged, ignoring his glare as she led the way to his door. "Honestly? I don't know. Just possessive, I guess." She stopped beside the door and waited for him to unlock it.

"We're not together," he bit out. "You have no right to be possessive."

She shrugged and tossed her curls over one shoulder. "Old habit."

As if that explained anything.

She pointed to the doorknob. "Are you going to let us in?"

With another weary sigh, he unlocked the door and ushered her in. The sooner she got in, the sooner she could leave. She walked through the foyer to the sunken living room and lingered there, trailing one hand over the back of the couch.

Part of him wanted to ask her what she wanted. She was clearly toying with him, leading up to something. But to ask would give her the edge. She'd see his curiosity as a win for her side.

That's what it had always come down to with the two of them. Games. Winning and losing. Had there ever been a connection? If so, it had never come close to the sort of innate bond he'd felt with Tamara from the first moment he saw her. A bond that continued to strengthen every time they spoke.

For him and Vanessa, that spark—if it had ever existed—had burned out long ago. They'd hurt one another too badly for there to be any connection left except for shared memories.

Vanessa reached the end of the couch and spun to face him. "You're going to hurt her."

Her voice was smug and she wore a smirk that he knew and hated. "Who?"

She shrugged. "Whoever it is you're seeing." Taking long, slow strides, she made her way back to him, the edge of her slinky dress riding up as she walked. "Whoever she is, she won't be able to handle you and your demons."

He gave a little snort of disgust. "Come on, V. That's a little melodramatic, even for you."

She didn't seem fazed by his snide remark. "But it's the truth. Face it, Gregory—you and I worked because I understand you."

God, he was too tired to deal with this. "I don't know what you're talking about, Vanessa. It's late. I need to go to bed."

"I'm talking about your father," she said, over-enunciating as though he were a child.

Gregory ran a hand over his face. He was too tired to fight, let alone hold a deep, meaningful conversation about his daddy issues. No thank you. "It's time for you to go, V."

She placed a hand on her hip and cocked her head to the side. "I think you should hear me out." Her smile was as cold as ice. "Before you go and hurt Tamara."

That made him freeze. His body tensed at the mention of Tamara. If she'd been digging into his new girlfriend, what the hell had she discovered? "Don't bring her into this."

Her eyes widened with false innocence. "You're the one who brought her into it, Gregory, not me."

Her words added to his tension, and much as he didn't want to get dragged further down Vanessa's rabbit hole, he couldn't help himself. This was Tamara she was talking about. "Drag her into what?"

"Your toxic little feud with your father." She radiated smugness from her pretty nose to her stiletto toes. "I know what you're doing, you know. It's so obvious."

He clenched his jaw. He would not give her the satisfaction of asking what the hell she was talking about. It seemed he didn't have to.

Leaning in so he was overwhelmed by the cloying scent of roses, she gave him that smirk he hated. "You're trying to get back at your father by dating that little nobody from nowhere."

Despite her nasty words, he felt a quick stab of relief. If she called her a nobody from nowhere, she had no idea that Tamara was a Vanguard from Boston. The relief was short-lived as she continued in a know-it-all tone.

"It's what you *do*, Gregory. You go out of your way to piss off your father like you're hell-bent on proving him right." She shook her head and crossed her arms over her considerable chest. "Everything you do is to spite him, regardless of who gets hurt in the crossfire."

Her pout made it clear she was talking about herself now. With Vanessa, the conversation always started and ended with her. And maybe she had a point as far as she was concerned. He could admit to himself that part of the reason he and Vanessa stayed together so long was because his father hated them as a couple. She was everything he didn't want for Gregory— always embroiled in a scandal. The woman lived for drama, on screen and off. So maybe in his own way he'd been playing games with her just as much as she'd toyed with him. Either way, they'd been bad for each other. Toward the end it seemed they'd hurt one another just for the hell of it.

But that wasn't him and Tamara. This was different. He would never hurt her. And despite what Vanessa might think, their relationship had nothing to do with his family issues. What they had was deeper and stronger than anything he'd felt before. Hell, it was more than he'd known he was capable of feeling. It was scary as hell, but it was real.

What they had was the real deal.

Vanessa moved closer, reaching out a hand to stroke his arm. "I can handle you and your issues, Gregory. Do you think this new little debutante of yours will say the same after she gets to know the real you? Admit it, Gregory—I get you. And you get me and my baggage. We always did have an understanding."

He nearly groaned at that twisted point of view. "We didn't have an understanding, Vanessa. We just saw each other's weaknesses and exploited them."

She pulled her hand back as if he'd stung her. "That's hardly fair."

"I don't know what's going on with you." He forced himself to gentle his tone. No need to make this any more unpleasant than it needed to be. "Maybe you're lonely, or maybe you're feeling nostalgic. But what you're trying to do here—it's not going to work."

Vanessa pouted at him, but some of the artifice slipped from her demeanor, and he found himself talking to the woman he'd originally fallen for and not the tough bitch she liked to pretend she was.

"I'm happy, Vanessa." The words came out without any thought, and he was nearly as stunned by the admission as she seemed to be. Holy shit. He was happy. Maybe for the first time in his life, he felt like he fit. Like he belonged. He was with someone who cared about him—not his money or his family name.

And he could be good for her. He'd gotten her to open up and was helping her face her fears. The swelling of pride was unexpected and unusual… but it felt *good*. He liked being needed, being a help to someone.

Once Vanessa recovered from her obvious surprise, those words made her smile—it was a sad smile that didn't reach her eyes. "Are you really?"

The doubt in her voice made him uneasy. "I am." He hated how defensive he sounded.

Vanessa moved past him, patting his arm as she went. "If you say so, lover. But don't come crying to me when you realize I'm right. You may think you're happy now, but you'll mess it up. You always do."

"Thanks for the vote of confidence," he muttered.

She stopped by the doorway and turned back to give him something close to a genuine smile. "I'm not being cruel. You can't help it. You'll never be able to commit to this woman, whoever she is."

"You don't know that." The anger in his voice was unmistakable. "I'm so sick of everyone telling me I'm unable to commit. You and I lasted two years, didn't we? That's not nothing."

Vanessa smirked. "We were more off than on for two years—not exactly a record to brag about. Besides, I'm the only reason we lasted as long as we did."

He let out a mirthless bark of a laugh. "Oh really?"

She nodded in all seriousness. "Sweetie, you've always run away the moment things get difficult. Blame it on your mom leaving you at such a young age, or maybe it's just in your genetics, but you're wired to flee in the face of real emotions."

If her intention had been to hurt him, she couldn't have aimed her blow any better. It was exactly what his father had been pounding into him his whole life. He was just like his mother. He would hurt the ones he loved. He'd leave because he wasn't strong enough to stay.

"You—that's—" He tried to come up with words to argue and failed miserably. Because the truth was, he *had* fled before. But he wouldn't now. It was different this time.

She came over and patted him on the arm. "Face it, Gregory, it was always me who came running back to you even if you were the one in the wrong." Her smile turned bitter and self-deprecating. "Like tonight, for example." She spread her arms wide. "Here I am, chasing after you. Again. For the millionth time." Leaning in, she stroked his chest and lowered her voice. "Face it, it's what we do. You run and I chase."

He moved back, away from her wandering hands. "Not anymore, Vanessa. This time we're over for good."

But even as he spoke, her words lingered, stinging old wounds—and she wasn't done. Though she wore a small smile, there was something frighteningly close to pity in her eyes. "You might have the best intentions, Gregory, but you and your new fling are doomed to fail. You'll never be able to commit and be happy until you face the fact that doing so will make your father happy."

Her words were a slap in the face. Exactly as she'd intended, no doubt.

It wasn't true. He went to tell her that, but she was already walking out the door. Whatever box she'd come to pick up—if there really had been a box—was forgotten.

# Chapter 9

Tamara critically eyed her reflection in the floor-length mirror for the tenth time as Marc paced the length of her bedroom. "Are you sure you didn't like the black one better?"

Gregory had been in DC all week for business, and though they had texted and talked on the phone every day in the week he'd been gone, she was anxious to see him again. She turned to check out her profile. She wanted to look good. This party had started out as a business date—she'd be his plus one just to gain entry. But now that they'd slept together, was this a real date? She sucked in a deep breath to quell an entirely different set of butterflies in her stomach.

The idea of facing this crowd was still enough to make her want to bolt, but the thought of having her first real date made her want to squeal with excitement. Whether this was a business outing or a real date— or maybe both—either way she wanted to make him proud when she showed up on his arm.

Plus, she needed the confidence boost. If she was going to walk straight into the lion's den, she sure as hell needed to look her best.

"You look hot in red," Marc said matter-of-factly. "Now let's get back to this dick of an ex." He plopped down on her bed and leveled her with a glare. "I cannot believe it took you six years to tell me that you have been living a double life."

She let out a snort of amusement. "Not a double life, Marc. I just didn't tell you everything about my past."

"You told me nothing!" The dreaded Billy conversation had come up again and again over the past few days. Marc dug for details, and Tamara found to her surprise that she didn't mind. The more she talked about that period of her life, the easier it was to put it behind her. Marc, however, was hung up on the fact that she'd waited so long to tell him. Now that his initial pity had faded, he'd been giving her hell over that.

His arms were crossed, and he was giving her a pout that she knew well. It was the same one he gave her when she watched *America's Next Top Model* without him. It meant he was pissed but not hurt. Thank God. She wouldn't have been able to take it if her silence had cost her his friendship.

"I told you I was a ballerina when I was young," she offered.

He rolled his eyes. "Yes, but not that you were this close to going pro. Oh yeah, and that your psycho ex went all *Gaslight* on your ass and nearly drove you insane."

She gave him an appreciative smile. "Nice reference."

He doffed an imaginary hat before going back on his rampage. "If you'd told me, I could have done something."

"Like what?" she picked up her makeup brush and added one more sweep of blush for good measure.

He hesitated for one second before saying, "I could have beaten him up for you."

She arched one eyebrow in disbelief—Marc was more of a "make love, not war" kind of guy. She couldn't imagine him fighting anyone, let alone her burly ex.

"Okay, fine. Maybe not that. But I could have made you feel better. I could have been there for you!"

She turned to face him, her hands on her hips. "Are you kidding me? You *have* been there for me, from almost my first day in the city. From the moment you answered my Craigslist ad and moved in, you've been there for me. I couldn't have moved on the way I have if it wasn't for you."

There was an awkward silence as he blinked at her in surprise, his eyes growing watery as hers started to spill over. But then he jumped off her bed and hurried over with a tissue. "Oh no you don't. Your eye makeup is perfect; you will not ruin it with silly tears."

She laughed and sniffled a bit as she dabbed away the wetness. "You're right. I need to get my game face on if I'm going to face this crowd."

He gave her his best pout. "I wish I could come with you."

"Me too." She sighed.

He patted her shoulder. "You'll be fine. Your sexy new boyfriend will make sure of it."

She bit her lip as Marc rolled his eyes. "The guy has been calling you constantly and is taking you home for the holidays. I think it's safe to say he's your boyfriend."

"This is business," she argued automatically. But even as she said it, her heart threatened to leap out of her chest with happiness at Marc's confidence that this was a real date. It was ridiculous that after everything they'd discussed, after being as intimate as two people could be…she still wasn't quite sure where they stood. He certainly hadn't brought up the topic—for all she knew, she was one of many women he was currently dating.

Besides, as excited as she was at the prospect of a real relationship with this man, the thought of being in another long-term commitment made her chest tighten with anxiety. She wasn't ready. Maybe she'd never be ready. It had been so long since she'd been truly happy, and the feeling was mixed with terror.

*Just enjoy it while it lasts.* Stay in the moment, wasn't that what the therapists always said? She could do that.

As if reading her mind, Marc slipped out of her bedroom and returned with a glass of wine. She modified her earlier thought. She could do that—with the help of wine.

"I cannot believe that my little Tam-Tam is sleeping with the city's most eligible bachelor."

She met his gaze and they both burst out laughing. It was ludicrous that *she*, of all people, was dating someone like *him*. Not only did they live in different worlds—now, at any rate—but she'd been swearing up and down to her friends that she didn't date. Ever.

But that was before she'd met Gregory…again.

\* \* \* \*

Gregory came to the door bearing a bouquet of roses. He'd been waiting all week for this moment, and when the door opened—the moment was better than he could have imagined.

Her long hair was curled, and her figure was shown off to perfection by the short, long-sleeved red dress. But the best part of all was her smile: wide, open, and genuine. "You look incredible."

She blushed at the praise, and it was all he could do not to draw her into his arms and carry her back to her bedroom to pick up where they'd left off before he'd headed out of town.

He might have done just that if her roommate hadn't appeared behind her.

After exchanging pleasantries with Gregory, Marc handed Tamara her clutch purse before taking her shoulders in his hands. Ignoring Gregory, he bent down a bit so he could look Tamara in the eyes. "You've got this, girl. Your history is history and you are goddamn Ingrid Bergman."

Gregory watched Tamara's brows shoot up as she bit her lip to keep from laughing. "I'm Ingrid Bergman?"

Marc nodded sagely. "You are. And you are about to make those rich people your bitches."

Now it was Gregory's turn to smother a laugh. "I don't need her to fight my parents' guests, you know. We just need her to speak on the theater's behalf."

Marc waved him off with one hand while never taking his eyes off Tamara. "You call me if you need backup, okay?"

Tamara nodded, and Gregory took her by the elbow and led her down the stairs to the street where he'd parked his car. As he helped her in, he took the opportunity to lean over and inhale her scent, feeling the warmth from her skin. "You look amazing, have I told you that yet?"

"Not yet." She smiled up at him and his heart stopped. God, she was perfect. Once he was behind the wheel he leaned over for the kiss he'd wanted to give her the moment she'd opened the door. Her lips were gratifyingly eager as they met his, and for a heartbeat he actually contemplated skipping the party altogether.

He pulled back slowly and took a deep breath, watching as she did the same.

But they couldn't skip it—this was a great opportunity for her to make the right connections for the theater, which was imperative to the theater's success.

And since the theater's success was imperative to shoving it in his father's face, it was a priority he couldn't dismiss. He watched his gorgeous date tidy up her lipstick in the mirror above the passenger seat visor. "You ready for tonight?"

She glanced over, and her emotions were written clearly all over her face. Fear mixed with resolve.

"As I'll ever be." Her smile was tentative, but it was a smile nonetheless. He reached out to squeeze her hand.

"I've got some good news," she said as he weaved the car through traffic to his parents' place on the Upper East Side.

"What's that?"

"I've booked an event at The Ellen."

When he looked over in surprise again, he found her smiling broadly, excitement giving her eyes sparkle in the dim light of the car.

"That was quick. What's the event?"

"It's for one of Alice's clients. She's organizing a fundraiser for the hospital's new children's clinic. It's a bachelor auction." He didn't comment, but she hurried on. "Before you say anything, I know how that sounds, but it will be classy, I swear. And Alice has invited all the biggest donors, so I figure—"

She stopped talking when he smiled at her. "That sounds perfect. Exactly the type of event we're hoping to get."

When she lit up at the praise, he added, "I have to admit, I didn't expect you to get results so quickly."

Even in the dark lighting, the pinkness of her cheeks stood out. "I didn't really do anything. It was Alice's idea. She came to me with it."

"Still," he said. "It's a good omen, isn't it? We're off to a great start."

She nodded, and her eyes were soft and tender, filled with a trust that made his heart hurt. "Maybe it's a sign that we make a great team."

He turned back to the road quickly. Something that sounded a bit like alarm bells went off in the back of his brain. That trust he'd heard—it made him tap the steering wheel, suddenly too antsy to focus on anything other than driving.

*You're going to hurt her.* Vanessa's words from the night before came back to him with utter clarity. *You're going to mess it up. It's what you do.*

It wasn't true. She was messing with him; that's what *she* did. And she did it well. She'd known exactly where to strike to bring about the most pain. Right now he couldn't imagine anything worse than causing Tamara more pain in her life.

*What if Vanessa was right?* He shook his head. He was a grown man who made his own choices. He didn't have to relive his mother's mistakes or let his father's low expectations define him.

But even as he told himself that, uncertainty had him shifting uncomfortably in the driver's seat, keenly aware of the delicate hand she rested on her lap beside him. God, she was so small, so...*breakable.*

Not for the first time this week, he remembered how fragile and vulnerable this woman was. Hadn't Ben told him she didn't date? And she'd all but said it herself. But here she was, giving him a chance. Looking at him like he might be the answer to her prayers. Like he was the leading hero in one of those old black-and-white romances she loved so much.

Him. The guy who hadn't been able to commit to anything, not for any length of time. Hell, his father had had to give away his pet fish because he'd forgotten to feed it one too many times. His father had given it to another family so he wouldn't kill it. He'd loved that stupid fish, but that hadn't stopped him from nearly killing it.

*He was his mother's son.* But no, that was his father's voice he heard, not his own. And the fish incident had happened when he was ten. He was a grown-up now. He could handle this.

He cleared his throat and focused on the car in front of them. "So, what was that Ingrid Bergman comment about? When Marc was saying goodbye?"

He heard her shifting beside him, and he glanced over to see that she was biting her lip.

"It's stupid," she said with a roll of her eyes. "I told Marc what happened and he thought it sounded like the plot from *Gaslight*."

"You told him," Gregory repeated. The fact that she'd glossed over that detail didn't fool him into thinking it had been a small deal for her.

She nodded. "I told him."

He brought the car to a stop at a red light and turned to look at her. "And?"

She met his gaze, and the honesty he saw there nearly leveled him. "And it felt good to finally get it out there. I can't believe it's taken me so long to tell my best friend."

"What was holding you back?"

She shrugged. "I guess I was worried that he'd pity me."

"But he didn't." He didn't phrase it as a question, because Marc's tone had been anything but pitying. He'd sounded like a confident coach sending his best player out onto the field.

"He didn't," she confirmed.

Good. The last thing she needed was pity. She needed… She needed… ah hell, who was he to say what she needed? He parked a few blocks from his parents' apartment and helped her out of the car. He just hoped bringing her to this party wasn't an epic mistake. In theory, it should help her overcome her fears. His stepmother and her friends would be tactful, surely, and Tamara could overcome her paranoia that she was still the scandal of the high and mighty.

Still, as he offered her his arm and he felt her hand slip through, petite and dainty just like her—he hoped like hell he was right.

One of the hired help let them into the apartment, and Gregory patted Tamara's hand, which had clenched his arm with enough force that he'd most likely bruise. She paused in the entryway, and with a quick glance, he could practically see her debating whether to run away.

"I promise I'll be by your side as long as you need me."

She responded with a grateful smile that had his chest swelling with pride.

His stepmother approached them, her face lit with a welcoming smile. "Ah, Gregory, I'm so glad you're here." She pulled him in tightly before giving him a kiss on both cheeks. When she released him, she turned her gaze to Tamara, who was still squeezing his arm so tightly he was just waiting for her to cut off the blood flow to his hand.

But when his stepmother's smile widened and her eyes grew soft and teary, Tamara's grip loosened slightly.

"Oh, my dear. How good it is to see you again." Elena pulled Tamara in for a hug that, by the looks of it, knocked the wind out of her. She whispered something in Tamara's ear before releasing her. Whatever she'd said must have helped, because some of the fear was gone from Tamara's face and she didn't cling to his arm for support.

He hoped the look he gave his stepmother effectively relayed how grateful he was. He'd known she would be an ally tonight, but it still warmed his heart to see her take Tamara under her wing.

On cue, she tucked Tamara's hand through her arm and led her off toward a group of women who were laughing near the bar the catering company had set up. "Come with me, my dear. There are so many people I'd like you to meet." She threw Gregory a wink over her shoulder as she led his date into the fray. "I trust you'll be all right on your own, my sweet?"

He waved them off in reply and gave Tamara an encouraging smile when she gave him a wide-eyed look over her shoulder.

He kept to the sidelines for most of the party, too distracted with keeping a watchful eye on his date to be much use at the small talk these events required. He needn't have worried, it seemed. After the first introductions were made, the tension in Tamara eased away, and with some urging from his mother, she started to take part in conversation.

By the time an hour had passed, Tamara looked like she was in her element. She still looked shy, but he caught glimpses of the mystery woman he'd first met. He grinned as he sipped his whiskey. By the time this night was over, she would be out of her shell. And he'd helped.

"That arrogant smirk doesn't suit you."

Gregory's smile melted at the sound of his father's voice behind him. "Father," he said. "Merry Christmas."

"What were you thinking bringing her here?"

*And happy holidays to you, too.*

His father's remark had an age-old anger simmering in his blood, adrenaline coursing through him as his body reacted to the harsh but familiar tone. He could hardly remember a time when his father didn't use that tone with him—the one that screamed "you're a disappointment" without him having to say a word. He should have known his father would react like this. Whatever had brought his father and stepmother together, it wasn't a shared sense of compassion.

"Is she your new girlfriend now?" his father demanded.

Gregory glared at him, unable to think of the right response. *Was* she his girlfriend? They hadn't discussed it, really, and he sure as hell didn't want to have "the talk" with his father before they'd had a chance to make things clear.

Apparently his lack of a response was answer enough, because his father sneered at him. "This is your problem right here."

Gregory looked around him before turning back to his father. "What problem? I don't see a problem."

His father continued as if he hadn't spoken. "You don't think ahead to the consequences."

Gregory rolled his eyes. He knew this speech by heart, but the words rankled every time he heard them. "I know, I know. You want me to be more respectable. More responsible. More like you."

And that was the crux of it, really. His father wanted Gregory to be his spitting image, but he'd gotten more from his mother than just her dark hair and eyes. He'd gotten her temperament, too. And that was unforgivable in his father's eyes. He would never approve of the man he'd become. He should have given up hope by now—Lord knew Gregory had given up trying to win his approval.

"You're not thinking this through, as usual," his father said.

Gregory's jaw clenched shut. His father never approved of the women in his life. He should be used to it by now. He had gotten used to it to some extent. With Vanessa, his father's snide remarks about her flighty ways had never really bothered him. Not like this. Maybe because Vanessa could stick up for herself, but Tamara was still fragile. The last thing she should have to face was his father's disapproval. "In case you've forgotten, I'm a grown man. I don't need your permission for the women I choose to date."

"Oh, grow up," his father said.

Gregory jerked back at that. His father's tone held more frustration than contempt, but the words still stung. He was in his early thirties and had done well for himself by anyone's standards. Anyone except his father, apparently. He forced back the anger—that would only encourage his father. Instead he kept his voice cool. "That's my point exactly, Father. I am grown up, which is why your opinion on who I date is not only unwelcome, it's out of line."

His father ignored him. He was too busy shaking his head. "You have to see that this is different, Gregory. For God's sake, the girl is an employee of The Blanchard Group now."

The fact that his father had a valid point rubbed his nerves, and he found himself losing the cool, calm tone his father detested. "It's not as though she's my assistant. She's running what amounts to a charity. And don't try and make it out that her employee status is what you find fault with. We both know better."

He met his father's stare, and the older man didn't try to look away. "No, that's not my only issue with you taking up with the Vanguard girl."

*The Vanguard girl.* Of course that's how he saw her. His father probably looked at her and only saw the disgrace that her parents went through.... The scandal that turned a "good girl" into a runaway.

His father leaned in and lowered his voice. "Do you really think you are good for her?"

Gregory's mouth fell open in surprise. A jolt of pain twisted his chest. His father had struck a nerve. *Well done, Dad.*

Was he good for her? Lord knew, he'd try to be. But Vanessa's words were plaguing him. She'd seemed so convinced that he would hurt Tamara, and Vanessa had never even met her. She had no idea how vulnerable Tamara really was. And now his father was saying what amounted to the same thing.

That he couldn't be trusted to be there for her. That he'd bail at the first sign of trouble. Yes, maybe he'd done that in the past. But this was different. Tamara was different.

Like a dog with a bone, his father kept going, his voice filled with scorn and disapproval. "What do you honestly think will come of this? Do you really believe that you are this poor girl's white knight? That you with your notoriety and your flashy ways can provide the stability that she needs?"

The words so closely echoed his own doubts that he couldn't ignore them. The fact that his father had touched on the truth only made his anger more intense. Rage flooded through him at his father's lack of faith in him and in his presumptuous statement about Tammy. As if this man had any idea what Tamara needed.

"It's just like you to want to play hero," his father continued. "But how long will it last this time?"

The words stung, but there was no way he would give his father the satisfaction of letting him see how accurate his aim had been with that barbed comment. The old urge to strike back came swift and strong.

"Don't act like you care about Tammy."

His father's lips tightened. He knew that look. Disappointment. "Of course I care about her. I remember her from when she was a little girl. Such a sweet young thing."

*And what about me?* His father had known him since birth, but that didn't automatically mean he cared about him. What about what *he* needed? What about what was good for *him*? Had his father ever cared about that?

"She was always such a good girl," his father continued. "Obedient. Dutiful."

Ah, there it was. That was what it all came down to. Tamara was the golden child in his father's eyes. She was everything his father had hoped Gregory would be. Until she'd caused a scandal.

His father's mind seemed to be going down the same track. He scowled off into the distance. "Such a shame she turned out to be quite troubled."

The urge to defend Tamara was nearly as strong as his disgust with his father. Now it all became clear. It wasn't concern for her that had his father balking at the idea of them as a couple. He just didn't want his precious family name associated with her scandal.

Of course, he should have seen it right away. He was attacking Gregory, making him doubt his ability to make Tamara happy...and why? To keep his precious pride intact. Heaven forbid his son's happiness take precedence over the family name.

The rush of age-old bitter anger was familiar and blinding. How many years had he heard his father say that he should be dating someone from within their circle? Well now he finally was and even that wasn't good enough. Oh no, not for the almighty Blanchards. It must be killing his father to know that he'd found the only upper crust debutante with a scandal. Well, too freakin' bad. His father might have an issue with her past, but he sure as hell wouldn't let family pride get in the way of true happiness.

His voice was gravelly with rage when he finally trusted himself to speak. "You're just pissed that I've finally done as you've asked—I've gone and found myself a sweet girl from a good family—and she's damaged goods." Gregory barely recognized his own voice. It was filled with years' worth of cynicism and hurt.

His father's brows lowered and his scowl intensified. "Gregory—" he started, his voice filled with warning. But Gregory didn't want to hear it. This was the last time his father would stick his nose in his personal business. The last time he'd speak of Tamara as if he knew her. Knew *them*.

The irony of it was too much, and it was the perfect weapon to throw in his father's face. "Admit it, Dad. It's driving you nuts. I found the perfect girl like you asked me to...and it turns out she's crazy. That's why you don't want me with Tammy. Admit it."

In his anger, his voice had gotten too loud. The ensuing silence felt equally loud. He nearly winced along with his father at the harshness in his tone, the bitterness and spite he hadn't even tried to hide.

But before he could say something to dispel the tension and salvage the conversation, they were interrupted by a voice behind him. A soft, sweet, unbearably sad voice.

"It's not Tammy anymore, actually. I prefer to go by Tamara now."

# Chapter 10

Tamara surprised herself by how much she enjoyed the party. This was her worst fear come to life, yet somehow…she found herself having fun.

With the help of Gregory's stepmother, Tamara had met everyone who was anyone, or at least that was how it felt. Several she remembered from her childhood, and they greeted her as warmly as Elena had. Whether their words were sincere didn't matter—they'd made her comfortable. Best of all, they didn't bring up her parents and her rift with them.

*Thank God.* It was hard enough seeing reminders of her family. If she'd been forced to talk about them, she might have broken down. Each time she saw someone she recognized, she couldn't help but wonder if they would tell her parents they had seen her.

Did she want them to? That was a question she was hard-pressed to answer. On one hand the thought terrified her. She had no idea what they thought of her at this point, or if their relationships were even salvageable. But, at the same time, the thought that they would get word that she was here in New York and doing okay…well, maybe it would be the opening they all needed to bridge the gap.

Thanks to years of practice, she didn't allow herself to dwell on her family issues too long, firmly shoving those thoughts out of her mind as she focused on the task at hand.

Besides, the majority of the people Elena introduced her to were strangers, and with them she was very nearly comfortable. Elena managed to steer the topic to the theater and their work there and stepped back as Tamara took over, explaining the theater's history, its mission, and the type of support they were looking for.

The guests were receptive and warm—whether it would lead to any money remained to be seen, but it was a start.

Best of all, Tamara had overcome a hurdle, and a massive one at that.

The funny thing was, after six years, this party marked the first time she actually felt like she'd moved forward in her life. As she listened and smiled as one of the guests regaled her and Elena with a story, Tamara found herself marveling at her own progress.

How crazy to think that after all this time, she'd finally taken a step in the right direction, and she'd done it by going backward, essentially. Because this was exactly the type of function—including some of the same people—her parents would have dragged her to.

She'd run away from all of this in the hopes that she could start a new life, but in reality she hadn't really been living at all. Oh, she'd had a job and she'd made some dear friends, but she'd kept herself so cut off from everyone. She'd hidden huge parts of her life, and there was no way to hide your life without cutting off a piece of your soul. She'd gotten so accustomed to it that she hadn't even realized what she'd been missing.

Not until Gregory.

She glanced over and saw him talking to his father. Not a terribly pleasant exchange, if Gregory's dark scowl was anything to go by.

Sneaking glances, she tried to look like she was paying attention to the elderly woman who was talking, but her eyes kept coming back to Gregory as if they had a mind of their own.

God, he was hot. *And he was hers!* Maybe. Sort of.

*Way to jump the gun, Tam.* They hadn't had "the talk"; nothing was official. But that didn't mean she couldn't hope. It had been so long since she'd let herself dream about finding love again—it was almost too terrifying to think about. But if there was anyone who could help her move forward, it was Gregory. Her hero. She bit back a goofy grin at the thought. But it was the truth. Until he'd come along, she'd been living in a bubble, isolating herself with her fears and her insecurities.

Taking a deep breath, she waited for a pause in the conversation before making her excuses and sidling toward Gregory. After everything he'd done for her, the least she could do was save him from an unpleasant chat with his father.

She'd nearly reached his side when his words struck her. She jerked back as if he'd slapped her across the face. *Damaged goods.*

Freezing in place, she struggled to catch her breath as the words ricocheted through her brain. Maybe he didn't mean it, maybe he wasn't talking about her, maybe—

But he kept talking, and she couldn't pretend he was talking about someone else. "...I found the perfect girl like you asked me to...and it turns out she's crazy."

The ground shifted beneath her feet as her stomach went into a free fall. Everything she'd been running from, it was all right here in front of her. The words coming out of his mouth mocked her for thinking that she'd moved forward, that her past mistakes hadn't followed her.

Hearing those words from anyone would have been painful...but coming from Gregory? The pain was brutal. His derisive tone cut her heart as surely as a knife. And then came the paranoid thoughts she couldn't bear to face.

Was that what this had been about from the beginning? Had Gregory been using her to spite his father? Because that was exactly what it sounded like. Gregory might not be able to take off in his father's car these days, but he could do much worse. He could date society's pariah.

He could pretend to care for her. He could make her think that he loved her. He could make her fall in love with him.

A sob choked her and made breathing impossible. Tears welled up behind her eyes, but before she lost it completely, she saw Gregory's father watching her over Gregory's shoulder, and some semblance of pride had her swallowing back tears.

*Pity.* She'd seen it clear as day in his gaze. That was one thing she couldn't bear. A second later Gregory turned and saw her. Guilt was written all over his face the moment he spotted her.

But she didn't want his guilt—that was one step above pity. He felt sorry for her. Sorry for hurting her.

Pride had her straightening her spine and finding her voice. She said the first thing she could think of, latching on to the anger she felt whenever she heard her old nickname.

"It's not Tammy anymore, actually. I prefer to go by Tamara now."

*Stupid.* It was a ridiculous thing to say given what she'd overheard. She should shout at him or slap him, even. But either option meant making a scene, and that meant drawing attention to herself. It meant whispers, rumors, and gossip.

She wouldn't give them the satisfaction.

So she ran away.

Turning and weaving through the crowd, she ran back toward the front door, shaking off Gregory's hand when he tried to stop her and blocking out the sound of his voice as he called after her.

\* \* \* \*

Gregory was in hell. Or rather, he was in a booth in the back of a dive bar sitting across from his best friend—but it might as well have been hell.

"It's been twenty-four hours," Gregory said, holding up his phone to Ben for proof. "I've texted, I've called, I've staked out the theater... I've done everything short of sending smoke signals, but she's avoiding me."

Ben didn't look at the phone. He nodded and shoved a handful of bar nuts into his mouth. "Yeah. Sounds like you really messed up, buddy." He didn't even pretend to flinch in the face of Gregory's glare. "You know it's true."

Gregory sighed and let his head fall back against the back of the booth. "Of course I know it. Why do you think I've been stalking her? I need to apologize."

Ben took a swig of his beer. "Yeah, you do."

He narrowed his eyes on his friend. "What do you know?"

Ben held up his hands. "Nothing." But Gregory knew him too well to fall for that fake innocence routine.

"You clearly know something. Tell me what you've heard."

Ben sighed. "All right. Caitlyn may have been a little put out that you hurt one of her closest friends."

Gregory groaned. *Shit.* Caitlyn was his best ally in Tamara's circle of friends. He'd been hoping he could convince her to plead his case. But if she knew what happened...

"Tamara told Caitlyn about...everything?"

Ben smirked at his attempt to be coy about her past. "Everything. Apparently she came home pretty upset last night, so Marc called for some reinforcements. Caitlyn and Meg went over and..." He shrugged as he took another sip of his beer. "From what I heard, there was quite a bit of booze and chocolate involved."

"Oh no." Gregory moaned. He knew he'd hurt her, that much had been obvious. But the thought of her crying to her friends, of the pain he had caused and had been trying not to think about, stuck like a knife in his gut.

"I've been given orders to kill you," Ben said. Then he shrugged. "Of course, Caitlyn was pretty drunk when she gave the order, so I'll give you a pass this time."

Gregory ignored the joking and leaned forward. "So what do I do? How can I make things right?"

Ben's brows shot up in surprise, and it was no wonder—up until a few weeks ago, Ben had been the one struggling with new-relationship woes. And prior to that, his friend had been a disaster when it came to love. But now, against all odds—Ben was the resident expert.

And apparently he took his new role seriously. Leaning back in his seat, Ben crossed his arms over his chest and blew out a long exhale. "All you can do is keep trying. Her first impulse is clearly to run...."

Gregory nodded. That was putting it mildly. This was a woman who'd changed her name and run away from her family to escape the pain.

And now he'd gone and hurt her as well. His heart plummeted into his stomach at the thought. He'd done the worst thing imaginable and hurt the one person he cared for most. And now she'd run far away from him. He rubbed a hand over his eyes as he cursed under his breath. Could he really blame her?

Maybe his father had been right all along. Maybe he wasn't cut out for a serious relationship. What if he always hurt anyone stupid enough to fall for him? Maybe he was better off with frivolous dalliances like what he'd had with Vanessa. At least in those relationships everyone had known the score. No one had gotten too close—certainly not close enough for him to hurt anyone the way he seemed destined to.

*Like mother, like son.*

The bitter thought was enough to make him slump down in his seat, suddenly exhausted. But his friend wasn't done dispensing advice, and he owed it to Tamara to apologize, at the very least. He couldn't let his issues with his father be the reason she retreated back into herself. She deserved better for her life.

*She deserved better than him.*

He shoved the thought away. That was his father talking. He could do better—*be* better.

Ben continued with his lecture. "I know she's running from you, but you need to find her. Show her that you care enough that you won't give up on her."

Gregory nodded. That he could do. He would never give up on her, but the best thing he could do was protect her from himself. Make sure he never hurt her again. He needed another chance to show her that she could trust him and trust herself.

"How do you propose I apologize and make things right when she clearly doesn't want to see me?"

Ben's grin was smug as he called the waitress over for another round. "Tomorrow is Christmas, my friend. A day of forgiveness and new beginnings. And it just so happens I know exactly where she'll be."

* * * *

Marc hovered near the front door, one bag slung over his shoulder and the other sitting next to the door. "Are you sure you won't come with me?"

Tamara bit back a sigh as she sank further into the couch and prepared herself for a cozy day of old movies. She was armed with multiple bottles of wine and the number for her favorite Chinese place.

Basically, she was setting up camp for a nice long day of not thinking about Gregory. An impossible feat since she couldn't stop thinking about how she didn't want to think about him. But maybe with a little peace and quiet she could ease the stabbing pain in her gut. Maybe with enough wine she could drown out the little voice that was screaming bloody murder at having been proved right.

She'd known all along that she couldn't leave her past behind. That Gregory's words about not caring about her history were too good to be true. Wasn't that why she'd left her family and that social circle all those years ago? Even then she'd known she wouldn't be able to be herself there, not without a constant reminder of those dark days with Billy.

Yet she'd stupidly thought Gregory was different. That she could trust him and that he actually cared about her.

*She should have known!* He'd openly admitted that almost everything he did was to get back at his father. Taking his father's car, buying a run-down theater…. Dating high society's lunatic. All part of the game.

She'd thought she'd cried until she couldn't cry anymore the night before, but just thinking about her stupidity and Gregory's painful words was enough to have her sniffling all over again.

Marc came over and moved a box of tissues from the kitchen to an end table next to the couch just in case. Wise man.

"Are you sure you don't want—"

"I'll be fine," she said, waving him toward the door. "Go have fun with your family. I'll see you in a couple of days."

Marc looked unconvinced, but he took hold of the doorknob before giving her one last look over his shoulder. "Promise you'll call if you need me? I can be back in the city in two hours."

She nodded and held up three fingers. "Scout's honor."

Less than a minute after the door closed behind him, she heard a knock. Marc had never once been able to leave for a trip without coming back for some forgotten necessity, and apparently this time it was his keys.

"I told you you'd forget something," she said as she pulled the door open.

The sight of Gregory in her doorway had her stomach twisting in agony even as her stupid heart threatened to leap out of her chest with joy.

Goddammit, why did he have to look so good?

Even with mussed hair and shadows under his eyes, he looked delicious. *Dangerous.*

And that's exactly what he was, she reminded herself. He was a danger to her peace of mind and to her sanity.

There was no way she could risk that again.

For a second she contemplated shutting the door in his face. She'd always hated confrontations. But she wasn't that girl anymore. This was her home, and he was the one in the wrong here. She pulled herself up straight and crossed her arms over her chest. "What are you doing here?"

She watched him suck in air and shove his hands into his pockets. What, had he been expecting a warm welcome?

His deep voice sent shivers through her despite her best efforts to guard against it. "I came to apologize."

Words left her. It wasn't that his proclamation was so stunning but the look in his eyes. The pain there was raw and genuine and… Oh shit, she didn't want to feel sorry for him.

Spinning on her heel, she all but ran into the kitchen. She couldn't face him, not yet. She needed just one moment to clear her head. Remember how badly he'd hurt her and how he would always hurt her. Hadn't she learned that lesson six years ago? This would only end in pain; that was how it worked for her. It was why she'd sworn off relationships. Falling for someone meant giving them control. It meant losing herself, something she'd vowed she wouldn't do a second time because the first time had nearly destroyed her. It had taken years to recover, to earn back the confidence Billy had stolen from her. It had taken starting over and reinventing herself for her to figure out who she was apart from his lies and manipulations.

Gregory might not be another Billy, but that didn't make him any less of a threat. The kindest man on earth still had the power to destroy her if she fell for him. Because falling in love intrinsically meant losing yourself, losing power, losing identity.

No, it didn't matter who the man was or how noble his intentions; she'd promised herself she wouldn't go down that path again. If only she'd remembered that promise earlier. Maybe then she wouldn't be in this mess and maybe her heart wouldn't be ready to shatter over this man.

She'd hoped to get some space to get her head on straight and remember why she had to be strong and stay away from him. But he followed right behind her. She felt the heat from his body as she came to a stop in the center of the kitchen.

"I'm sorry," he said, his voice little more than a whisper.

Her throat closed up; she was choking on tears. Forcing them down with a swallow, she kept her back to him. She didn't trust herself to face him. "I understand."

And she did, that was the worst part. It had been too tempting.

"What do you mean, you understand?" He walked around so he was standing in front of her, so close she smelled his aftershave. Maybe if she held her breath her body would stop craving the feel of him. Despite her heartache, she found herself resisting the urge to move forward and lean against him.

"Tamara," he said gently, insistently. "What is it you think you understand?"

A flash of anger shot through her, and she did look up then. Her gaze met his, and his head jerked back at whatever emotion he saw there.

"I get it," she said. "You've never lied to me about your feelings about your father—your need to get back at him and spite him." She swallowed again and forced her voice to remain steady. "No matter who gets hurt in the process."

Gregory's face fell, and the pain in his eyes was so convincing that it must have mirrored her own. "It wasn't like that."

"Wasn't it?" She stared at the collar of his leather jacket, unable to meet his gaze any longer. "Because that's how it seems. Like you found out my secret and realized you had the perfect weapon to get back at your father. He was always giving you a hard time over the women you dated, right? He wanted you to date someone in his social circle, I'm sure of it. I know your dad, remember?" She forced a laugh and it came out sounding as bitter as she felt. "So what… You met me and realized I was exactly the type of woman he'd been trying to force on you. But what luck! You found the one debutante who'd lost her mind, who'd caused a scandal. The one you could shove in your father's face and make him—"

"Tamara, no!" His voice was loud and filled with anger as he cut her off. Taking her by the shoulders, he softened his tone. "It wasn't like that. I never intended to hurt you. I didn't set out to use you—"

"But you did." That silenced him. The only sound was the hum of her refrigerator and her breathing. She tried to slow it but it sounded harsh, like she'd just run a marathon.

His gaze never left her face, but his hands dropped from her shoulders and her breathing came a little easier now that his touch wasn't scalding her. She took a step backward and then another, wrapping her arms around her waist as her body grew cold.

"I never meant to hurt you," he said again.

Her breath escaped in a short burst—nearly a laugh but not quite as she repeated herself. "But you did."

* * * *

Gregory would do anything to take away the pain that etched her delicate features, making her appear more fragile than ever before.

*He'd done that.* His gut twisted in agony. He'd known he'd hurt her, but seeing it with his own eyes made it so much more real.

She deserved better, so much better. Shit, had he really thought he could make this up to her? That she would give him another chance after he'd shoved his foot in his mouth and exposed her to the kind of humiliation he'd sworn to protect her from?

He couldn't protect her. His father had been right. Hell, even Vanessa had been right.

He watched her walk away from him, her shoulders slumped. The right thing to do would be to walk away—avoid hurting her any further. Because he would; he couldn't help it. His father was right—he didn't know the first thing about commitment. He'd devoted his adult life to this feud with his father and now he thought he could just flip a switch and somehow be the kind of man Tamara deserved? It didn't work that way.

If he was being honest with himself, a future with Tamara would end one of two ways—he'd bail on her when she needed him most or he'd hurt her again. Even if he could make a commitment—and that was a big if—there was no way he wouldn't disappoint her eventually. She'd get caught in the crossfire between him and his father, and there was nothing he could do to protect her.

"I'm sorry," he said again. Because really, there was nothing else to say. He'd been a fool to think he could make this right. Oh, he could probably find words to make her feel better, maybe even make her forgive him. They could start over… But then what? Every past relationship flashed through his mind. It was time to face facts—he was a failure when it came to love.

His father was right. He wasn't cut out for anything serious—and until he realized that, anyone he dated would be collateral damage.

She didn't respond to his apology, and he took a few steps closer. He saw her stiffen and stopped. Frustration lanced through him like a knife. He wanted to promise her he would never hurt her again—but that would be a lie. For the first time in his life, his father's words finally made sense. He didn't have what it took to be serious. He'd never had a healthy relationship, and he couldn't ask Tamara to hedge her bets on him. To take the chance that maybe, just maybe, her love would be enough to change him.

"I understand if you don't want to see me anymore."

He heard her short, humorless laugh. "That won't be easy, since we work together."

Right. *Crap.* This was exactly why he never got involved with women he worked with. Now he'd gone and muddied the waters at the theater in addition to everything else.

*Great work.*

There were so many things he wanted to say. Namely, he wanted to beg her for another chance. But even if she agreed to forgive him for the stupid remarks to his father, he couldn't guarantee that he wouldn't hurt her again.

There was nothing for it but to move on. Move forward. Make this as painless as he could for her and for him. So even as his chest tightened with a sickening ache, he forced himself to think rationally.

"I trust you to run things at the theater. I'll have one of the company's accountants take over looking at the theater's financial history."

She spun around, and her face was deathly pale. Her lips were pressed tightly together and her eyes were filled with pain. "So that's your answer to this? Just run away from your commitments?"

It might as well have been his father he heard and not Tamara. Calling him out on his inability to see things through. He'd been so sure he could change. That his father was wrong and he was nothing like his mother, who had walked away the moment that things turned difficult.

And now here he was, about to do the same thing.

But it was for the best. He would protect her from future pain. He would only hurt her worse if they grew any more entangled. Maybe sometimes walking away was the right decision. Maybe it was for the best.

Looking at the pain so evident in her eyes, it was obvious—walking away was the best thing he could do for her. But to walk away, he had to shove his own emotions to the side. If he let his heart decide, he would be on the ground groveling for another chance.

He steeled his features and met her gaze. "Did you really expect anything else?"

She studied him in silence for a moment before her lips twisted into a cynical sneer that was totally out of character for his sweet, genuine Tamara. Not "his" anything, he reminded himself.

"So you're trying to live down to your father's expectations now, is that it?"

His jaw tightened. He was trying to save her from making a mistake, dammit. "Just giving in to the inevitable."

Some of the bitterness faded from her expression, and her defensive stance deflated slightly. For a minute he swore she saw through him—past all of the defenses, the years' worth of games he'd been playing with Vanessa and the others. Even through the spite his father brought out in him that seemed to shape the course of his life. "What are you doing, Gregory?"

He opened his mouth to reply. *Saving you from me. Giving you a chance to find someone worth your time—someone who can help you heal old wounds and not cause you even more pain.* But nothing came out. He couldn't bring himself to admit that he was pushing her away for her own good.

And then he lost his chance. Her eyes grew shuttered at his silence and her body stiffened once more, her arms wrapping around her waist.

She was going back into her shell—the one she'd spent years building around herself to keep her from having to face the wounds from her past and the risk of pain in the future.

*He'd done that*, he thought again.

He choked on a bitter laugh. His father would love this. He'd finally gotten it through his thick skull that his father had been right all along. All it took was breaking the heart of the one woman he'd ever truly loved.

*Loved.* The word reverberated through him and left him weak.

Holy shit. He'd fallen in love.

She was staring at him, but her gaze was unreadable. Did she feel the same?

He stumbled backward toward the door at the thought. Panic swept through him. All the more reason for him to get out now, before they were both crushed.

"I'm sorry," he said once again as he made his way toward the door. He was keenly aware of her gaze on him. She saw too much. Knew him too well. He had to get out of there.

"I think it's for the best," he continued, his back to her. "We'll keep things between us professional. It will be for the best."

He was repeating himself. Babbling, almost, in his desire to escape.

Risking one more glance back at Tamara, he instantly wished he hadn't. The hurt on her face was a silent condemnation.

He'd screwed this up, as he should have known he would. He never should have gotten involved with her in the first place, but now it was too late. He'd caused her pain, just like his father had told him he would.

# Chapter 11

Days passed with no contact from Gregory. Not after that bizarre performance in her kitchen—the one where he all but ran away after telling her what a mistake he'd made in being with her. And he was right…wasn't he?

She and Marc were the last to leave the theater after what was sure to be one of the last meet-ups for Operation Petticoat. And what a meet-up it had been.

"I still can't believe that Alice—our little anti-love Alice—finally figured out that she's in love with the good doc," Marc said.

Tamara pushed away the nagging thoughts about Gregory. For a little while there she'd managed to forget about him entirely—especially once Alice had opened up to them about her own love life dilemma.

But somehow Alice's dilemma had turned into a conversation about Gregory and there was no avoiding the topic. Her friend needed her help—or rather, Gregory's help—and there was nothing for it but to help her.

Which meant talking to Gregory.

Her stomach did a backflip, but it was impossible to tell if it was out of dread or excitement. Because as badly as he'd hurt her, it had hurt far worse to watch him walk out of her apartment. She missed him, pure and simple.

Marc interrupted her thoughts. "What are you going to say to him?"

She blinked up at him as they trudged through a snowbank to cross the street.

"Are you just going to outright say, 'Hey stud, we need you to be the bachelor'?" He lowered his voice to a sexy baritone, making her laugh.

"I don't know what I'm going to say," she said in all honesty. "This isn't exactly a typical request."

Alice's boyfriend—or whatever he was—was supposed to be the star prize for a bachelor auction to raise money for the hospital where he worked. But Alice was having second thoughts about offering the man she loved to the masses of single women who would surely want to snatch up the handsome doctor.

So she'd asked Tamara if Gregory would be the star instead. In Alice's defense, she had no idea what drama had been going on between Tamara and Gregory. She'd been so caught up in her own love life mess that she and Tamara hadn't had a chance to talk. And when she'd asked this morning, Tamara hadn't been able to bring herself to say no, not when it meant so much to Alice.

Besides, the decision wasn't up to her. She would just be the messenger.

"He'll say yes," Marc said with full certainty.

"How do you know?"

He grinned down at her. "Because you're the one who's asking. We both know he won't be able to say no to you."

She gave a snort of amusement. "Marc, did you not listen at all when I told you what happened between us the other night?"

Marc put a hand to his heart. "I'm hurt, *ma Cherie*. Of course I listened. I just know something you don't know."

"What's that?"

"Gregory Blanchard is in love with you."

Tamara stopped walking. Unfortunately they were in the middle of the street, which meant Marc had to tug her arm to get her across before the light turned and she was run over.

And honestly that was how she felt—like she'd just been run over by a truck. Questions flew through her brain. Was Marc right or was he being nice? And if he was right, what did that mean?

And maybe most importantly, did she love him?

She was dimly aware that Marc had paused next to her on the corner. "Are you breathing?"

She nodded. Breathing, but still dizzy. "Why did you say that?"

"What? That he loves you? Because it's true."

"How do you know?" she demanded.

"Because I have eyes." He laughed. "It was completely obvious in the way he looked at you. Like you hung the moon and every star in the sky."

He waited for her to digest that before adding, "Is that good news or bad?"

When she glanced up, he was giving her a knowing smile.

"What do you mean?"

He sighed and threw an arm around her shoulder, leading her back toward their apartment. "I mean, are you ready to admit that you love him, too?"

Her response was to gulp for air. No, she was definitely not ready to admit that. It might even be true, but the idea of being in love again, of making herself vulnerable and leaving herself wide open to pain… She was definitely not ready for that.

Marc seemed to read her mind, and he sighed once again. "You'll get there, Tam-Tam. You'll get there."

They walked in silence for a while, and it wasn't until they were only a block from the apartment that Tamara broke it. "What am I going to do, Marc?"

He grinned. "You're going to ask him to be the bachelor, of course. It's the perfect excuse to get the two of you talking again."

"And then what?" She honestly wanted to know, and Marc seemed to have all the answers.

"True love can't be denied, my sweet. You two will figure it out."

She didn't know whether to laugh or cry at his romantic ideas. Up until her brief fling with Gregory, she'd been convinced that love was not in the cards for her. Not after everything that had happened with Billy. As if she'd had her chance and lost it. But what if what she had with Billy hadn't been her only shot? She'd loved him once, but it had never been the kind of love she'd wanted or needed. It had been a childish infatuation that had grown twisted and toxic far too quickly.

Maybe there was a chance for her to experience real love—the kind Meg had found with Jake and that Caitlyn had found with Ben. It was possible, wasn't it?

The hope that flickered in her chest had her fighting to catch her breath. Hope was a tricky thing—a beautiful emotion in and of itself. But terrifying, too. Because if she allowed herself to hope and then those hopes were dashed…she didn't know if she could take it.

Marc, as usual, seemed to know exactly what was going through her head. Coming to stand in front of her, he took her hands in his. "You have to talk to him, Tam. Literally, you *have* to if only to help Alice. So why not take the opportunity to really talk to him? You owe it to yourself and to him to give this thing a second chance."

She blinked up at her best friend, whose face was set in an unusually serious expression. "When did you get so wise?"

He threw his head back with a laugh. "I have always been wise, my dear. You've just never needed my counsel before."

She gave a snort of disbelief as they headed up the stairs to the apartment.

A little while later she found herself once again looking completely out of place in the cushy offices of The Blanchard Group. The same blonde greeted her and told her that Gregory was in a meeting but that she should wait in the lobby.

Wonderful. Just what she needed. More time to sit and stew and get anxious as hell. What if he didn't want to see her? What if Marc was wrong and he didn't have real feelings for her? What if, what if, what if…

She let out a slow exhale, hoping to calm her nerves. Nope. Slow breathing was not helping. Distraction, that was what she needed. The coffee table in the lobby was littered with newspapers, and she picked one up at random.

She flipped through it absently, her mind unable to focus. Marc's words kept echoing through her skull. What if Gregory really did love her?

When she let herself consider that possibility, the overwhelming swell of joy fell flat in the face of reality. They barely knew each other—not as adults, anyway. It had been a brief whirlwind of an affair, nothing more. The alternative seemed far more likely.

Maybe she'd found the kind of love typically reserved for fairy tales… or maybe she was just an idiot. A romantic who'd read too much into sex. Maybe she was no better at choosing men now than she had been as a teenager. He could have been laughing at her all along.

He'd seen her as a way to get back at his father, nothing more. The laughingstock he could shove in his father's face.

*No!* A small voice in the back of her mind didn't want to believe that. She wanted to believe his apology. But then, he hadn't asked for a second chance. He'd said he was sorry, but he hadn't offered another explanation.

If he truly wanted her, wouldn't he have fought for them? Maybe he was embarrassed by her history after all. What if she'd served her purpose in his life and he was ready to see it come to an end?

So many what-ifs, so many maybes. It was impossible to know what was going on inside his head. Only his actions mattered. And he'd ended things between them, plain and simple. Maybe that was all she needed to know.

She had her answer.

The blonde poked her head into the waiting area, and her chipper smile grated on Tamara's nerves.

"Mr. Blanchard is ready to see you now."

She followed the woman back to his office despite the heavy weight in her gut that begged her to run away. She was here on business, that was all.

*Liar.* The little voice she tried to ignore mocked her. She wasn't just here on business—she was here because she was hoping to be proven wrong.

Despite everything he'd said and done, a small, stupid part of her still wanted to believe that this was all a misunderstanding. That he truly did care about her and was only trying to protect her.

*Fool.* How many excuses had she made for Billy over the years? How many times had she let him off the hook because the truth wasn't what she wanted to hear or see?

That was exactly what she was doing now. Repeating her old mistakes. Believing what she wanted to be true and then rearranging facts to make it so.

Not this time. She wouldn't be that idiotic ever again.

Gregory stood when she walked in. He looked terrible, from the bags under his eyes to the mussed hair—the man standing before her bore little resemblance to the Gregory she'd had a crush on from afar.

His eyes lacked the laughter that made him so charismatic, and his sexy smile had been replaced by a scowl. "What are you doing here?"

Her heart fell into the pit of her stomach. After all that self-talk about not getting her hopes up, she'd done exactly that. Without even trying, the stupid optimist in her had been holding out hope. That he'd changed his mind, that he'd want to fight for her, that he truly had cared about her.

More than anything, she'd been hopeful that she could trust her gut. The intuition that had told her she could believe this man. That he cared about her. That he was different—worth being vulnerable for and worth risking her heart over.

She'd been wrong. Gregory didn't love her. She'd made a fool of herself over a man.

Again.

Good God, when would she learn?

"What are you doing here?" he asked again.

Good question. Straightening her spine, she shoved away the hurt feelings and the wounded pride—and the broken heart.

"Don't worry, I'm just here on behalf of The Ellen. I'm not looking for another scene." Even she was stunned by the ice in her tone. The harsh coldness covered up all the emotions jostling for attention beneath the surface.

He raised one brow. "Is something wrong at the theater?"

She shook her head. "Not an issue. But we could use a favor."

"I'm listening," he said as he resumed his seat and stared at the computer screen. He might be listening, but he was ignoring her presence as if she was a lowly peon and not a business partner. Certainly not a lover.

She briefly explained the situation—how their star bachelor could no longer participate in the fundraiser. How it was for a good cause, how the organizers had hoped Gregory might step in... She spoke as if on autopilot, her voice oddly even.

When she was done, Gregory looked up with a weary sigh. "So they want me to sell myself to the highest bidder." He met her gaze, and for the first time she thought she saw a flicker of emotion. "And is that what you want?" he asked.

To see him paraded around and handed over to some other woman to be her dream date? *No!* He was *hers*.

But of course that wasn't true. It had never been true. Just a figment of her imagination—what she wanted to be true.

Maybe she was crazy after all.

She shrugged as if it meant nothing to her. As if *he* meant nothing to her. Maybe if she acted like he didn't matter, it would come true. "It's in the best interest of the theater. So yes, this is what I want."

"Fine. I'll do it." He dropped his head to continue reading whatever was on the screen in front of him.

She had been dismissed.

As she walked out of his office building, a numbness stole over her. He didn't care about her. He truly didn't care. She'd been foolish enough to trust a man with her heart for a second time, and for a second time she'd had her heart broken as a result.

She shivered as she stepped outside into the frigid air.

She knew the truth now, she told herself, that was something. Better late than never. And yes, her heart had shattered into a million pieces, but she would recover in time. That much she knew from experience.

At least this time she had friends and the theater to help her through. She supposed it could have been worse.

She pulled her phone out of her pocket and turned it on so she could call Alice and let her know that he'd agreed. She'd had the sound off to avoid being disturbed during their meeting and when she glanced at her phone she saw she'd missed a call. She stopped in the middle of the sidewalk, thoughts of Gregory pushed out of her mind at the shock of seeing this phone number pop up on her screen.

It was quite possibly the only number she still knew by heart. The first one she'd ever learned.

She'd missed a call from her parents.

# Chapter 12

Gregory had to assume there was a special place in hell reserved for people like him. But then again, maybe he was already there.

"You, my friend, are an asshole." Ben was sprawled across his couch when he stated the obvious.

Gregory was determined to not look up from his book. Ben had long ago decided that he was always welcome at Gregory's and never bothered to call before dropping in. Most of the time he was right. Not today. Today, Gregory wanted to be alone with his misery. His voice was clipped when he finally asked, "Is there a reason you're here?"

Ben's laugh irritated him. It was hard enough being around his old friend these days thanks to Ben's new fantastically irritating love of life. Which had clearly come as a result of his even more annoying love of his girlfriend.

Gregory's head shot up, and he studied his friend. "Did Caitlyn send you?" And by that, he meant, had Tamara talked about him? He fought the urge to roll his eyes at his own ridiculousness. Here he was, the cold, heartless cad...and he was about ready to fly out of his chair at news of his ex.

If he could even call her his ex. They hadn't been together long enough for that. So what did that make her? His former lover? Too callous. That didn't come close to defining the way she'd burrowed through his defenses and taken up residence in his heart.

Ben's answer cut through Gregory's romantic nonsense. "No one sent me. I came because it's obvious your head is so far up your ass that you're going to require some assistance getting it unstuck."

Gregory glared at his friend. "Very funny."

"I know." Ben's mirth grated on his last nerve.

Gregory sat in stony silence as he debated whether to throw his best friend out onto the street or get this conversation over with and avoid all future talks about his emotions or lack thereof.

He opted for the latter. Mainly because knowing Ben, if he failed on his current mission, he would recruit his girlfriend to help with future interventions. Ben he could curse out and even strike, if need be, but if Caitlyn were drawn into this? He'd be unarmed. For all he knew she would use her honesty and tough-love tactics to reduce him to a whimpering puddle of tears.

He caved with a growl. "Fine. Say what you came here to say and then get out."

Ben grinned. "So you can get back to moping in peace?"

Gregory fell back in his seat. "Exactly." What use was there in denying it?

Ben leaned forward on the couch and starting rubbing his hands together. Donning an over-the-top American accent, he launched his sales pitch. "What if I were to tell you that you never need to mope again. Yes, sir, the answer to all your problems is so easy you'll slap yourself silly that you didn't think of it yourself."

Gregory refused to smile despite his friend's ridiculous antics. "Let me guess. I should pull my head out of my ass."

"Wrong!" Ben dropped the accent as he met his friend's gaze. "All you have to do is admit you love the girl."

Gregory's heart dropped into the pit of his stomach at hearing the word said aloud. He opened his mouth to deny it but couldn't. Not just because this was his oldest friend and he never lied to him, but because lying about it seemed like yet another betrayal against Tamara.

So he kept his mouth shut. Ben seemed content to wait for a response all day, if need be, but their heavy silence was broken by the sound of the doorman buzzing to let someone up.

When the doorman announced his visitor, Gregory cursed under his breath. "Send him up."

He returned to the living room to find a smug know-it-all still lounging on the sofa.

"I'll say this once and then this conversation is over." He drew in a deep breath. "I do love her, but sometimes that's not enough." He held up a hand to stop Ben from interrupting. His ears were ringing from hearing the L-word come out of his own mouth, but now wasn't the time to agonize over it. Not when he had an unwanted visitor on his way up.

"Sometimes love is not enough," he said again.

"Since when?" Ben shook his head. "Do you even hear yourself? Look, I get it, mate. I understand better than anyone that your intentions are good. You think she's better off without you."

"It's the truth."

"No!" Ben's voice was loud in the otherwise silent apartment. "It's not. Take it from me, I had to learn the hard way. You're only hurting her more, and that girl doesn't deserve any more pain in her life."

Guilt lanced through him. "I already hurt her once. I won't do it again."

Ben's face twisted in confusion. "You hurt her *once*. And yeah, that sucked, but it was a slip of the tongue. One mistake, hardly unforgiveable. To end everything based on that? Talk about throwing the baby out with the bathwater."

Gregory's jaw clenched. How could his friend not understand? He knew him better than anyone. "It's not what I said, but why I said it."

Ben raised one brow. "To piss off your dad, right?"

Gregory gave a jerky nod. Humiliating that his father still held so much power over him. "Don't you get it? She'd be a pawn between us." Ben opened his mouth, but Gregory wouldn't let him interrupt. "And it's not just that, Ben. You *know* me. I don't do commitments. I don't do serious. And I sure as hell don't do love."

Ben stood, and his look of disappointment spoke volumes. "You know who you sound like, don't you?"

Gregory sighed as a knock sounded on the door. "Yeah, I know."

Ben kept talking as he followed him down the hall to the front door. "Just because your father repeats himself over and over doesn't make it true. You know that, don't you?"

He ignored him, pushing down the question he wanted to ask. *But what if he's right?* What if he did take after his mother? After all, every failed relationship he'd ever had only bolstered that theory. And what if he was destined to run away every time shit hit the fan?

No. Tamara deserved better. Someone stable, reliable, and capable of giving her the support she needed.

Ben reached from behind and placed a hand on the door, not letting Gregory open it until he said his piece. "You see the ridiculousness of your actions, don't you? You have to see that you're being a complete and utter ass."

"Ben, I don't have time—"

But Ben refused to budge, and Gregory was forced to let him speak and get it over with—otherwise they would be standing there all day. "All right, Ben. Just say what you want to say."

Ben shook his head, his eyes filled with something disturbingly close to pity. "You're so hell-bent on protecting her from yourself that you don't even see. In trying to protect her, you're proving your father right. It's a fucking self-fulfilling prophecy—you're hurting her to avoid hurting her."

Gregory stared at his friend. The words made sense. Goddammit, it took everything in him not to cave then and there and go running to her, begging for her forgiveness.

A knock sounded again, louder this time.

"I should go," Ben said, finally lifting his hand from the door. Gregory opened it for him and they both turned to stare at his father, who was wearing a deep frown, most likely from having to wait.

Ben shot him a look over his shoulder. "Good luck." He moved past Gregory's father with a small nod, and even that was more of an acknowledgement than he normally gave the older man.

His father ignored Ben in response—it was a typical interaction between those two. No love lost there.

Pushing past him into the apartment, his father dove right into business, which was the only reason he was there.

"I need your signature on those documents."

He bit back a nasty retort. He never particularly wanted to see his father, but now he would have done just about anything to get rid of him. He needed time to clear his head after Ben's lecture. It had stirred up every weighty emotion he'd been trying to avoid this past week.

Guilt. Pain. Loss. Yearning. Now that Ben had stirred it all up, he needed time to get himself under control. So rather than argue with his father, he simply said. "Fine. Do you have them with you?"

But his father kept talking as if he'd argued. "I don't know why you're holding us up on this. We've done our due diligence and—"

"I said I'd sign." He couldn't even remember why he'd been arguing with his father about this deal in the first place. And at the moment, it didn't seem to matter. It was just a deal—an exchanging of money. What did he care?

His father either didn't believe his sudden concession or was looking to pick a fight, because he narrowed his eyes at Gregory and swept him with a look that seemed to take in everything from his mussed hair to his ratty old jeans. "What's wrong with you?"

"What do you mean, what's wrong?"

"Are you sick?"

*Just heartbroken.* But his father wouldn't want to hear that, even if he could believe it.

After a lengthy silence, his father dropped the folders he was holding on the end table near the couch. "I suppose you've heard about Tammy…"

He straightened automatically at the sound of her name, panic coursing through him. "No. What? Did something happen to her?"

His father's brows drew together for a moment as though he was trying to figure out a puzzle. "Nothing happened to her, unless you think being reunited with her family is a tragedy."

Gregory stared at him in shock. "Tamara spoke to her family?"

"From what I understand, she's planning to visit them soon." His father walked toward the window and looked out at the view.

A million questions raced through his brain at the news. None of which his father could answer. How was she holding up? Was she happy to reconcile with them? Were they looking out for her best interests this time around? Had they apologized for the way they had treated her six years ago?

Instead he settled for something his father might be able to answer. "How did they find her?"

His father turned back with a small smile that was a rarity. "Me, of course."

Anger swept through him swift and fierce. "You had no right to interfere—"

"Of course I did." His father walked toward him. "The Vanguards are some of my oldest friends. Not having contact with their daughter was killing them. They had a right to know—"

"It should have been up to Tamara."

His father shrugged. "Maybe, but she might never have taken that step. Sometimes people need a shove."

Gregory let out a bark of humorless laughter. "Is that how you would describe your parental style? All this time you've just been giving me a shove?"

His father frowned. "We weren't talking about you."

"No, we were talking about Tamara and how she is none of your business."

"But you made her my business when you brought her to my house. When you bought the theater that she works for with the family's money." His father took a step closer. "You couldn't possibly expect me to keep it a secret when her parents have been desperate to see her."

"Desperate to see her or to smooth over any further scandal?" His voice was filled with bitterness and anger on Tamara's behalf, and his father had the good grace to flinch.

"It's true," he said slowly. "They didn't handle the situation well all those years ago."

"You think?" His voice dripped with sarcasm. Despite his best efforts he couldn't seem to summon the cold, detached amusement he typically used to hide his emotions around his father. Not after that conversation with Ben and definitely not now when the conversation had turned to Tamara.

His father regarded him. His expression was blank, but his eyes were calculating.

Gregory shifted beneath that stare. "What?"

"You care about her." It wasn't a question, and Gregory couldn't read his tone.

"Shocking, isn't it?" Gregory mocked.

His father was quiet again. Folding his hands together, he walked closer. "You know, I never approved of the way the Vanguards handled that fiasco."

Gregory let out a disdainful snort. *Fiasco.* Only his father would call it that.

His father ignored him. "I always liked Tammy. But as much as I didn't agree with the way they handled the situation, I understood it."

"Of course you did," Gregory muttered under his breath. Sweeping family secrets under the rug was a Blanchard specialty. But his father's next words took him by surprise.

"They may have made mistakes, but they were only trying to protect their daughter. Just like I always tried to protect you."

Gregory's mouth fell open in shock, and for a moment he didn't know if he was going to laugh or shout. Laughter won out, but it was dark and bitter. "*You,*" he said, "protecting *me?*"

His father blinked, the only sign that he was taken aback by Gregory's response. "Of course. I wanted to protect you from your mother's reputation. I needed to instill in you a sense of responsibility to your family and to the people you care about."

"By constantly berating me and telling me how similar I am to her? By making sure I always knew that I shared her blood and that I was always going to hurt the ones I loved?"

Now it was his father's turn to stare with his mouth slightly open. "That's not... That was never my intention."

Gregory stared as if the mere act of looking at him might help solve the riddle that was his father. Finally some of the anger seemed to ebb and he leaned against the desk, depleted of energy. "Maybe not, but that was the end result."

His father's brows furrowed, and he opened his mouth to speak but shut it just as quickly.

Whatever he had to say, Gregory didn't want to hear it. His mind was too fixed on Tamara and her situation to fight with his father.

Maybe it would be good for her to see her family again. They could help her heal old wounds so she could start fresh with someone worthy of her.

"Gregory, your mother..." His father's voice trailed off, and Gregory was grateful. They'd never really spoken of her. She'd become a ghost after she left—haunting them with actions that would never be explained and leaving only her legacy of failure in the form of her son.

"You're not her," his father finally said. "You never were."

Gregory raked a hand through his hair. "You don't know that, Dad. Maybe you were right all this time."

He didn't know who was more surprised by that statement. But his pride was no longer standing between them. After losing Tamara, the confrontation with Ben, and now this news from his father, he felt gutted. There was no room for blustering indignation. It was about time he gave his father what he'd always wanted to hear. "I mean, look at my track record—in business and relationships. I don't exactly have a history of hanging in there for the long haul, now do I?"

His father didn't answer right away. When he did, he didn't outright answer. "Your mother hurt me when she left."

Gregory's eyes widened in surprise, but he kept his mouth shut. His father rarely mentioned his mother, let alone spoke of how he'd felt when she'd walked away.

"But, more importantly, she hurt you." His father cleared his throat. "I didn't want you to repeat her mistakes. You idolized her as a child, and I didn't want..."

When his father trailed off, looking at a loss for the first time in his life, Gregory took pity. "I get it. You didn't want me to hurt people the way she hurt us." His mind flashed on Tamara and the pained look in her eyes the last time he'd seen her. "And I won't."

He'd stay away from her, for her sake. It was the least he could do to make up for hurting her.

"That's true," his father said. He dipped his head and scratched the back of his neck in a rare show of uncertainty. "But I also wanted to keep you from getting hurt again. It's possible that I went too far."

Gregory gaped at his father. Never in his life had he heard his father admit he might have been wrong about anything, let alone him.

His father turned away. "You see, when your mother left, she didn't just hurt me. You were devastated."

Gregory stared at his father's back and tried to comprehend what he was hearing. His father was talking to him like they were equals. Peers. Hell, he was talking to him like he was his son.

"You were so much like her." His father's voice was almost pained.

Gregory bit back a sigh. "Yeah, I know. You've made that clear."

His father turned around. "No, that's not what I meant. Not in your ability to hurt people or to run away from commitment. Like her, you cared so much. Too much."

Gregory stared at his father, speechless, afraid to interrupt lest his father stop talking. This was more than his father had ever spoken about his mother or their past.

"I always knew that was why she left. She was so emotional. She wore her heart on her sleeve. What I could give her was never enough."

For the first time in his life, Gregory felt a pang of sympathy for his father. At this moment, the cold, callous businessman looked lost and confused.

*Welcome to the club.*

His father sighed. "I guess what I'm saying is, I know I've been too hard on you. And yes, I was trying to help you so you wouldn't make your mother's mistakes and run from commitment and difficult situations."

A bit of his father's normal know-it-all tone returned, and Gregory was oddly relieved. It was disconcerting to see his father less than one hundred percent confident.

His father straightened. "You have to admit you had a tendency to choose women who were…unworthy. You gravitated toward relationships that were easy to deal with, ones that didn't put you outside your comfort zone. Relationships where you could walk away."

His father's voice grew hoarse—this was probably the most talking he'd done all year. To his son, at least. "You deserve better than that. So did your mother. You deserve to be with someone who loves you the way that you are capable of loving."

*Tamara.* There was no question who his father was talking about. Gregory cleared his throat, partly out of discomfort at having such an emotional conversation with his father and partly for lack of anything to say. Finally, he told the truth. "I'm going to hurt her. You know it as well as I do. I couldn't even keep a fish alive, let alone—"

"Oh Christ," his father groaned. "It was just a fish. You couldn't keep it alive because you didn't truly care about it. The fish was a compromise— what you really wanted was a puppy."

The hint of laughter in his father's voice had him looking up in surprise. "You remember that?"

"Of course I remember that. You wouldn't stop talking about that damn puppy you'd seen at the pet store. But Elena was allergic, so we figured we'd start you off with a fish and see if you could handle it."

His father was back to his normal self, full of his usual swagger. "Son, if we'd gotten you the puppy, you would have loved it and I'm sure you would have taken care of it."

"But you always said—" He stopped, too annoyed to continue. His failure with that goddamn fish had been thrown in his face for as long as he could remember. It was one of many irritating lectures his father had given him his whole life to convince him that he didn't have what it took to commit.

His father took a step toward him. "This situation with Tamara has made me reevaluate how I've handled things with you in the past." A flicker of uncertainty passed over his face. "I realize that I've been too hard on you. I've only ever wanted the best for you, and if I pushed too hard...I'm sorry."

Gregory gave a grudging nod. All was not forgiven or forgotten, but he could appreciate the older man's attempts to make things right. Besides, this new insight into his mother's temperament and his father's fears was eye-opening.

For the first time in a long time, he started to feel a flicker of hope. If Tamara could forgive him for putting his foot in his mouth—if she could give him another chance...

His father put a hand on his shoulder. "If you truly care about Tamara, don't let my fears or your mother's actions be what stop you from pursuing her."

Gregory nodded. He didn't trust himself to speak. Maybe his father was right. What he had with Tamara was different than anything else in his life. He might not have been able to see things through with Vanessa or the other women he'd dated, but that didn't mean he had to repeat his mistakes with Tamara.

Everything was different with her. *He* was different. He could be the man she needed...if she gave him a chance.

Excitement and a glimmer of hope had his heart racing. She was planning to visit her parents, his father had said. Which meant she was still in town. And maybe, just maybe, there was still hope.

He half pushed, half led his father toward the front door, making some excuse about how he had places to be. He'd tell her what an idiot he'd been and he'd tell her the truth. That he wanted her—no, he *needed* her in his life.

# Chapter 13

Tamara's bags were packed and waiting by the door, but she was not entirely sure she was ready to go. She couldn't believe that after six years she was about to see her parents and brother again. She'd talked to them each individually on the phone, but seeing them in person was a whole other matter.

A jumble of emotions threatened to overwhelm her—and not all of them had to do with her family. It had been more than a week since she'd seen Gregory, and each day she had thought it might start to get easier.

Somehow it only seemed to get worse. Losing Gregory was like losing a limb. Even when she was distracted by work or planning to see her family, there was something missing. There was a hole where her heart should be.

The worst part was that she could feel herself going back to the dark place. She found herself doubting every decision she'd made, everything from agreeing to work for Gregory to telling her friends about her past. Most of all, she kept berating herself for falling for Gregory. She'd done this to herself. Despite all her promises and vows to make her own peace of mind her priority, she'd gone and broken every self-made rule. And look where that had gotten her.

She was right back where she'd started.

The fact that she would be facing her family soon didn't help. It brought the past into the present, and she'd been forced to deal with it in a way she hadn't in far too long.

Marc had noticed the change in her and had called her out on it in typical Marc fashion. There was no beating around the bush with her best friend. "You look like shit," he'd said, coming into her bedroom and flopping down at the edge of her bed. "And you're not acting like yourself."

She'd scowled at him over the blanket she'd been happily buried under as she watched a Charlie Chaplin movie on her laptop. "Oh yeah, and how am I acting?"

He'd dropped the teasing tone and turned serious. "You're acting like you did way back when I first met you." He patted her leg as if to ease the pain of his statement. "Like you're scared of your own shadow."

He'd been right. Not that she was scared of Gregory. No, she was scared of herself. Of how quickly she'd lost herself. Of how quickly she'd given someone else the power to hurt her. Again.

She'd started to think she was safe. Immune from that kind of pain. She'd become overly confident. So yeah, she was scared. Which was why, when Marc had offered to come home with her for moral support, she'd been all too happy to take him up on it. If nothing else, maybe he could keep her from obsessing over Gregory.

She heard him packing his bag in the other room when the sound of the buzzer had her running for the door. "Did you order lunch?"

Marc's "no" reached her just as she flung open the door.

For a second time she was speechless and confused, facing Gregory on her doorstep. "What are you doing here?"

As quickly as hope rose in her, she squashed it down. He was probably here on business.

Or...maybe not. His mouth was set in a firm line, and there was a tautness around his eyes that mirrored her own. There were also bags under his eyes, and he sported a five o'clock shadow.

He looked miserable. Her heart went out to him, and she fought the urge to go to him, wrap her arms around his waist and tell him everything would be okay.

She gripped the edge of the door to keep herself from doing just that. Instead she repeated herself, since he seemed to be similarly frozen, despite the fact that *he* had come to see *her*. "What are you doing here?"

Then the spell was broken and he took a step toward her. "I made a mistake."

She blinked up at him, certain that she'd heard wrong. "You... What?"

He licked his lips and moved even closer until she backed up, scrambling to get some distance lest she lose all control.

"Tamara Pierce, you are the best thing that has ever happened to me." At her shocked silence, he added, "Ever."

Her mouth gaped open but no sound came out. That was so not what she'd been expecting. Her heart threatened to burst out of her chest with joy while her mind went in an entirely different direction. *Don't trust him. He hurt her once and he'll do it again.*

As quickly as her heart leapt with excitement, it stopped. The instant flood of joy was replaced by a cold sensation. *Fear.* More like terror. Whatever it was, it held her in its grip. His ability to send her emotions spiraling out of control with one simple sentence...that alone was terrifying. The fact that he could destroy her entirely if he broke her heart for a second time left her trembling before him.

He closed the distance between them, crossing into her apartment and shutting the door behind him before reaching for her.

She stiffened but didn't pull away. She couldn't—not yet. The feel of his arms around her was too sweet. His scent and touch flooded her body with warm sensations that left her aching to press against him, to get as close as humanly possible.

"I'm sorry." His voice was slightly muffled as he spoke into her hair, but she heard him.

The best she could manage was a short, jerky nod. It wasn't like she thought he'd intentionally hurt her. And she was sorry too. Sorry she'd ever let him get close in the first place. She should have known better—she *had* known better. There had never been any doubt that she would get hurt, but she hadn't expected him to get hurt as well.

But it was clear they were both in pain and she could have avoided it—she could have kept them both safe if she'd followed her own rules. The ones she'd created to avoid this exact situation.

He pulled back to look at her, and the depth of emotion in those warm brown eyes made her heart ache. He cared about her, he truly did. Which made what she had to do that much harder.

"I'm so sorry I hurt you," he said. "I'd give anything to go back and tell you exactly what you mean to me."

She nodded. "I'm sorry, too. For everything."

He went to pull her back into his arms, but this time she had the strength to resist. "Gregory."

His gaze moved from her eyes to her lips and back again. What he saw there made his hands loosen their grip on her waist.

She swallowed back tears and tried to keep her voice even. "I accept your apology...but nothing has changed."

His eyes narrowed on her, their brown depths filled with pain and confusion. "I promise I won't hurt you again, Tamara, just give me another chance."

She shook her head and tried not to hear the pleading in his tone. This was hard enough; she didn't need any more guilt or second-guessing. One thing was clear—this man held too much power over her.

A searing pain sliced through her, but she forced herself to stay strong. It might be painful, but better to deal with the pain now than to spend a lifetime vulnerable. And that's what she would be if she went back to Gregory now. She'd be at his mercy, and slowly but surely she'd lose herself in him. She'd drown in her love for him and he would have complete control. It had happened before, and she wouldn't let it happen again.

He might be sorry, but he would hurt her again. Unintentionally, most likely, but the pain was the same. She'd been so caught up in having fun with this man that she'd nearly missed the fact that she'd been on the verge of losing herself in him. She couldn't risk that.

First she'd be happy, then she'd start caring more about his wants and needs than her own. Soon she'd be so dependent on him that she wouldn't survive a breakup.

His gaze was fixed on her, his eyes pleading.

"I'm sorry," she said. "I can't do this. I can't risk it."

"You can trust me. I won't hurt you again."

The words sounded eerily familiar. How many times had Billy promised the same thing? But this was different—Gregory wouldn't set out to hurt her. She knew he hadn't set out to hurt her, but he'd hurt her nonetheless.

"I can move past my issues with my father," Gregory said. He took a step closer and reached for her, but she jerked back, out of his reach. He let his hands drop, but his gaze stayed on her, challenging her. "You've made me realize that. We can start fresh. I promise you, I can be strong enough for both of us. I should have fought for us before. I shouldn't have given up without a fight. It won't happen again."

Tears stung the back of her eyes. "I know you'd be strong. And I know you'd try not to hurt me." Couldn't he see? He wasn't the issue. It was her. It had always been her.

"Tamara—" He went to touch her hair, but she knocked his hand away. She could barely think straight as it was. His touch would undo her.

"You might be strong enough to give this another shot." She dropped her gaze, unable to see the hurt in his eyes. "But I'm not that strong. I can't risk falling apart again."

The silence lasted so long that she finally looked up to find him staring down at her. The pain in his eyes was unmistakable. "Fine." He backed up and reached for the doorknob. "If that's your final decision, I'll respect it."

She gave a jerky nod, not trusting herself to speak.

* * * *

She needed space, so he would give it to her. Hell, she needed more than just space—she wanted nothing to do with him. Pain sliced through him, familiar now but no less painful than the moment she'd told him it was over. For good.

And maybe she was right. It was her decision, and who was he to say she was wrong? He might be ready to try again, but could he really ask her to take that kind of chance on someone like him…someone who had a terrible track record and one strike to his name? No, she'd made her choice, and if he was being honest with himself, he could admit it was probably the right one. She seemed convinced that he'd hurt her again, and he couldn't promise that wasn't true.

So he'd do right by her. He'd respect her decision and he'd keep his distance. But staying away proved more difficult than he'd imagined. He might not have known her for long, but she'd gotten into his system. Her absence in his life felt like a gaping hole. By the time his weekly dinner with Elena rolled around, Gregory was a mess.

"Darling," Elena called as he headed toward her table in the back of the restaurant. Her expression shifted from joy at seeing him to concern as she eyed him from head to toe. When he reached the table and leaned down to kiss her cheek, she murmured, "Should I be worried?"

He played dumb. "About?"

She lowered her chin and pursed her lips in a rare show of disappointment. "You, of course." Waving a hand toward his mussed hair, five o'clock shadow, and wrinkled shirt, she added, "You look like a hobo."

"Thank you, Elena," he muttered as he took a sip of his water. "Always a pleasure to see you, as well."

She leaned forward and lowered her voice. "Is this about your girlfriend?"

His jaw clenched, but he kept his tone even. "I don't have a girlfriend."

Elena's lips thinned as she rolled her eyes. "Fine. Is this about Tammy?"

He flinched at the sound of her name. God, wasn't time supposed to heal all wounds? Why the hell was he feeling worse by the second?

"Are you worried about her reunion with her parents?" She pulled an olive out of her martini and popped it in her mouth. "Don't be. Her parents are delighted to be back in her life. They can't wait to get their little girl back—if one can be considered a little girl at her age."

At his frown, she quickly added, "Not that she's old, darling. But she's not a girl, you know. She's a grown woman."

Oh, he knew. She was preaching to the choir on that one. But the frown wasn't at the use of the term "girl" so much as it was that Tamara was going through this ordeal alone. Reuniting with her family after all this time had to be bringing back painful memories. She shouldn't be on her own.

Ah hell, who was he trying to kid? She didn't need him, she'd made that clear. Not only did she not need him, she didn't want him.

"She needs you, you know."

For a second he thought he'd made up the words—that they'd come from God or something. But no. It was just Elena watching him with a sad, knowing smile. Almost…pitying.

Crap. Was he that obvious?

"She doesn't need me. It sounds like she's doing just fine on her own."

Elena nodded. "That's true. I think that girl is finally coming into her own. She held her own at the holiday party, that's for sure. And from what her mother tells me, she's been the picture of maturity and understanding when it comes to her family and making amends. But I do think the timing is pretty telling, don't you? This new and improved Tamara didn't come forward until she met you."

He let out a short, humorless laugh. "Yeah, because I forced her."

"You pushed her," Elena amended. "We all need a push sometimes. Someone to challenge us and help us to grow."

He studied Elena for a moment as she toyed with the stirrer in her drink, looking far too innocent.

"Stepmother, dearest," he drawled. "Why do I get the impression that we're no longer talking about Tamara?"

"Because we're not, dear," she said gently.

"Wonderful." He muttered it under his breath, but she clearly heard him considering the twinkle of amusement in her eyes.

"Bear with me, Gregory. Somebody has to step in and tell you when you're acting like an ass, and as your stepmother, it's my burden to bear."

His mouth fell open, but before he could speak, she added, "I swear, sometimes you are just like your father."

"I'm nothing like him," he bit out, a little too loudly judging by the stares he got from the table next to them.

Elena, however, looked unfazed. "Of course you are, dear. Why else do you think he's so hard on you?"

Was she kidding? The answer to that was obvious. "Because I'm just like *her*."

"Your mother," Elena clarified, as if it wasn't a known fact. She tipped her head to the side and studied him. "I knew her, you know. Before she left you and your father, of course. Back when she was a young debutante like Tamara once was."

He stared at his stepmother, too surprised to comment. He and Elena had never talked about his mother, just like he and his father never spoke her name.

Honestly it had never occurred to him that Elena might have known her. He put them in such different categories in his brain—the one who left and the one who stayed—somehow it seemed odd that they could have interacted in the real world. As if he was the only thing between them.

Well, him and his father, of course.

"She was a lovely woman," Elena said. "You look just like her, that much is true."

That much he'd always known. Even if he hadn't found the occasional picture of his mother around the house, he remembered her well enough to recognize the black hair and brown eyes he saw in the mirror every day.

"She was also very passionate—very emotive—just like you."

He tried not to roll his eyes. That was also nothing new.

Elena leaned forward and captured his hand in hers. "But you have your father's sense of loyalty and ethics."

He stared at her, waiting to see if she was serious.

Deadly serious if the look in her eyes was anything to go by.

He pulled his hand back gently. "That's sweet of you to say, but—"

"Don't you 'but' me, young man."

He blinked in surprise. She hadn't used that tone—or called him "young man," for that matter—for longer than he could remember.

Still using her no-nonsense tone, she barreled on, ignoring his wide-eyed stare. "Now, your father has a lot of wonderful qualities. Loyalty is one of them. But any trait taken to extremes can have a negative side. For your father, the flip side of loyalty is stubbornness."

He raised one brow. It wasn't like he could argue with that.

"When you were small, your father looked at you and saw your mother." Elena took a sip of her martini and set it back down. "He saw her looks and her passion in you, and it scared the shit out of him…. Excuse my language."

Gregory swallowed a laugh.

She met his gaze. "You inherited some of your mother's traits—her best traits, I'd say. But you're also your father's son. Just like him, you are loyal and trustworthy. A good man—one who looks out for the people he loves and the ones who rely on him, like his employees."

Gregory opened his mouth to interject but she hurried on. "But he's stubborn. He got it into his head that he had to beat your mother out of you, not understanding that there were good parts to her as well—the parts he fell in love with."

He found himself too stunned to form words. For some reason he'd never once imagined his father in love with his mother. It seemed too crazy that he could ever have loved the woman he so clearly despised.

"Your mother's emotions weren't her downfall," Elena said softly. "Her love for you and your father didn't make her fickle or faithless. Her love was what made her such a wonderful woman. Kind, charismatic...the woman your father fell in love with."

He went to argue. Not because he didn't see the truth of what she was saying but because his father's voice was so ingrained in him. "But—"

She cut him off with a wave of her hand. "That's not to say that she didn't have her faults. Of course she did. No woman leaves her family lightly, and something tells me your mother had some demons she was fighting. Demons that had nothing to do with you."

This last part was said so gently and with such tenderness that his chest constricted with emotion.

Elena's tone lightened as she added, "Heck, it may not have had much to do with your father, for that matter, not that he'd believe it."

He stared at her, temporarily speechless at seeing his family from an objective point of view. Well, not totally objective, but Elena clearly had a dramatically different take on his mother's leaving than his father did.

Before he could thank her for the insight, she continued. "Like I said, your father has his wonderful traits. You know I love him dearly."

He could feel the "but" coming, and he wasn't disappointed.

"But your father can be a stubborn ass."

He blinked in surprise before letting his head fall back in the first genuine laugh since he'd walked away from Tamara.

Shaking her head, Elena fixed him with another fierce glare. "Sometimes that man is stubborn to the point of blindness. Though I think lately he's finally started to open his eyes and see what's right in front of his face." She reached over and took his hand. "Like how you grew up to be a loving, loyal son. One that any woman would be lucky to have at her side."

"Tamara doesn't think so." The words were difficult to get out. It had been hard enough to hear, but to admit it aloud was torture.

Elena's gaze turned mildly pitying. "Oh darling, Tamara has been through quite a lot these past few weeks. She's not thinking clearly."

He shook his head. "You don't know that's true." Staring at the glass in his hand, he forced himself to admit the truth. "She might be right. There's always a chance that I'll hurt her and—"

Elena's irritated sigh cut him off. "This is exactly what I mean. You didn't inherit your mother's fickle ways. If anything, you've gotten your father's stubborn streak. You've clung to his fears as if they were your own. Even though they're not true and you know it." She leaned over the table. "If you let that old way of thinking interfere with what might be the best thing to ever happen to you…" She paused as if waiting for a response.

The best thing that had ever happened to him? His mind flashed on Tamara's kind eyes, her mischievous smile, the way she'd opened up to him and trusted him and put her faith in him…like he deserved it. He looked up and nodded. Yeah, she was definitely the best thing in his world.

Elena's lips twitched up in a knowing smile before she forced another scowl. "If you let her push you away without a fight, you're stupider than you look."

But when he opened his mouth, fear spoke. "I don't want to hurt her."

Some of the gut-wrenching fear must have been clear in his expression, because Elena's look softened. "Oh, Gregory. You really are your father's son. You and he both get an idea in your head and you stick to it." She patted his hand. "Even when you're wrong."

The hope that she was right was painful. Because what if she was wrong? If he could convince Tamara to give him a second chance, he couldn't go through the heartbreak of walking away again. If she gave him another chance, she would be stuck with him, flaws and all.

Once again, Elena seemed to know what he was thinking. Leaning back in her seat, she folded her hands primly in front of her. "I know you worry about Tamara, but she's a big girl and she's stronger than you give her credit for."

"I know she's strong," he argued.

She raised one brow. "Do you? If you did, you wouldn't try to protect her—you would fight for her. Prove to her that she's wrong and that you belong together."

And if her heart said that she wanted him as badly as he wanted her… He couldn't let himself hope that was true. For all he knew she had moved on. "I—I—" He looked up to see an amused Elena trying not to laugh at him.

"Yes, dear?"

"I've been an idiot."

Her smile was gracious. "I know, dear."

"What am I going to do?"

"You're going to fight for her, of course."

\* \* \* \*

Tamara lay by the indoor pool, Marc next to her. They had cocktails in hand, despite the fact that it was only noon. But, as Marc pointed out—reuniting with family was as good of an excuse to drink as any.

Besides, she'd earned it. Over the last few days she'd had a tear-filled heart-to-heart with her parents and her older brother—one that was long overdue. But maybe the time had helped in a way. The bitterness and anger she'd felt so strongly six years ago had faded, and she found she was able to talk to her parents about how she'd felt back then with a perspective that kept the conversation from turning accusatory.

Apologizing had been the hardest part. She'd seen with her own eyes how much they'd aged over the past six years, and she knew she'd added to their worry and pain in a way she could never make up for. But saying the words *I'm sorry* had been a good start.

"Sweetheart, when you said you came from a wealthy family, you were being modest." Marc took a sip of his margarita and adjusted the sunlamp that was giving them the illusion of being on vacation somewhere warm and not in her parents' pool house in the middle of winter.

She shrugged. "I guess I forgot just how rich they are. I mean, I kind of took it for granted, I suppose." Glancing over at Marc, she added, "You know, before I had to pay my own way in Manhattan and all."

Marc laughed. "Mmm, that's quite the reality check for a spoiled little rich girl."

She gave him a smile that almost felt genuine. If it wasn't for the ache in the area where her heart used to be, she would have said she was happy. The drink was celebratory, since overall the reunion had gone well. Better than anticipated.

Marc raised his glass to hers. "Here's to you kicking Billy Braden's ass last night." He clinked his glass against hers as she giggled. "Metaphorically, of course."

"Of course," she repeated. She hadn't really kicked his ass, but she'd come pretty damn close. In an effort to make amends and forge a new bond with her family, she'd agreed to tag along to one of the charity events they loved so much. Her brother had gone back home, but Marc tagged along as their fourth wheel and Tamara's personal cheerleader.

Billy had been there, looking bloated and more miserable than ever. It was funny—if someone had asked her just weeks ago, she would have said having to face her ex was one of her greatest fears. But when he was standing right in front of her it wasn't fear she felt. There was revulsion, contempt, maybe a little leftover hatred, but the emotion wasn't nearly as all-consuming as it once was. There was a mix of emotions, but none of them was fear.

His eyes lit up when he spotted her, and before her parents or Marc could intervene, he was at her side. "Tammy, good to see you."

He sounded…pathetic. Too eager, too fake. His nice guy act was so transparent it was almost funny. Almost. She couldn't bring herself to smile, let alone laugh. She'd looked him up and down, taking in the little things that made him so very human, not at all the terrifying figure she'd made him out to be in her mind's eye.

She felt her parents tense beside her, but her mother put a supportive hand on her shoulder as her father made a move to step in front of her and shield her. Years ago she would have been grateful, but now? She didn't need it. She gently moved her father aside as she stared up at her ex.

She wasn't worried about embarrassing her family, but this man didn't deserve a scene, and that was exactly what the gossips in this crowd expected. He didn't deserve to see her true emotions…. He didn't deserve anything from her.

"Billy," she said quietly, calmly. She thrust her shoulders back and summoned her best Ingrid Bergman impersonation. "We didn't expect to see you here."

Maybe it was her confidence, or her utter lack of excitement at seeing him, but a familiar nasty smirk replaced his friendly grin, and he moved closer and dropped his voice so only she could hear. "Yeah, I'm surprised to see you, too. I heard they were keeping you locked up these days."

Years ago, he might have intimidated. Now, he just pissed her off. But again, she reminded herself that this man wasn't worthy of a scene. His words couldn't hurt her anymore, and there was no way in hell she'd allow herself to be in a position where he could hurt her physically. With that thought, she leaned in closer and kept her voice soft and even.

"You heard wrong, Billy. I'm a changed woman. I left the institution years ago a far healthier and happier woman, thanks largely in part to the help I got there."

He blinked at her in surprise, and she couldn't resist adding, "And the fact that I'd finally gotten you out of my life once and for all was the best change of all."

He opened his mouth as if to retort, but nothing came out. He never had been terribly clever. As far as she was concerned, this conversation was done. He'd been out of her life for ages, and she was more than ready to let go of the memories and pain as well. She looked through him as though he were invisible and walked past him without a second look.

As far as encounters went, it wasn't exactly dramatic, but it felt damn good to walk away with her head held high. *If only Gregory had been here to see it.*

That thought rang out clear as day as she walked away from Billy, and it kept coming back to her throughout the night and all morning. She'd had her epic run-in with Billy and she'd walked away unscathed, feeling stronger than ever. But it didn't seem to matter because nothing seemed to matter without Gregory to share it with. After all, he'd been the one to push her out of her shell of a life. He'd made her face her demons. She had him to thank for her newfound confidence…but she couldn't. Because she'd pushed him away.

As she walked away, her confidence was high but her chest felt hollow. All this time she'd been so afraid of Billy—that fear had followed her everywhere, even into her new life. But that fear had been baseless. She'd been afraid of ghosts and shadows. The fear had taken on a life of its own, probably because she'd never properly dealt with it.

Seeing Billy hadn't magically erased that fear. The fear had disappeared a long time ago as she'd built her new life, as she'd reinvented herself at The Ellen and among her new friends. As she'd faced her past by telling her story to Gregory in the dark of her apartment.

*"We didn't expect to see you here."* Marc imitated her imitating Ingrid Bergman as he sipped his drink, his eyes narrowed dramatically, making her laugh. He fell back against his seat. "God, I'll never get tired of replaying that scene. I can't wait to get back to New York so I can tell the crew all about it."

Now that several days had passed, she and Marc were starting to find a bit of a rhythm with their kinda-sorta vacation, and Tamara was actually sorry to be saying goodbye again. But this time, not for long. Her parents and her brother had already made plans to visit her in the city the following month.

"Can't you leave me here?" Marc asked. "I mean, I could play the part of the dutiful daughter if it means getting to live in the lap of luxury for the rest of my days."

Tamara laughed, and Marc glanced over with a grin. "It's nice to see you like this."

"Like what?" she asked, even though she was fairly certain she knew the answer.

"Happy," he said, studying her as if seeing her for the first time. "You seem…lighter. Like you've stopped carrying a massive burden."

Tamara gave another laugh, this one breathless with wonder. "You know, that's exactly how it feels. Talking to my parents about all that crap that went down…it feels like I unloaded a giant weight off my shoulders." She drew in a deep breath and let it out with a sigh. "I can breathe again."

They sat in companionable silence as Tamara reveled in the new sensation. Sitting there sipping a margarita with her best friend, with the secrets and burdens of her past laid to rest…life was perfect.

Almost.

It would have been perfect if her heart wasn't broken. What a stupid phrase. Broken heart did nothing to describe the pain, the emptiness. It didn't explain how nothing in her world felt right.

And it wasn't just the pain of the broken heart that had her stewing when she should have been celebrating. It was the fact that it felt so *wrong*.

Not having Gregory in her life was wrong.

She sat up straight, adrenaline rushing through her as the missing pieces clicked into place and she finally listened to what her heart had been trying to tell her. Not having Gregory in her life was wrong. Not having the love she deserved was wrong. Closing herself off from love to avoid making another mistake…wrong, wrong, wrong.

Gregory fit into the missing piece of her heart; he made her whole. So why was she letting him walk away?

She didn't realize she'd gasped until Marc sat up too and looked over at her. "Are you all right?"

She nodded, staring unseeing at the pool. Then she shook her head. "No, not really. I made a mistake."

Marc waited patiently.

Finally she looked over at him with wide eyes. "I shouldn't have let him walk away."

Her best friend raised his brows in a look that said "tell me something I don't know," but he didn't say anything.

Slumping back in her chair, she groaned as she thought about their last encounter. Why had she turned him away? Why hadn't she fought for him?

Because she'd been scared, that was why. Scared of being hurt again. More than that, she hadn't been able to trust herself. If she'd learned anything over the past few days with her family it was that what hurt most about that awful time in her life hadn't been their lack of trust in her—it had been her inability to trust herself.

"How do I start trusting myself again?" she asked, her voice little more than a whisper.

Luckily Marc seemed to know exactly what she was thinking. "Oh, my little buttercup," he said with a sigh, "I don't think it's something you can turn on and off with a light switch. If you want to start trusting yourself again, you have to dive in headfirst." He pointed to the pool. "Jump right into the deep end, girl, with no floaties and no life preserver."

They both stared at the pool for a moment before Tamara finally spoke. "You're right." There was no easy way out. There was no running away, not this time. If she learned anything from this homecoming, it was that running hadn't solved her problems. It might have given her perspective, but the only way to deal with a fear was to face it head-on. Life was giving her a second chance to face her fears. She was getting a second chance—or maybe a first chance—at love, and she sure as hell wasn't going to let it go. Not without a fight.

Swallowing the fear that threatened to strangle her, she turned to him. "So…how do I show Gregory that we're worth fighting for?"

# Chapter 14

Tamara hovered near the exit of the theater. "Have I mentioned that I hate parties?"

Alice, the organizer for the bachelor auction, patted her arm. "Relax, you're going to do great."

Marc stood on her other side, and his sympathy was nowhere to be found. "Who are you trying to fool, princess?" He'd been calling her princess ever since he saw her childhood home. "You have gone to several parties, and you are knocking it out of the park. Do I need to remind you of how you put that ass of an ex in his place?"

A smile tugged at her lips at that memory. It had been thoroughly satisfying to see that man and realize that he had no power over her anymore. Face to face, she'd seen exactly how weak he was—how weak he'd always been. It was that weakness that had led him to bully her. And while she couldn't bring herself to forgive him or even pity him, for that matter, some of the anger and pain receded at the pathetic sight. Seeing him in person had made it clear that he was just a bad story from her past—there was no way he could ever have power over her now. Not when she was strong and knew her own mind, not to mention was surrounded by people who loved her.

And Marc had a point about her recent stint of parties. First Gregory's parents' party, then all the social engagements her parents had dragged her along to. While she'd never been thoroughly relaxed at any of them, she had gotten her anxiety issues under control.

But this was different—this was in another ballpark entirely.

She heard Alice's new boyfriend, Nicholas, approach and ask Alice, "Is she okay? She looks like she's going to be sick."

"She'll be fine," Marc and Alice said in unison.

Tamara attempted a smile despite the churning pit in her stomach. "Glad to know you guys have confidence in me."

"Always," Alice said.

"You've got this, girl." Marc threw an arm over her shoulder and steered her none too gently toward the bar in the center of the lobby. Aside from the fact that she was wearing a simple cocktail dress and not a costume, this night felt way too much like the night she'd met Gregory. Or met him again, rather.

And tonight? Tonight would be the night she threw it all out there. Tonight would decide if she and Gregory had a future.

*Right. No pressure.*

Just then her phone dinged with a text from Caitlyn, who was in the theater area helping corral the bachelors.

*He's here.*

She breathed a sigh of relief even though her nerves grew more frayed by the second. A little part of her had been worried he would bail on the fundraiser, even though it was for a good cause and would benefit the theater. But no, he was here. Which meant she was really doing this.

"Are you sure there isn't another way?" she asked, even though she knew the answer.

"This was your idea," Marc reminded her. They'd reached the bar, and he turned to her with a look of concern. "Do you need a drink?"

She shook her head. Tempting as it was to down some liquid courage, she needed to be fully present tonight. There was no softening this or making it easier. She was going to put herself out there for him, and she would do it stone cold sober.

But this was what had to be done, she reminded herself. She'd spent too long expecting others to fight on her behalf and be strong for her. It was time she fought for herself—for what she wanted. She needed to prove to Gregory—and to herself, if she was being honest—that she was well and truly rid of her ghosts. That she was strong and didn't need him to protect her, especially not from his love.

Because she *was* strong. Over the past month she'd done all of the things she'd spent years running from because she'd thought she was too weak.

She'd confronted her parents, she'd returned to her former world—she'd even given her heart for a second time and risked having it shattered all over again.

And even with their setback and the pain it caused, she hadn't broken. She could see that now. She'd given her heart and she'd made herself vulnerable—and she was that much stronger for it.

Being vulnerable wasn't the same as being weak. And to trust others she had to trust herself.

Two simple lessons—but lessons she would never have learned if not for Gregory.

He'd helped her to heal, even when he was hurting her. The least she could do was fight for him.

The rest would be up to him. She couldn't learn his lessons for him—she couldn't make him take a chance. She knew better than anyone how hard it was to trust yourself, and Gregory had to take that leap on his own.

Smoothing her hands over the silk of her dress, she took a deep breath. She couldn't make him leap, but she could lead him to the edge of the cliff.

Another ding of her phone had her smiling. Meg and Jake were home with their baby but rooting her on from the sidelines. Apparently Caitlyn was under strict orders to report back immediately.

Taking a deep breath, she let it out slowly. At least she had her friends around her for support. If the worst-case scenario happened and Gregory didn't appreciate her grand gesture—well, at least she wouldn't be alone.

Marc grabbed her arm again and started heading for the theater. "It's time."

"Don't say it like that," she said, pulling her arm from his grasp. "I feel like I'm walking to the gallows."

"Dead man walking," Marc called out, causing everyone around them stop and stare but also making her giggle, which she assumed was his intention.

"Thank you."

"Anytime."

They walked into the theater and there he was. Gregory stood at the front of the theater by the stage, one among many of the eligible bachelors up for auction. Tamara breathed in deep. She could do this.

With Marc by her side, she headed down the aisle toward the stage. She knew the moment he spotted her; all of the air in the room seemed to disappear. His gaze burned into her, but she refused to look his way. She couldn't. If she did she might lose her courage, and this was it. Her chance to show Gregory she was strong enough to stand on her own. Strong enough to stand by his side.

When she drew close to the stage, she paused and waited as Alice and Nicholas took to the stage to kick off the event. Tamara barely listened as they addressed the crowd—a crowd made up of the city's most influential, its wealthiest, its most famous.

These were the people she'd been afraid of for so long. Now it was hard to remember what she was so scared of, because now she had so much more to lose. Now it wasn't her ego at stake, or her wounded pride. It wasn't her image that was in danger of being shattered.

It was her heart on the line.

She was dimly aware of laughter from the crowd as Alice and Nicholas teased the contenders.

She made the mistake of looking in Gregory's direction. His gaze clashed with hers, and her heart squeezed painfully at the agony she saw there—a pain she knew was reflected in her own eyes.

But maybe his grief was a good sign. It meant he was as heartbroken as she was. So maybe he'd believe her when she told him she was ready to admit that what they had was worth fighting for.

*I'm here*, she wanted to scream across the theater. But shouting wouldn't achieve anything. It was time to show him that she was ready to fight. For him, for them...for herself.

Tearing her gaze away, she forced herself to concentrate on what was happening on the stage. Marc took her hand and squeezed it as Alice started to wrap up.

"Our bachelors will be stepping up on stage in a moment. We've asked them each to prepare a few words about what makes them such a catch and why you should bid on them." Dropping her voice an octave, she added, "And remember, folks, all money goes to charity, so bid high even if you think he's a dud."

More laughter and applause as the crowd settled in for the entertainment of watching the city's most eligible bachelors humiliate themselves for a good cause.

"But first," Alice continued, making Tamara's stomach do a backflip. This was it—no turning back now.

"First we have a surprise contestant—a bachelorette!"

Applause echoed in Tamara's ears, and she reminded herself forcefully that she was not allowed to get out of this by fainting.

A few minutes. She just had to be courageous for a few moments, and then it would all be over. Either Gregory would have come to his senses and realized they were meant to be...or he wouldn't.

Either way, she would survive and she would be just fine.

With that thought, she pasted a smile on her face as Alice announced her name. "Give a hand for Ms. Tamara Pierce."

She tried not to pay attention to the whispers as she walked the last few steps to the stage and allowed Nicholas to help her up the stairs.

The theater took on a dreamlike quality—or maybe that was just her perception. But from up on that stage, with the dim lighting and the buzz of hushed voices—the nerves subsided and a calm swept over her.

Only then did she let herself look in Gregory's direction again.

"Hi, everybody, I'm Tamara Pierce. Or you might know me better as Tammy Vanguard." Tamara stopped. If anyone gasped or whispered in the crowd, she didn't notice. She was too focused on Gregory to hear or care.

Standing by the edge of the stage, she could make out his features in the dim lighting. His eyes were wide with shock and confusion. She nearly laughed aloud. Maybe she would have if her heart wasn't in her throat.

Smothering a nervous giggle, she forced yourself to continue. "Some of you may have heard of me, some of you may not. And honestly it doesn't matter. Whatever you heard, whatever you think you know, it has no relation to the truth." Tamara drew in a deep breath. "The truth is, years ago I was hurt. Badly. And it took me a long time to recover, and not just from the physical and emotional injuries."

She had to stop speaking, because Gregory's look of confusion disappeared and what replaced it was unbearable to see. Pain was etched on his features as though he was hurting on her behalf. She gave him a small smile to let him know she was okay.

Truth was, she was better than okay. Speaking these words aloud only confirmed what she knew to be true in her heart. "I had to recover my trust—in others and in myself. That's not an easy thing to do, but I was lucky."

She paused, holding Gregory's gaze. She needed to be sure he was listening. Truly listening. "I was lucky because I had help. Someone came into my life who showed me what it was to be fearless. He showed me what it was to trust."

Tears were burning in her eyes, but she forced the words out. "He showed me what it was to love."

Gregory's eyes were filled with emotion, filled with tears. He made his way through the crowd of bachelors so he was at the edge of the stage. When she realized he was going to jump up on stage, she stopped him with a shake of her head. She wasn't done.

She hoped he understood. If he came to her now he would be saving her, rescuing her. And that wasn't what she wanted or needed. This wasn't about being saved; it was about proving to herself and to him that she had the strength to put herself out there—back in the world that used to terrify her. But most importantly she had to prove that she trusted him.

He loved her, she knew he did. And she understood him well enough to understand that his reservations had been based on false beliefs about his own worth and capacity to love.

If anyone could understand doubts—how hearing lies and misconceptions about oneself could lead to believing them—it was her. And maybe that was why they were meant to be together.

They understood one another, believed in each other. And she hoped, given time, they could come to truly trust themselves not to hurt or be hurt. But no one was perfect, and if they hurt each other, then she hoped they could learn to forgive.

For the first time since she started speaking, she let herself look away from Gregory and faced the rest of the crowd. From where she stood, all she could see was smiles of encouragement. She even spotted a few women who had tears in their eyes as they smiled up at her.

Funny to think she'd been so afraid for so long, and for what?

Gripping the microphone a little harder, she started speaking again. "Alice says I'm supposed to talk about what makes me a great catch and why you should bid on me." She let out a little laugh as she made eye contact with Marc, who was beaming at her like a proud mama.

"Why am I a good catch? Because I'm strong. I may have had my struggles, but because of that, I am stronger now than I ever could have imagined." She smiled at the crowd and saw a hundred smiles in return. "That makes me a great catch, I'd say, because I don't need to be saved. I'm not some princess in a tower, and I'll slay my own dragons, thank you very much."

This was met with a scattering of applause and a few shout-outs from some women in the crowd.

"As for why you should bid on me..." She looked off to the side and saw Alice giving her a thumbs-up, and she laughed. "Well, because it's for a great cause, obviously. But to be honest, that's not why I'm standing up here making a fool of myself."

Turning back she met Gregory's gaze for one long second before facing the crowd with a smile. Something Marc had said to her days ago came back to her now, and she found herself fighting back a laugh at its truth. "It always starts with someone who says they don't want love. But you know what they say—love finds you when you're not looking for it." Her courage gave out, and she couldn't turn to face Gregory, instead focusing on the crowd before her who were no longer a threat. "There's only one person here who I'm hoping will take a chance on me. But to do that he'll have to trust me and trust himself—not an easy feat, I know." She swallowed the sudden onset of nerves. "I'm hoping he'll do it, though, because... because I love him."

Her voice gave out on her as nerves and adrenaline made breathing nearly impossible.

A man in the crowd shouted out, "I'd bet on you, Tammy!" Followed by other good-natured calls. She tried to smile, but the silence coming from the crowd of bachelors had her frozen in place.

This was it. Speak now or forever hold your peace. What if she'd put it all on the line and he couldn't do it? Maybe love wasn't always strong enough.

* * * *

Gregory was frozen in place. Shock and awe made it hard to think. But he could feel.

After all this time trying to keep his distance, the need to run to her, to embrace her, to claim what they had—it was nearly unbearable.

He was distantly aware of some male voices calling out that they'd bid for her.

*Like hell they would.*

Not stopping to think it through, he sprang forward, finally unleashed from his shocked stupor. Striding up the stairs and onto the stage, he called out, "Thanks so much, gentlemen, but you can put away your wallets. This bachelorette is mine."

Whoops and whistles followed that announcement, but he was too focused on the woman standing before him on the stage to take much notice.

And holy hell was she gorgeous. Radiant with strength and confidence, she turned to him with a look of such pleasure that it nearly crippled him. It wasn't just pleasure, but pride—in him. In the fact that he'd stood up and claimed her despite his insecurities and fears.

God, he loved this woman.

Then he was at her side, and he swept her into his arms and crushed her lips beneath his, ignoring the raucous applause. All he cared about was right here on this stage, in his arms.

He pulled back just long enough to smile down at this woman who'd conquered her worst fears and showed him he could do the same.

"I hope you're sure about this," he said between kisses. "Because now you're stuck with me."

He could barely hear her laugh over the din from the crowd, but he could feel it reverberating through him and decided right then and there that it was the best feeling in the world.

As he was leaning in for another kiss, a hand on his arm had him looking up. One of the organizers of the event was firmly but gently leading them off the stage. For the first time, he became truly aware of his surroundings and the fact that he and Tamara were giving this crowd the show of the night.

He saw the moment Tamara realized it too and her cheeks turned a brilliant shade of red. Catcalls and whistles followed them off the stage. He gave the crowd a wave as Tamara ducked her head and all but ran offstage, dragging him with her.

Once there she turned to him and laughed.

"I cannot believe you just did that," he said.

"Believe it." She grinned up at him. "Meet the new and improved Tammy Vanguard."

He arched a brow as he wrapped an arm around her waist. "I thought you only answered to Tamara Pierce these days."

She shrugged, her eyes alight with a joy that made her radiant. "I'm learning to embrace both names."

Brushing a long blond lock from her face, he leaned down until his lips were tantalizingly close to hers. "Then I guess it's a good thing that I love them both."

He heard her gasp of surprise, but he captured it with a kiss before she could respond.

A pang of fear had him pulling back, cupping her face in his palms. "You know I'm new to this whole intimacy thing, right? It may take me a while to figure out how to be a good boyfriend."

"I trust you," she said. And with those three words he got a glimpse of what his life could be. A warmth filled his chest as this tiny slip of a woman knocked down the demons that had been tormenting him for as long as he could remember.

The voices of doubt turned to words of hope. His father was wrong. His intentions might have been decent, but he'd been wrong all along. He didn't have to be like his mother. He could choose to be a better man. Loyal like his father, passionate like his mother. Take the best of both and leave the rest behind.

Before he could tell Tamara any of this, Alice came up beside them. She was grinning at them, but she had a slightly harried air about her. "You guys, I'm so happy for you."

"Thanks," Tamara said, her gaze never leaving his.

"And I hate to rain on your parade," Alice continued, laughter in her voice. "But the bachelor auction is still going on, and we are missing one very important contender."

Tamara's eyes widened, and he was sure his surprise matched hers. He'd forgotten all about the auction...and the fact that he was supposed to be the star. The city's most eligible bachelor up for grabs.

Giving Tamara a light peck, he turned to Alice. "Let's get this over with."

Alice led him back onto the stage, where he was met with loud applause. Giving a small bow, he saluted the audience. There was no avoiding the fact that he and Tamara had created quite the scene in front of this influential crowd. Might as well make the most of it.

Alice gave a brief, unnecessary intro before handing the mic over to him.

"Look," he said. "I think most of you know who I am and what I'm about. And now, after that performance you witnessed earlier, I'm sure you can imagine what I'm about to say."

He glanced over and spotted Tamara, surrounded by her friends, smiling up at him. All the faith in the world shone in her eyes.

"When I signed up for this auction, I was a bachelor. But now, I'm happy to report that I am a taken man."

Laughter and whistles greeted that comment.

"I think we all know how important this charity is, so I hope you can still find it in your hearts to bid on me. In return, I can offer stellar financial advice and maybe even tell you the tale of how this eligible bachelor fell head over heels."

Apparently everyone loved a good love story, because the bidding started high and the end amount was the most raised all night. The woman who won him was old enough to be his grandmother, and she told him when he left the stage that she couldn't care less about his business acumen. She just wanted the exclusive story on how he'd swept that beautiful young woman off her feet.

That, he realized as he made his way through the crowd and to the love of his life, was something he was still trying to figure out. Because much as he'd love to take the credit, he wasn't the hero of this love story—Tamara was.

Before she came along, he'd been clueless. An overgrown child who was still trying to rebel against his parents. Always out to prove something— that he wasn't like his mother. That he was better than his father. But like an idiot, he'd been fighting because he was afraid it was true. Deep down he'd believed the hype, the story his father had spun from the moment his mother left. Just like Tamara had fallen victim to the lies Billy had told to keep her down. But she had woken up, faced the truth about herself, and come out stronger than ever.

So strong she had the courage to show him what a fool he was and wake him up, too.

Holy shit, she really was his hero.

His love for her was overwhelming in that moment. A short laugh escaped, and he gave her a quick hard kiss. When he pulled back, she lifted her brows in question. "What's so funny?"

"You. Us." He shook his head. "When we first met, I had this crazy notion that I was helping you. Saving you." He laughed again, and she tilted her head to the side.

"You did help me," she said. "You helped me to face my ghosts. If it wasn't for you pushing me, who knows how long I would have stayed hidden in the shadows, hiding from my former life."

She wrapped her arms around his neck as she said it, tugging him down for another kiss.

After another lengthy kiss that drowned out the fact that they were still in public and still the center of attention, he pulled back and rested his forehead against hers. "That may be so, but I can't thank you enough for being strong enough for both of us."

He nodded toward the stage. "That, what you did… It took guts. You put yourself out there and risked your pride for me."

She shrugged as if it was no big deal. "You're worth a little wounded pride. And besides, it all worked out the way I'd hoped."

"Mmm," he murmured as he leaned down for another kiss. He pulled away just enough to meet her gaze, to make sure she could see how serious he was. "I'm going to do my best to live up to your faith in me. I'll do everything I can to be the man you deserve. Because you deserve the best, you deserve—"

"I deserve *you*," she said, her voice solemn. "I want *you*. I need *you*. I love *you*."

He forced himself to let it in. The love, the commitment, the new life. It wouldn't be easy—redefining himself was an undertaking that might take years. But he could do it with her at his side. "Then you have me."

Now it was her turn to let out a short, choked laugh. "What's so funny, my love?"

She shook her head, glancing around at the packed theater and her friends, who were watching them with gleeful grins. "This. All of it. It's like the happily ever after I only dreamed about. The happy ending that only happens in black-and-white movies. It almost doesn't feel real."

He pulled her closer in his arms and held her tight. "That's because it's not an ending." He leaned down and planted a kiss on the tip of her nose. "This is just the beginning."

# Epilogue

The theater looked the same, but different. The restorations Tamara and Gregory had paid for and implemented over the past two years had brought the theater back to its former glory. It had taken a couple of years, but the theater's popularity had caught on, and it had become the "it" spot. They had a regular crowd of moviegoers on the weeknights, and the theater was booked out for the remainder of the year for events during the weekends.

All in all, she'd call it a success. She knew his father thought so. Gregory teased him on a regular basis about how he'd won the challenge and turned a small pro bono project into a moneymaking success. At that point, his father typically pointed out that Gregory should be glad he'd pushed him—if he hadn't, Gregory might never have won over the woman who would become his wife.

And now the mother of his child. She absently smoothed a hand over her rounded belly as Alice and Nicholas, laughing, rehearsed their opening speech onstage. The doors would open any minute for the third annual bachelor auction, and the only person missing was the star bachelor.

"Sorry I'm late," Gregory called as he made his way down the aisle toward her.

The sight of him made her smile and brought a flutter of butterflies—or maybe that was the baby kicking? All she knew was that she still had a schoolgirl crush on this man, on top of loving the hell out of him.

"Are Caitlyn and Ben with you?" she asked.

Meg and Jake walked in. Her friends were always the first to arrive for these big functions at the theater. They said it was for moral support, but she had a sneaking suspicion that they all missed the Operation Petticoat meet-ups as much as she did. Of course they all still hung out, but there was something about working together at the theater that held a special place in their hearts. Now, instead of scraping gum and scrubbing floors every other Saturday, they settled for volunteering at all of the charity fundraisers.

"Their babysitter was running late," Meg answered. "But they're on their way."

Gregory had reached her side and wrapped a possessive arm around her waist, placing his hand against her belly. "How's our boy?"

"He's fine," she said, leaning back against him and closing her eyes for one blissful moment as she let him take some of the weight off her aching feet. "His mother, on the other hand… She could use a nap."

His laughter was soft and low and sent shivers down her spine. "After all the work you've put into tonight, I'd say you deserve a back rub, a hot bath, and then a good night's sleep. What do you think?"

She moaned softly at the tempting image. "Don't tease me," she said. "You know we can't leave. Not until you're done with your part."

He rolled his eyes but didn't argue. He'd been such a hit at the first bachelor auction that he'd continued to star as the "bachelor" at these events. Of course, everyone knew he was taken—he'd made that very clear at the first auction. But the elderly woman who'd won him raved to all her friends about the incredible financial advice he'd given her, and now he was the catch of the night for his brain rather than his body.

"They only love me for my mind," he said with a melodramatic sigh.

"Yes, it must be hard to be objectified like that," she teased. "Thank goodness you have a wife who loves you for the whole package."

"That's right. For better or for worse, for richer or poorer… You promised."

"Mmm." She turned in his arms so she could face her husband. "And so did you. You know, for someone who was so afraid he couldn't commit, you leapt into that whole 'till death do us part' thing awfully fast."

He shrugged. "I'm a quick study."

"Thank God," she said with a laugh. "This baby will certainly be glad his daddy finally worked through his demons."

"Thanks to his mommy," he added. She didn't try to argue that it was the other way around—he'd saved her. They'd agreed ages ago that they each played a part in helping the other heal. There wasn't just one hero in this relationship.

"Did I tell you that Marc wants to throw the baby shower here at The Ellen?"

"Fitting," he said. "Since this is where it all started."

She ran her fingers through the hair at the base of his neck. "Marc says I still owe Alex for forcing me into that ridiculous Veronica Lake costume."

"I would have spotted you in that crowd no matter what you were wearing." He leaned down to whisper in her ear. "Although, I wouldn't mind seeing you in that costume again."

She laughed as he nibbled on her ear. "I hate to break it to you, but it'll be a while before I fit into that dress again."

He pulled back to give her a seductive grin. "Have I mentioned that I like you even better without the dress?"

Her answering kiss was cut short by Alice's announcement that they were ready to open the doors for the auction. Which meant her husband was due up on stage at any moment.

As she watched him walk away to his assigned waiting area, she couldn't help but smile. Thank God this bachelor wasn't up for grabs—he was all hers.

He'd promised.

And don't miss Maggie Dallen's A Chance Romance series.

*The Accidental Engagement* and *The Accidental Boyfriend* are now available!

### Oops...

It started as a regular night for New York City restaurant hostess Ivy Sinclair, until a rowdy customer turned out to be world famous playboy Jack Everett. Thanks to the paparazzi, now the world thinks they're a couple—which couldn't be further from the truth. But when a brooding, sexy businessman offers her a simply irresistible proposition...

### Uh oh...

Just when cutthroat venture capitalist Daniel Gladwell thought he'd never close the deal with an Italian conglomerate, a simple mistake becomes the perfect opportunity. All he has to do is convince Ivy to pretend to be Jack's fiancée while on a business trip to Italy to offset Jack's bad boy reputation. As long as Daniel doesn't sabotage the plan by claiming the tempting waitress for himself...

### Oh yes!

It was supposed to be a business only arrangement. But in the magic of the Tuscan countryside, neither Ivy nor Daniel can fight the attraction building between them. In the world's most romantic setting, the line between business and pleasure is one that begs to be crossed...

# Chapter 1

Ivy Sinclair thought she'd seen it all as a hostess at a hotel bar—but when a young man came running up to her with a look of panic before diving behind her hostess stand—well, now she'd really seen everything.

"Excuse me, can I help you?" she asked, looking down at the top of his head as he crouched beside her.

The young man barely looked at her. He was too busy peering around the edge of the stand toward the door. He muttered a curse as a large, brutish man wearing an intimidating scowl walked in.

"I'm not here," the young man at her feet whispered.

"Excuse me?"

"Please," he added. His eyes widened and filled with panic. Ivy couldn't help but take pity. The large man who looked ready to kill zeroed in on her. "Where is he?" She swallowed a lump of fear at the aggressive tone.

"Where is who?"

Ivy tried to keep her voice innocent but it came out as a squeak. She cleared her throat and tried again. "I'm afraid I don't know to whom you're referring." He leaned in closer and Ivy fought the impulse to run. "Where is Everett?" he growled.

Ivy stared down the oversized thug who was leaning over the hostess stand. She tried not to flinch even as his hot, rancid breath hit her square in the face.

"As I said before, sir, I have no idea what you're talking about."

Several guests had paused in the hotel lobby, on route to the restaurant, to watch the drama unfold. The giant didn't seem to mind the attention but this job was Ivy's only source of income and she could repeat the manager's lecture on courtesy and service verbatim. But above all else, her job was to be discreet.

Ivy had to believe that meant covering for the well-dressed, albeit rumpled young man who was currently crouching behind the hostess stand, uncomfortably close to her legs. She didn't know what the hidden man had done but she couldn't blame him for hiding from the heavyset giant who loomed over her—he looked like a man who was capable of causing serious pain.

And at this particular moment he looked like he would throttle her given the slightest provocation. Ivy was a good foot shorter than the brute, with a petite frame—not exactly an even match. She tried to keep her voice soft but stern—the same tone she used to cajole Otis, her parents' German shepherd, into his cage when it was time to visit the vet.

"I don't know what this Mr.—uh—"

"Everett. Jack Everett," the man sneered. The name caused even more passersby to stop in their tracks. *Why did that name sound familiar?*

"I don't know what Mr. Everett has done, but I assure you I have not seen the man you described come into this restaurant."

His frown deepened into a menacing glare and she added, "If Mr. Everett comes looking for you, I'd be happy to pass along a message, Mr.—"

He leaned in even closer. "You tell Jack that if I see him with my wife again, he's a dead man."

Ivy's hands clenched at her side. That was it. She couldn't have people making death threats in her restaurant. She drew a deep breath and mustered her courage. "If you don't leave immediately, I'm afraid I'll be forced to call the police."

The burly man slammed a fist against the podium. "Listen, lady, I'll do whatever I—" His voice cut off abruptly when she snatched up the phone and started dialing, keeping eye contact all the while.

The man muttered a curse, shook his head, and backed toward the door. "You tell that little bastard I'm coming for him."

When she was certain the man was gone from view, Ivy let out a deep breath and looked down at the young man.

"You are my hero," he said with a grin.

Ivy rolled her eyes and reached out a hand to help him to his feet. "You're Jack, I presume?"

The young man paused on his knees, a lock of floppy brown hair partially covering eyes that were filled with mischief.

"If I were you, I would get out of here quick, before he comes back," she said.

He ignored her advice and grasped her hands in his. "I'm serious, I owe you my life. That guy was going to kill me."

Ivy stifled a laugh at his melodramatic tone. He looked to be around the same age as her—most likely in his late twenties—but everything from his laughing eyes to his mussed hair said he was a little boy in a grown man's body.

"In case you didn't hear, that nice gentleman would prefer that you stay away from his wife. I hope you take his advice," she added, allowing honesty to outweigh discretion for a moment.

His look was sheepish and he gave her an adorable lopsided grin but he made no attempt to deny the accusations. The man had the face of a movie star and clearly the charm and confidence to go with it. She shouldn't be surprised that he was a ladies' man. Working in a hotel restaurant she'd witnessed more than her fair share of adulterous rendezvous. She'd thought she was worldly-wise when she'd first started working at the hotel. She was no longer fresh off the bus from her tiny hometown in Ohio, but she'd still been shocked by the constant and casual affairs. Now, after two years in one of New York's swankiest hotels her scandalized disgust had given way to weary disapproval.

The young man was still on his knees and resisted her insistent tug. She was horrified to realize that the crowd of people who'd gathered to witness the earlier scene were now watching *her*—with more than a little amusement. Heat flooded her cheeks and she dipped her head. "Please stand up," she muttered.

He flashed her a wicked grin. "Not until you accept my sincere gratitude—"

"Fine, you're welcome. Now stand up, please."

"And tell me how I can repay you," he finished.

"You can repay me by standing up." Whether it was her pleading tone or the red cheeks, he did stand up—and planted a sloppy kiss on her lips. Sputtering with surprise and embarrassment, she pushed him away and turned her face from the people who were now laughing and clapping. Ivy ducked her head, trying to hide her flaming cheeks behind a curtain of hair. She grabbed Jack by the hand and dragged him into the hallway leading to the restrooms, away from the prying eyes of strangers. "What do you think you're doing?"

"Sorry," he drawled. "I just wanted to say thank you." His eyes were wide with innocence but the unapologetic grin told her that he found her distress entertaining.

"You've said it," Ivy said with a scowl. She tugged her hand out of his and crossed her arms into her chest.

His lips twitched in what she assumed was a valiant attempt to keep from laughing. "Do you know who I am?"

Ivy blinked at the sudden turn in conversation. "According to your friend who was just here, I'd assume you're Jack Everett."

He crossed his arms and leaned back, his eyes searching her face, waiting for something—some sort of recognition, no doubt. The hotel where she worked was one of the most exclusive in the city; nearly every guest thought they were famous as well as rich. They were almost always wrong.

"Should that mean something to me?" she asked.

"Nothing," he said with a laugh. "Nothing at all. So now that we've established my name, why don't you tell me yours?"

"Ivy Sinclair."

"As in poison ivy?"

"As in 'The Holly and the Ivy'." At his raised eyebrow, she explained. "My mom has a thing for Christmas."

"Don't tell me you have a sister named Holly," he teased. She gave a sheepish shrug and he burst out laughing. He gave a jaunty salute as he walked back toward the hotel lobby.

"Thank you for saving my life, Ivy Sinclair. I'll be in touch."

* * * *

Word had spread quickly in the hotel and less than twenty minutes after Jack left, Ivy had been summoned to the manager's office. Franklin Webster was known for being a tough boss but he kept his mouth shut through the entire tale, giving her a chance to fully explain her side of the story.

Ivy cleared her throat and forced herself to continue despite Franklin's intimidating frown. "So you see, sir, I really didn't intend to cause such a scene. I was trying my best to keep the situation under wraps. But this young man...well, I'm afraid he was a bit of a ham and he sort of made me—er, *us*—the center of attention."

When she'd finished explaining, he took his time polishing his glasses and made a show of straightening his tie. Ivy tried not to squirm in her seat. Every time she was called into Franklin's office she couldn't help but feel like she'd been called in to see the principal. More nerve-wracking since the only times she was called on to speak to the principal were when her sister Holly was in trouble.

"Ivy, do you have any idea who Jack Everett is?"

Ivy's eyes widened in surprise. "Uh, no sir."

Franklin sighed. He handed her a copy of one of the tabloids that were sold in the hotel's gift shop.

Ivy stared at the front cover, momentarily speechless. There he was—the man who'd huddled by her feet while she fended off an angry husband. He was flashing the camera that now-familiar cocky grin, one hand on the back of a supermodel as they made their way toward a waiting limo. "Tech Mogul Out on the Town," the headline read. Ivy had never taken much interest in gossip columns or celebrities and today her willful ignorance was on display.

When she looked up she saw that Franklin was watching her with a tight-lipped look of disapproval. "I'd say your Mr. Everett has a tendency to find the spotlight. Or rather, the spotlight has a tendency to find him."

Ivy let out a pent up breath. "So you're not angry?"

"No, I'm not angry. I think you handled the whole thing quite well, considering...."

"Oh, thank you, Mr. Webster," Ivy interrupted.

Franklin's lips twisted into a rare hint of a smile. "Of course. And if Mr. Everett should be true to his offer and come back to the hotel, I know you will do everything in your power to keep him...*entertained*."

The suggestion made Ivy's skin crawl but her smile didn't falter. It remained frozen in place as her stomach churned. She had heard stories about coworkers being urged to dress more provocatively or to flirt with the guests but she never believed them to be true. She struggled to keep her voice even. "Excuse me?"

His expression remained coy. "I think you know what I mean, my dear." His gaze lowered and he studied her figure as though appraising a piece of art at auction. "My sources tell me you were quite a hit with the young man."

She forced a joking tone as she held the tabloid up before her. "From what I gather, most women are a hit with that young man."

Franklin let out a cackle that made her jump in her seat. Franklin Webster did not laugh. Everyone knew that. But at least he wasn't eyeing her like a piece of meat anymore.

He settled back into his seat. "I like you, Ivy. You're smart and you're a go-getter. This is a tough business and there aren't a lot of openings in the areas where you show an interest..." his voice trailed off and he seemed to be weighing how best to phrase the next statement. "You'll soon learn that to be considered for promotion, an employee must show that he or she is willing to go above and beyond for the company."

Bile rose in her throat. She was going to be sick. She knew exactly what he was insinuating but feigned confusion. "Mr. Webster, are you suggesting that I get involved in a romantic relationship with Mr. Everett for the sake of my job?"

Franklin's mouth opened and closed to resemble a guppy as he protested the coarse accusation. "Of course not. I would never suggest such a thing."

"Of course not," she repeated—*because that would be illegal.*

Feeling a twinge of success at having the last word, she made a move to leave the office but he stopped her.

"No one would ever make such a crass suggestion at this hotel," he said. "But I hope you keep in mind, my dear, that there are a limited number of jobs at this hotel and there is no room for employees who aren't team players."

She stopped in her tracks halfway to the door with her back to the manager. The threat could hardly be called "veiled".

Panic warred with disgust. She needed this job.

She heard the crinkle of the tabloid when he picked it up. "We're willing to overlook your antics this afternoon because we know that you are a team player. Am I making myself clear?"

Ivy resisted the urge to spin around and tell the old man where he could shove the tabloid and her job. But that couldn't happen. She could barely afford to pay this month's rent and she was drowning in debt from her stint on unemployment. And there was no way she could turn to her parents. They had enough on their plate trying to keep their house. The last thing they needed was another mouth to feed.

It was only the thought of having to run back to her parents that gave her the strength to turn around and force a smile. "Understood, Mr. Webster."

* * * *

Ivy's studio apartment in Brooklyn was tiny, but it was all hers, and for that she was eternally grateful. Particularly that evening when all she wanted was a hot bath and a glass of wine.

Hours had passed and she still couldn't get rid of the disgusted feeling. Not even a hot bath could wash it away. For what felt like the millionth time that week, Ivy considered quitting. Oh, it would feel so good. She sank further into the tub and let herself daydream about all the ways she could give her notice. In reality, she would go to bed, wake up, and do it all over again.

She'd moved to the city right after college because she'd landed a great job in an up-and-coming ad agency. But less than two years into the great new job, the recession had hit, and Ivy's entire office had been liquidated.

Hers was a small branch of a large company and the closure of their office had been a necessary sacrifice for the greater good—or so she'd been told.

The hostess gig wasn't exactly her dream job but it paid the bills and it was steady work after a series of temp jobs. And it wasn't *all* bad. More and more lately she'd been called in to help the assistant manager with event planning for the hotel and she'd discovered it was something she really enjoyed. She knew there was an opening for an events manager at the hotel. If she could just keep her head down and hold her tongue with Franklin, the job could be hers.

She sighed and sipped her wine. That was a very big "if."

The front door buzzer rang just as she was stepping out of the tub. Her elderly neighbor Edith liked to stop in for a cup of tea and a chat often and she always seemed to show up at a time when Ivy craved solitude. Sleepy and wet from the bath, she threw on a robe and went to answer the door. She tried to summon a smile for her elderly friend.

"Hi Ed—" The name stuck in her throat as she faced the stranger in her doorway.

This visitor was *not* a harmless old woman.

Ivy's mouth gaped as she took in the tall man with dark hair and even darker eyes. His shoulders were broad and he wore a well-tailored suit that looked incongruous in the dingy hallway of her apartment building. Behind him stood a nondescript man with an earpiece and ramrod posture.

"Miss Sinclair?" The tall man before her smiled, causing his eyes to crinkle and eased the intimidation factor only slightly.

"Yes?" Ivy cinched her robe tighter. She was keenly aware of the fact that she wore nothing beneath her flimsy robe.

"I'm Daniel Gladwell, I work with Jack Everett. I believe you met him this afternoon?"

Ivy nodded, unable to take her eyes off of the man before her. He had the kind of chiseled features that were usually reserved for statues or actors portraying James Bond. She made a futile attempt to swipe away some of the unruly auburn curls that had escaped from the loose bun atop her head.

She closed the door a little behind her and took a step into the hallway, wary now that the surprise of finding a gorgeous man in her doorway had worn off

"Can I help you with something?"

The man's smile grew and he tilted his chin in a charming sort of aw-shucks way, but it was all show—the look in his eyes was strictly business. "Actually, I believe you can. May I come in?"

Ivy hesitated; her small town politeness warred with practical street smarts. "I'd rather not invite strange men into my apartment."

"Of course." If he was surprised to be denied, he didn't let on. "I apologize for the late hour. Jack just informed me of this afternoon's *interaction* and I wanted to speak with you immediately."

Now Ivy was truly intrigued. "Is something the matter? Is Jack okay?"

"Oh no, he's fine. Thanks in no small part to you." Heat flooded her cheeks under his watchful gaze. Despite his warm smile and easy demeanor, his eyes were calculating and observant. They seemed to take in everything, from her bare feet to the damp tendrils clinging to her neck.

"That's actually why I'm here, Miss Sinclair."

"Call me Ivy, please."

"I wanted to thank you in person for your assistance today. I'm sure you're aware of Jack's fame and fortune—he's easy fodder for the tabloids."

Ivy nodded, but she was sure some of the confusion she felt was evident. *Where on earth was he going with this?* She shifted from one foot to the other.

"I came here tonight because I'd like to show you how appreciative we are...."

"We?"

"My business partners and I. There is a lot invested in Jack, and his reputation."

"I see," Ivy said politely.

"We'd like to show you our appreciation for your help today and for your discretion in the future." He was watching her closely for some sort of reaction and it took several moments for Ivy to fully grasp what he was implying.

"You want to pay me to keep my mouth shut?" The words slipped out before she could stop herself.

Only a slight widening of the eyes revealed Daniel's surprise at her outburst but he recovered quickly. "Well, that's one way of putting it, I suppose."

Daniel gave her a lopsided grin, the first genuine smile she'd seen, and Ivy was very nearly charmed off of her feet.

For a moment she just stared at the man before her, unsure of how she should react. She didn't know whether she was offended or amused. Amusement won out and she startled both men in her hallway when she burst out with a great peal of laughter.

She slapped a hand over her mouth and let out a little snort as she tried to contain her giggles. "Oh, I'm so sorry, this is just too much." She waved her hand toward Daniel and the silent man behind him who was watching her with no expression. "I feel like I just stepped into a movie or something. I mean, are you seriously trying to pay me off? If I don't take it am I going to swim with the fishes?" She giggled again at her own joke.

"Ms. Sin—Ivy, I hope I haven't offended you."

"No, no, why would I be offended?" she said, still smothering a laugh. She took a step back into her apartment and started to close her door. "Thank you for the laugh, Daniel, but you don't need to pay me. I won't say a word." She held up three fingers in salute. "Scout's honor."

His forehead creased in concern as he gave her a doubtful look that said he wasn't convinced. He opened his mouth to protest, but she held up a hand to stop him.

"Look, I understand where you're coming from, I really do. But believe me when I say I have absolutely no interest in that sort of fame. And if you don't believe that, then maybe you'll understand this—the hotel has very strict rules about not speaking to the press about their guests. If I break that rule, I'd be out of a job. If you don't trust my girl scout's honor—which is sacred, by the way—then believe me when I say I would never jeopardize my job."

He studied her for a moment longer and was apparently satisfied with whatever he saw there. "I'm sorry I disturbed you, Ivy. Have a good night."

\* \* \* \*

Ivy didn't even have a chance to hang up her coat when she arrived at work the next day; she was summoned to the manager's office the moment she walked through the door.

She was stunned to find Daniel there, leaning against the manager's desk when she walked in. Both he and Franklin turned to look at her when she entered. Ivy's stomach sank. This could not be good.

Franklin was the first to react to her arrival. He threw down a copy of that morning's paper and beckoned her over to take a look. She cautiously edged toward the desk and glanced at the paper spread before her—it was open to the gossip section. Both men seemed to be waiting for a reaction so she took a step closer and looked down.

Ivy's stomach dropped and she leaned in closer, unable to believe what she was seeing. It couldn't be. There was a large color photo in the center of the page that showed Jack on his knees before her with a caption that read, "Renowned bachelor Jack Everett may finally have found his bride. Everyone wants to know—who is the lucky lady?" As if that wasn't bad enough, there was another picture just below that perfectly captured Jack's ridiculous kiss. "Brilliant billionaire smitten with his mystery woman," the caption read.

There was a little blurb beside the pictures but Ivy couldn't tear her gaze away from the image of herself looking like a woman in love. Like a woman being proposed to, no less. This couldn't be happening.... A rush of adrenaline flooded through her, leaving her shaky and lightheaded. The words blurred before her eyes. She had a feeling she didn't want to read whatever they'd printed anyways. There was no way there would be one hint of truth to any of it.

"Franklin, may I have a private word with Ivy, please?" Daniel asked.

It wasn't so much a request as an order. Ivy couldn't believe anyone would dare to kick the old manager out of his own office but Daniel seemed to be the type to take control of every room he was in. The older man, who normally put the fear of God into Ivy, looked weak and nervous beside him. Franklin nodded and hurried toward the door. Daniel's face gave nothing away but Franklin's tight-lipped grimace was more than enough to tell her that she was in trouble. When he passed her on the way out of his office he shot out a hand and gripped her arm roughly. "You will do whatever he says to make this right, do you understand me?"

Ivy nodded and swallowed. This was it—she was going to lose her job.

Daniel leaned against the desk, one leg crossed in front of the other. He was wearing another perfectly tailored suit. This one was a dark gray as opposed to the jet-black suit he'd worn the night before in her hallway but it fit just as well. He was perfectly groomed from the tidy hair to the shined designer shoes. Unlike most men she knew, he looked like he was as comfortable in formal attire as though he had been born and raised wearing designer business suits.

He was watching her. His dark eyes scrutinized her every move, and despite his relaxed posture, or maybe because of it, Ivy grew unbearably tense until she had to do something.

The words came spilling out of her mouth. "I had nothing to do with that," she said, pointing to the newspaper. Her shaking hand seemed to betray her, making her look guilty rather than what she was—horrified. She instantly regretted the outburst. She hated how defensive she sounded.

Daniel nodded, his expression unreadable. "I know."

Ivy shifted uncomfortably. Well, at least he knew she wasn't the enemy here. "If you'd like for me to call the newspaper, explain what happened...."

Daniel shook his head. "Unfortunately, the situation is a little too complicated for that."

Ivy's face scrunched up in confusion. "Too complicated for the truth?"

She thought she saw a flicker of amusement in his eyes but it was fleeting. He gestured to the chair in front of him. "Please, have a seat and I'll explain."

Ivy hesitated for a moment before squaring her shoulders and perching on the edge of the chair. She tried to discreetly pull down the hem of her skirt, which suddenly felt much too short under his scrutinizing gaze.

He sat across from her and leaned over the desk with his hands folded. Every gesture, every move, was precise. This was a man who thought through everything—nothing was unintentional or improvised. Everything was planned. And the way he was looking at her now? It was clear he had a plan for her.

"As I mentioned last night, my company has a lot at stake, and it's all riding on Jack. He is the face of EverTech and his reputation has a direct impact on the business."

Ivy nodded and tried not to shift in her seat. *Just get to the point already.*

"I won't beat around the bush, Ivy."

*Oh God, could he read minds?*

"I am in the middle of negotiating a very sensitive merger with a company that could either make or break EverTech." When he paused Ivy wondered if she was supposed to speak. She opened her mouth, about to ask what any of this had to do with her but he continued before she could get the words out.

"The owner of the other company, Gianni Brunelli—well, he's a bit old-fashioned. He's made it clear that he doesn't approve of Jack's current lifestyle and this latest stunt...."

He gestured to the newspaper with a pained look. When he turned back to her, she was caught in his gaze. His dark eyes were focused on her with an intensity that was frightening. She couldn't look away.

Ivy squirmed in her seat. Was he trying to torture her? She had no idea what he was getting at but the way he was looking at her, you'd think she single-handedly maneuvered the latest "stunt," as he put it. Ivy gripped the edge of her chair to keep calm but she was growing impatient with nerves. She'd already offered to call the newspaper, to try to explain the situation.

"I'm not sure how I can help you," she hedged.

"The only way Brunelli will move forward with this is if I can convince him that Jack has changed. That he's a new man."

There was a brief pause and Ivy wondered if she was supposed to know what he was getting at. She found herself holding her breath as she waited for him to continue but he was either extremely fond of awkward silences or was waiting for her to respond. His eyes were studying her expression though his face was a polite mask, no emotions to be found. He was waiting for a reaction of some sort, that much was clear, but she had no idea where this was heading—only that it couldn't be good.

"Okaaay..." she stalled.

Silence broken, Daniel stood and moved to the front of the desk so he was looming over her. He crossed his arms in front of his chest and fixed his eyes on her. "You see, Brunelli doesn't want to get into bed with someone who's 'not faithful in his private life'—those are his words not mine," Daniel said.

Judging by his smirk, it was clear that this man didn't put much stock in Brunelli's beliefs or his old-fashioned values.

She blinked up at him in the silence that followed. "So, what do you want from me?"

Daniel's laugh took her by surprise. It was a deep rumble that Ivy could feel all the way to her toes. Her breath caught in her throat at the genuine smile that caused his eyes to crinkle and made him seem less intimidating but far more dangerous.

"You're a straight shooter, Ivy. I like that."

She wished his words of approval didn't affect her but she couldn't deny the warm glow that spread through her chest and left her slightly breathless.

He looked her straight in the eye. "I want you to go along with a lie, Ivy. I want you to tell the world that you and Jack are engaged and I want you to play the part of the happy fiancée until this deal is signed."

Ivy found herself staring up at Daniel and for the life of her she was unable to come up with any words. Her brain had turned to mush in her shock and she had the odd sensation that time stood still. The hum of the air-conditioner was temporarily washed out by the sound of her own heartbeat in her ears.

Daniel was eyeing her warily, his gaze fixed on her, and for a moment she thought she saw a hint of concern in his eyes. Those dark eyes that still held her captive.

*He was gorgeous.* Now was not the time to be thinking about this man's sex appeal, but there it was. Her heart was racing and she was no longer certain if that was due to shock or sexual attraction.

*Focus, Ivy.* This man wanted her to lie for him—about her entire life.

His voice startled her back to the moment. "I can see my proposition has taken you by surprise." He relaxed his intimidating stance and leaned against the desk with his hands in his pockets as though they were discussing the weather and not her life. "Don't get me wrong, we are not asking you to do anything illegal or anything that would jeopardize your values. You will be handsomely rewarded in return—my investors and I are more than willing to ensure that you are very comfortable financially in return for this favor."

"Other than lie." The words slipped out of her mouth.

Her words put a dent in Daniel's perfectly poised sales pitch. She couldn't help it. Her mother's face loomed in her mind's eye at the mere thought of lying. Her parents had thoroughly ingrained their children with the need to tell the truth, the whole truth, and nothing but the truth.

He paused and raised his brows in polite inquiry. "I'm sorry?"

She cleared her throat. "I said 'other than lie'. You said 'we're not asking you to do anything that would jeopardize your values.' And I said 'other than lie'."

Oh Lord, she was babbling. She was repeating their conversation like a court reporter. His forehead wrinkled as if in thought for a moment but again she couldn't tell if he was amused or annoyed. Or both.

"Yes, you have a point there. I'm sure lying to your friends and family will not be pleasant but unfortunately, we can't afford to take any chances on anyone slipping up. It would be more difficult for you as well if the truth were to come out. It would not paint you in a flattering light, I'm afraid."

Panic made Ivy's heart rate accelerate. He was talking as though she'd already agreed to go along with this stunt. She shook her head. "I'm sorry, Daniel, but I'm really not a very good liar and I'm not much of an actress. I don't think I could pull it off."

"Unfortunately for us, we don't have much of a choice in who will play the lead in this particular farce." He gestured toward the newspaper. "But you will have a team of people at your beck and call to help you—I am absolutely positive you will get through this little façade with flying colors."

Ivy bristled at his know-it-all tone. Was he really trying to steamroll her into telling a life-altering lie just because it was convenient for him?

He wasn't even pretending to frame it as a question—as though it was understood that she would comply.

"Do people always do what you say?" she snapped.

The charming smile faltered. It was slight but she caught it. His perfectly poised demeanor slipped—just for an instant, but it was enough to give Ivy a sense of triumph. She had a feeling that Daniel Gladwell was rarely taken by surprise.

He recovered quickly though and his answer was brutally honest. "Yes, Miss Sinclair. They typically do." *If they know what's good for them*. He didn't say the words but he didn't have to.

Gone was the polite smile and Ivy found herself face to face with Daniel Gladwell, the ruthless business tycoon. His jaw clenched and his eyes hardened, holding her captive yet again in a disarmingly direct glare. He looked like a gladiator ready for battle. The look he gave her was so intense, she swallowed her clever retort—this was not a man to mess with.

"Honestly, Mr. Gladwell, I'd really rather go back my job—"

"Your job will not be waiting for you should you refuse my offer." He stood up straight and moved to stand behind the desk. His tone was cool and collected, at odds with the harsh words.

She tried to ignore the uncomfortable sting of unshed tears as his words sank in. She couldn't go back to being unemployed. She'd worked so hard to get where she was. She couldn't start over. And she couldn't go home. Bad investments and a housing market collapse had left her parents teetering on the edge of bankruptcy at an age when they should be planning for retirement. If she lost her job they'd feel compelled to help her but they could barely help themselves.

"That's not fair, you can't do that." Ivy's voice shook. She swallowed and tried again. "The hotel has no reason to dismiss me. I've been a great employee. Ask anyone, ask Mr. Webster."

"It's not a matter of how well you've done your job, Miss Sinclair. The hotel can't keep someone on who acts irresponsibly with the hotel guests. Not to mention, employees here are expected to be team players."

"I am responsible. And I *am* a team player." She tried to keep the tremor out of her voice. She felt like she was on the wrong end of a steamroller. She had to regain control.

She tilted her chin up and straightened her shoulders. Who did he think he was to come to her place of work and threaten her job? Maybe Franklin wasn't in her corner, but there had to be people above him.

Standing, she faced Daniel who had returned to his seat behind the desk. "You can't fire me, Mr. Gladwell. I'm sure Mr. Webster doesn't even have the final say and you have *no* say in the matter so—"

Daniel cut off her tirade before she could even gain steam. "Actually I do have quite a bit of say. My company is the majority owner of this hotel."

His words were like a punch in the gut. Her mind struggled to make sense of this new information. It couldn't be possible—could it? Maybe he was kidding. But even as she thought it, she dismissed it. The man before her clearly didn't have a sense of humor. She stared at him with wide eyes, trying to think of something to say, but she was rendered speechless. She flopped back in her seat like a deflated balloon.

With astonishing speed his cold businesslike demeanor was once again replaced by the charming smile that Ivy was beginning to know well. It was the smile of a predator before it ate its prey. "Listen, Ivy, it doesn't have to be this way. I don't want to lose you as an employee. But I also can't allow yesterday's incident to ruin a multi-billion dollar deal that I've been working on for the past two years. You can understand that, can't you?"

Ivy just stared back at him. Her mind was racing as she considered her options. She could try her luck in an unemployment office once again and pray that she'd find a new position before she lost everything. She could go back home and try to find a job there—but no, that wasn't an option. The job market in her hometown was far worse than the city and she couldn't allow her parents to help her.

"How much?" she asked. "How much would you pay me if I go along with this?"

For a moment she thought he was ignoring her. He picked up a pen and jotted something down on a piece of paper. He pushed it her way and when she picked it up, a series of zeros stared back at her. The six-figure number took her breath away. That was enough to pay her rent for the year and still have plenty left over to help her parents.

"And of course you'll get a promotion, which comes with a raise," Daniel added.

"I don't want a promotion if I haven't earned one," Ivy said, sitting up straight. She may be desperate for money, but she still had some morals.

She thought she saw a hint of a genuine smile again. Good Lord, this man's lips were hypnotic.

"On the contrary, Miss Sinclair. I've had a long talk with Franklin and it seems you have been long overdue for the promotion. I plan to have a talk with him about that." His look of disapproval actually made Ivy nervous on Franklin's behalf.

"So, do I take it we have a deal?"

Ivy swallowed down the feeling that she was taking a leap off of a high dive without checking to see if there was water below.

"We have a deal."

# Meet the Author

**Maggie Dallen** is a huge fan of happily-ever-afters. She writes contemporary and YA romance and has been known to rewrite the endings to classic love stories to ensure that they end on a happy note. In Maggie's version, Ingrid Bergman does not get on the plane. She lives in Northern California and works at a yarn store to support her knitting addiction. For more info please visit maggiedallen.com.

Follow her on Twitter @Mag_Dallen.
Or connect with her on Facebook.